MARGARET'S PEACE

"A powerful and compelling novel...a marvelously crafted work."—*The Daily Gleaner*

"Linda Hall's characters are intriguing and complex.... She weaves the mysteries of the past nicely with the painful realities of the present.—*Bangor Daily News*

"A mystery novel that promises and delivers."—*Inspirational Market News*

"A dramatic and powerful story...highly recommended."—*Library Journal*

"*Margaret's Peace* goes deeper than most novels into spiritual issues of loss and trust. Linda Hall is definitely in the first rank of Christian writers."—Laurel B. Schunk, author of *The Voice He Loves*

ISLAND OF REFUGE

"Linda Hall weaves a riveting tale of mystery and murder in Island of Refuge. You know you're into a good book when it's difficult to put down after the first chapter—and that's how it is with *Island of Refuge.*"—*Northside News*

"*Island of Refuge* would make a great movie. It incorporates excitement, intrigue, mystery and romance with characters who are interesting as well as believable."—*The Daily Gleaner* (New Brunswick)

"Put Linda Hall's latest near the top of your list of good books."—*Bangor Daily News*

"A smoothly written romantic adventure."—*Library Journal*

Katheryn's Secret

"Suspenseful and compelling."—*Mennonite Brethren Herald*

"*Katheryn's Secret* is the best Christian novel that I have read to date. Ms. Hall delighted me with her ever-surprising tale and the completeness of her plot. I must read more of her works!"—a reader in Germantown, TN

"*Katheryn's Secret* is a powerful and humbling story. We need more mysteries as well written as this one."—a reader in Cincinnati, OH

"Linda Hall is a great mystery writer. I could not turn the pages fast enough."—a reader in Amarillo, TX

"Writing is a gift, and Linda Hall has it! *Katheryn's Secret* is rich indeed. I cannot recommend it highly enough."—a reader in Birmingham, AL

Sadie's Song

A Novel

LINDA HALL

Multnomah Publishers *Sisters, Oregon*

SADIE'S SONG

© 2001 by Linda Hall

published by Multnomah Publishers, Inc.

International Standard Book Number: 1-57673-659-8

Cover image by Carolyn Bross/FPG International, LLC
Cover design by Chris Gilbert/Uttley DouPonce DesignWorks

Printed in the United States of America

Multnomah is a trademark of Multnomah Publishers, Inc.,
and is registered in the U.S. Patent and Trademark Office.
The colophon is a trademark of Multnomah Publishers, Inc.

FOR INFORMATION:
Multnomah Publishers, Inc., Post Office Box 1720, Sisters, Oregon 97759

Library of Congress Cataloging-in-Publication Data
Hall, Linda, 1950–
  Sadie's song / by Linda Hall.   p.cm.   ISBN 1-57673-659-8 (pbk.)
  1. Women detectives–Maine–Fiction.   2. Missing children–Fiction.
  3. Maine–Fiction.   I. Title.
  PS3558.A3698 S24 2001 813'.54–dc21   00-013148

01 02 03 04 05 06 07 08 09 — 10 9 8 7 6 5 4 3 2 1 0

Acknowledgments

A special thanks to Sociology professor Nancy Nason-Clark of the University of New Brunswick, Fredericton, NB, Canada, for meeting with me and talking about abuse within the evangelical church. Her book *The Battered Wife: How Christians Confront Family Violence* (Westminster John Knox Press, 1997) was a tremendous help in writing *Sadie's Song*.

I would also like to thank the many women who shared their stories with me. I belong to a Christian women's Internet listserve, and for part of my research I asked if women who had been abused by Christian husbands would like to share their stories with me for this novel. I expected no replies; I received dozens of private e-mails, many with stories more heart wrenching than my fictional Sadie's. To all of you, thank you for being so honest.

I would like to thank my editor, Rod Morris, for helping me work through the various incarnations of this book, and to my husband, Rik, for his guidance, suggestions, and patience.

Dedication

To my husband, Rik.

Chapter One

I was ready. Well, just about. It wouldn't take me long to change out of these mayonnaise-stained sweatpants and into something presentable. Simon had been fed and bathed and was gurgling placidly in his baby seat. Gavin, my five-year-old, was sitting under the kitchen table playing quietly with his Game Boy. The twins were setting the table above him, and my eldest child, Mary Beth, who is eight, was on tiptoes stirring the spaghetti sauce with a wooden spoon. I wiped the kitchen counter and watched her plaid cotton school dress swish around her knees with each determined stir. Mary Beth never wears pants, even though all the other girls in her class wear scruffed jeans and T-shirts with sayings on them. My husband prefers his girls in dresses, so I never say anything about Mary Beth going down the slide in her Sunday dress or straddling the muddy logs down by the wharf. I looked at her, at her twig-thin arms stirring the sauce as if it were a school project, something that must be done before something else can be gotten to.

My seven-year-old twins were chattering to each other in half-sentences and partial words, giggling. Always giggling, those two. In front of their own places they grouped little dessert bowls, a separate one for each food item. This is something new with them. A couple of months ago they decided they didn't like their food to touch, and it has become an ongoing battle. I looked at their white-blond hair, soft and curling around their ears, the same cowlicks in exactly the same places. Pamela Jo and Tabbitha Anne, they were named at birth, but now they are just PJ and Tabby.

I once saw a television program about multiple births. A mother of quadruplets bounced them, two on each knee, while she talked about the challenges of breastfeeding and scheduling. "But what I want to know," said the interviewer, "is how can you *possibly* tell them apart!"

"Oh," said the smiling, perfect television mother, "a mother can *always* tell her own children apart."

When PJ and Tabby were babies I kept their hospital bracelets on for months until they were in danger of cutting off their circulation. Then I made up little bracelets of my own, ribbons where I scrawled their names in permanent felt-tip marker, a red one for Tabbitha and a pink one for Pamela.

Lately they have begun dressing alike, advice that goes against every book I have ever read on the subject (and I have read lots). "Never refer to them as 'the twins.' Celebrate their differences." But instead of becoming different, they seem to be growing more alike, if that is possible; growing inward toward each other instead of outward and away.

"We're having spaghetti." I kept my voice steady. "You won't need your little dishes."

"We want plain spaghetti in one," Tabby said.

"And sauce in the other one," PJ said.

"Then we can dip the spaghetti into the sauce…"

"One at a time."

"Then it doesn't get so gloppy."

"We hate gloppy food."

"Gloppy food is gross."

I could hear the beeps, the growls, and the cheers from the Game Boy under the table. It is useless to get Gavin to help with chores around the house, even though Troy thinks I should try. "That's part of his problem, Sadie," he tells me. "That boy has no responsibility, none whatsoever."

"But he's only five," I always argue.

One doorknob of a knee protruded from his torn jeans. He was not changed, not cleaned up, teeth not brushed, and there were smudges of dirt on his cheeks. Gavin is the prettiest of my children with his freckles and gold-flecked hair. When he laughs, his entire face lights up. But none of my children laugh much. Even Simon doesn't grin the way other babies in the nursery do on Sunday mornings when nursery helpers hold them out in their arms and coo and ahh.

The phone rang. It was Phyllis Carter from church with a prayer chain request. "Do you have a pen?" she asked.

I scrabbled for one in a kitchen drawer, found nothing, finally spotted my Bible case on the counter underneath an unopened box of cereal. I always keep a pen in there although I'm usually too busy worrying about keeping the kids quiet on Sunday mornings to take notes on the sermon.

"I'm ready," I said.

"There's been another missing girl. Irma and Bud Buckley's granddaughter, Ally."

I sat down at the kitchen table.

"They just moved here, well, about a year or so ago. Anyway, the request, and this is really sad, is that Ally has gone missing and to pray that she'll be found quickly."

"Oh no."

"It's still early so there's no reason to think this will be like the other one. She could have just wandered off. Kids are always doing that, you know. So, just pray that they'll find her."

"How long has she been gone?"

"As far as anyone can tell, she left school at the proper time, just never made it home. They phoned the school, of course, and nobody's seen her since she walked around the corner from it, so Irma decided to put it on the prayer line."

I asked if there was anything we could do.

"Maybe just pass it on to Troy. They might need the men later."

After I got off the phone, I rifled through drawer after drawer trying to find the prayer list that would tell me the person I was supposed to call. I couldn't find it. In the kitchen junk drawer, I piled up old phone books, note pads, calendars, endless scraps of paper, and enough pens and pencils to outfit an entire grammar school. But no list.

"Mommy." Mary Beth was talking. "Mommy."

"Hmmm?" A dozen pens fell to the floor.

"Mommy. Mom-EEEE!"

I turned to her. "Mary Beth, what *is* it?"

"PJ and Tabby are putting little dishes on the table again."

"I told them they could." I found the list, folded in quarters and stuck in the front of the church directory. I was supposed to call Ruby Fisher, an elderly widow who sat in a row of white-haired ladies near the front of the church. Gavin was adding his own sound effects to the Game Boy now; Simon was beginning to screech; and Mary Beth was sucking on the sides of her hair and shifting from foot to foot.

When I did finally get through to Ruby, Simon's screeching was so loud that Ruby had to say, "What? What?" several times before I was able to get the message to her.

After the call I looked at the clock. Simon and his screeches would have to wait. Dealing with the little bowls would have to wait. I needed to change my clothes and run a quick comb through my hair. A shower would be nice, but there would be no time for that. There were still toys on the living room floor, two laundry baskets full of clothes to fold, Kool-Aid spills on the coffee table, and the day's stickiness still on the kitchen floor. Troy hates a sticky floor, the squooshing sound it makes under his brown loafers.

I hurriedly brushed my teeth, sopped a cold washcloth on my face, and combed my hair up on the sides into the two barrettes Troy bought me. They are gaudy, I think, with blue stones that stick out, but he likes them, so I wear them. I pulled off my T-shirt, stepped out of my sweatpants, and threw them both into the hamper. I applied plenty of deodorant and a sprinkling of Simon's baby powder. Since I recently lost three more pounds, I was able to squeeze into a new pair of jeans from Kmart. Troy would be pleased with me for that.

I put on a white ruffled blouse and carefully tucked it into the jeans all around. I am far more comfortable in baggy sweatshirts. Troy says they make me look fat, but I say they cover it up. I straightened the collar of my blouse. Earrings. I should put earrings on. The little hearts, maybe. I stood in front of the mirror and frowned. Maybe I should really put on a dress…

A piercing scream came from the kitchen, and I was instantly there, lifting Simon from his baby seat and saying, "No, Gavin, no, we don't hit." I was talking quietly, firmly, the way you're supposed to; firm but loving. I was in the middle of a thick book on child rearing that I had taken out of the church library. Firm but loving.

"I could hit YOU! I could squish you like a worm!" Gavin screamed at me and waved the plastic Game Boy in my face.

"No, Gavin, you don't hit Mommy. That's a bad boy."

He threw the Game Boy across the room, and it clanged against the bottom of the refrigerator. I put Simon down and lunged for it.

"I want that!" Gavin yelled.

"You broke it, Gavin. You broke your toy," I said examining the crack that ran around the battery compartment like a stray hair.

"I don't CARE!"

"If you break things, you can't play with them."

"I WANT it."

I could see the little arms stiffening. His legs. His cheeks puffing out. The redness there. I reached for him, held on to him, but he thrashed his way out of my arms. I let him go. I knew his screaming would make my chest tighten, make my stomach hurt. When he got started he could scream for hours, thrashing, throwing things, and there would be nothing I could do. I handed the Game

Boy back to him, and he threw it again. Don't come home now, Troy, I prayed. Please not now, not yet…

I touched his hair. "Gavin," I said.

"I HATE you!"

"Gavin…"

"GET IT FOR ME."

I did. I handed it to him and he trotted into the living room. I was able to breathe again.

"You be good now, Gavin," I called after him as a kind of benediction. He didn't acknowledge me.

"But you can't *have* the little dishes," I heard Mary Beth say. "It's wrong!" And I wanted to grab this daughter who of all my children is most like me and say, "Mary Beth, can't you just be quiet? Can't you just do what they want? Let people have what they want. Life is so much easier when you just let people have what they want." But I can't say these life lessons that I have learned to her. I know that much, at least.

One of the twins said, "We can have separate dishes if we want. Mommy said."

"But it's WRONG. Daddy says." She was running a clump of her dampish hair through her fingers over and over.

"You're such a crybaby," PJ said.

"Crybaby. Crybaby," Tabby said.

"You have to *change* it." Mary Beth reached for the bowls.

"You're not the boss of us!"

"Mary Beth," I said, "it's okay. Just leave them be." And I held out my arms to her. She came, the way she always does, the way none of my other children do.

"But Daddy will be mad. He will, Mommy, you know he will."

I stroked her hair, felt the damp strands near her face. When I let go of her, she fled to her room. I said to the twins, "Why torment your sister? Why make her cry?"

PJ said, "But Mommy, she's such a *baby*."

And Tabby said, "Everything has to be *her* way."

"We're *hungry*, Mommy," PJ said. "Can we just eat without Daddy?"

"Please? He's always late."

"No, we have to eat together."

In the living room, Gavin was sitting cross-legged under the piano bench and had turned the television volume to a deafening level. Some program about aliens. From the coffee table I pocketed the remote. As soon as I heard the van pull into the driveway, I would flick off the television.

Simon was screeching; Mary Beth was wailing in her room; and the twins were unsetting the table, removing the dishes one by one and putting them on the counter in neat stacks.

"What are you *doing?*"

"We don't want to eat," PJ announced.

"We changed our minds," Tabby said.

I quickly reset the table with a plate each for Tabby and PJ, and raced to change a screaming Simon. His diaper was dirty; his nose was running; his clothes were a hopeless mess. Were there any clean ones? He could use a bath. When Simon was clean again, I strapped him back into his baby seat. My stomach hurt; my jeans felt too tight. I caught a glimpse of myself in the full-length mirror and wondered, *Whatever made me think I looked good in these jeans?* One of my hair clips had slipped down, so I took them both out and brushed my hair back into a blue scrunchy.

Troy was still not home. The sauce was now overdone, the top of it crusted with dark red bubbles. I switched off the burner and sat down at the table across from Mary Beth who had emerged from her room and was hugging Miss Piggy and sucking on her hair.

"Mary Beth, shouldn't you leave Miss Piggy in bed? And how about taking your hair out of your mouth, hmmm?" I tried to sound gentle but firm.

She kept sucking, kept hugging.

"Do you have homework you can get started on?"

"But I'm hungry."

I grabbed some crackers from the cupboard. "Here, have these. Do you have any homework?"

She shook her head. "I can't do it, Mommy. I can't!"

"Why not?"

"I always get it wrong."

"But you only got two wrong on your quiz."

"Yeah, but Jason next to me got a hundred and said I copied. But I didn't." She was shaking her head, and strings of her hair like wet yarn flapped across her cheeks. "He told Mrs. Barry."

"Don't chew on your hair, Mary Beth."

"I can't Mommy. I can't do it."

"Why don't you bring your questions down here and we'll have a look at them together."

I hate this early evening time of the day when the children are all at home and cranky, and everyone is hungry and tired and waiting for Troy, and I'm trying to make supper and make sure everything stays clean. My favorite time of the day is early afternoon when the four older children are at school and Simon is down for his nap. I climb into bed and read books from the church library. I read all sorts of things, books on how to be a better wife, how to be a better mother, but I especially enjoy novels, imagining myself in all those places, living lives I never will. I used to play the piano when the older children napped. It never seemed to bother them. But I haven't touched my piano for a long time. Now, I just read.

Mary Beth returned with her books, and I picked up a whimpering Simon, held him wheezing in the crook of my arm while I bent over the kitchen table with Mary Beth and her arithmetic problems.

Half an hour later I heard Troy thundering, "What in the name of blazes is this kid sitting in front of the TV for? I've half a mind to get rid of this idiot box once and for all!"

I rose, dropping one of Mary Beth's books onto the floor.

"You're late." It was all I could think to say. I bent down, still holding Simon, and retrieved the book.

"You're late? That's the first thing I get when I come home? You're late? Not, hello. Not, how was your day? But, you're late?"

"I'm sorry."

"I work all day. I come home, I want a little bit of peace and quiet. I walk in the door and the TV's so loud I can hear it halfway down the street. Kids yelling. And what's this disaster in the kitchen, now?"

"I was helping Mary Beth with her homework," I said.

"And you let her throw every pen and pencil we own onto the kitchen floor where people can trip over them?"

"That was me. I'm sorry." I bent to gather them up, still holding Simon. "There was a prayer request. I couldn't find a pen."

"All that junk and you couldn't find a pen? I see at least a dozen on the floor."

"None of them work."

"Then throw them out. For Pete's sake, just throw the blasted things out!"

"I'm sorry."

Huddled into herself across the table, Mary Beth was vigorously sucking on her hair, two hanks of it, on either side of her face.

I put Simon into his plastic seat, ignoring his cries. Troy carried in a wriggling Gavin and sat him down. The twins had still not emerged.

"Mary Beth," Troy said, "go get your sisters."

"How was your day?" I said, ladling out the overcooked noodles.

He grunted and sat down. "Fine, Sadie, just fine. You've got spaghetti sauce all over that shirt of yours, by the way."

I looked down. "I'm sorry. I'll go change."

"Don't bother now. Not for my sake."

"PJ and Tabby don't want to come," announced Mary Beth from the doorway.

"They don't want to eat?" I asked.

"They said they don't want to eat with us anymore because they don't like the sound of people chewing."

Troy threw back his chair. "I'll go get those two. If they think they can get away with—"

"No, no." I put up my hand. "You eat. I'll get them. You just sit. Relax. Sit."

Chapter Two

The following morning I was up in the attic going through boxes of summer clothes. There were shorts and shirts of Mary Beth's that would fit the twins; baby things of Gavin's that would fit Simon now. Things of Simon's to pack away.

My sons were with me. Simon in his baby seat sucked on a plastic toy, and Gavin in a dusty corner was crashing cars together. There is a small hexagonal window in the attic and it's the only place in our house where one can get a glimpse of the ocean. Ours is a tiny house, one of a series of look-alike row houses built around the turn of the century. Our road runs perpendicular to the water and we're the corner house at the end, farthest from the ocean. The house has low ceilings and a narrow enclosed staircase to the second floor where there are four small bedrooms. Actually there are three bedrooms; Mary Beth's is a converted closet. A set of pull-down stairs into Mary Beth's room provide access to the attic.

I am often embarrassed by the smallness of the place and the junk that gets piled on the kitchen counters and the living room floor, the bedspreads I throw over the couch and chairs to hide the rips.

About the only thing I like about this house is the doors. There are doors everywhere. Doors close the kitchen off from the living room, and there is even a door at the bottom of the stairs. Modern houses are all open archways and big rooms. I don't think I would like that.

We had grand plans for this place when we moved in. Troy and

I wanted to build a family room up here in the attic. We would enlarge the window, perhaps even add a deck of sorts. But when the babies started coming, we just never found the time nor the money. Now, it's just a hot, musty-smelling, plank-lined dormer room where we store things, a place for outgrown clothing and things we've finished with.

We live only a few blocks from a little beach, a sheltered place between rocks where in the summer children toddle in warm pools left by the outgoing tide. I used to take Mary Beth there when she was a baby. When the twins were born, I would pack everyone up, put the twins in a borrowed double stroller, while Mary Beth rode her tricycle alongside. When Gavin was born we never went. If three children was difficult, four was impossible. Every spring when I'm up here and look out the window, I make summer plans. This year we will have picnics on the beach. Even Troy will come. The sun, the warmth, the freedom—they will calm Gavin down, will be a poultice for Simon's wheezing, will leach the fear from Mary Beth. But when summer comes we never get there. I won't make any promises this spring. I have quit making promises.

I sat down on an old folding chair and began my morning's work.

Last night when we were in bed, Troy asked me to forgive him.

"It's work," he had told me, leaning up on his arm. He was so close that I could see tiny red lines in his eyes. "We have this new boss, he's making life miserable. You have no idea. You don't know the half of it. Sometimes I feel I can't deal with it. He kept me late. Talking to me. Lecturing me, more like. That's where I was. I know I come home and take it out on you and the kids. I don't mean to. Sometimes I just can't help it."

I looked at the fists he was making, running his fingers through the bedsheets, fisting them in hunks, and said nothing.

Troy is a hard worker. I can't fault him that. He's on the church board; he tithes faithfully. When there is a need in the church, Troy is right there. Saturday workbees at the church or at the church camp, Troy is always there in a pair of old jeans, his tools on his belt, a smile on his face. A hard worker, Troy is. No one could ever call him lazy.

"I'm sorry, Sadie." He was rubbing his eyes. "If only you knew what it was like for me, the things I have to go through at that place. Every single day. Every single blooming day. And now with this takeover thing, everybody, and I do mean everybody, is on edge. No one knows what's happening."

I had nothing to say to him. He sighed and turned away from me.

Within minutes he was asleep, but I had lain sleepless, listening to my thoughts. I was thinking earlier about favorite times of the day. The night is not one of them. I often can't sleep, even though I am dead tired so much of the time. Even though every cell in my body demands sleep, my thoughts twirl around in almost visible circles above my head. I think of my children, and I know I shouldn't, but I compare them to other children who sit well-behaved in the pews and get points for all the Bible verses they know. Sometimes I pray, and that helps, but even then I can't concentrate for long.

And then I thought about the missing girl. I never told Troy. He would have wanted to know. He would have called our pastor, been concerned. He would have gone over there, maybe. Ally Somebody. I couldn't even remember her name. And I never even prayed. I got the request, passed it on. Never even prayed.

It had been in the paper this morning. I had watched Troy bend his head over the article, running his finger down the page. She was still missing. It would be like the other one, and I had never even prayed.

His other arm was around Mary Beth, and he was smoothing her long beige hair between his fingers while he read. She was basking in the attention and chattering happily about a new girl in school and a school party. The twins were swirling their spoons in their Cheerios and giggling. I was jiggling Simon on my hip, and he was grabbing at his ears and whining.

"I can't remember one month," I said, "one month out of the seven he's been alive that this baby hasn't been on antibiotics."

Troy looked up from the paper. "Did you say something?"

"It's Simon. I think I'll have to take him to the pediatrician again."

"Do you want the van today?"

I sighed, shook my head. "I'll see how he is tonight. I'll call you at lunch if I need you to come home. Could you hold him for a minute while I pack up your lunch?"

"I would, but I've got my good suit on, Sadie. An important meeting with you-know-who, and what I don't need right now is for him to puke all over me."

I strapped Simon in his baby seat and tried to ignore his whimperings, but they grated on me.

The twins looked at each other, their faces close together and giggled. "Puke," PJ said. "Daddy said puke."

"Puke, puke, puke," Tabby said. And they made puking noises over their cereal.

"You girls," Troy said, "if you know what's good for you, will shut up right this very minute."

"PJ, Tabby," I said brightly, "finish your cereal. Quickly now. The bus will be here soon. You too, Mary Beth."

The twins giggled into each other's faces and made puking noises no louder than whispers.

"Stop it, Gavin!" It was Mary Beth now. "Mommy, Gavin's bugging me."

"Gavin," I said, "quit teasing your sister."

"He's touching me, Mommy. Quit TOUCHING me, Gavin."

"That's enough!" said Troy rising. "Get out from underneath that table this instant."

Gavin wiggled his way across the floor. "I'm a worm," he growled.

I handed Troy his lunch, kissed him quickly on the cheek. "I'll take care of Gavin. You go. You'll be late for work."

He pulled me close in a sudden embrace that made me gasp. "Things will be getting better for us soon," he whispered. "There's a lot riding on this meeting today. Pray for me, will ya?"

I laid a hand-knit sweater of Mary Beth's on my lap and looked out the attic window. A sailboat was making its way across the horizon, and I watched it and prayed for Troy. I heard a thundering noise behind me and jumped.

"Gavin." I stood. "Get down! Now!"

He was sitting on top of a wooden folding table. Boxes, games, photo albums, and scrapbooks lay in a heap around him. My old oboe case was in his lap.

"Not that!" I wrested it from his hands and opened it. All there, nothing disturbed or broken. I fastened the clasps and placed the case high on another shelf behind a pile of jigsaw puzzles. When I turned back, Gavin had a small, hinged wooden box open on his lap.

"Gavin, give that to Mommy."

"No!" He would not let me pry it out of his fingers. Those are mine, I kept saying. Mine. I could feel tears clouding my eyes.

"No" was all he said. Our match ended with the cover of the box being cracked down the middle and the contents strewn all over the dusty floor: loose photographs, pebbles, pennies, shells.

I bent to pick them up, crying openly now. "Gavin, why do you always do this? Why don't you ever listen? Why do you always disobey? Why does it always have to be like this?"

Across the bottom of the cracked cover, *Indian Head Lake* was burned into the wood. My brother and I had been camping with my parents when I bought this box in a gift shop that featured a lot of little wooden trinkets and Indian jewelry. I was about thirteen and fascinated with boxes. I still am. I still like the feel of things placed neatly inside them. I ran my fingers over my little wooden box, the top broken in two, the hasp bent. I began retrieving the contents and placed them neatly back inside. I picked up a small rock from a long-ago Indiana beach when I had thrown a stick into a campfire and given my life to God. I gathered up a bunch of old photographs of camp friends and rubberbanded them back together. The close-up snapshots, taken with our instamatics poised just under our chins, were mostly toothy grins, our faces wide-jawed and clownish. Maybe we all made decisions for Christ at the same time. Maybe that's why I was keeping these pictures. I couldn't even remember now.

There was a shell in the box, too, a more recent addition. I had picked this one up on Coffins Reach beach when Troy and I had walked hand in hand and everything was new and full of promise. I held the shell in my hand and felt the smoothness of it.

Chapter Three

*T*roy and I met in my third year of college and his last. I was studying music at a Christian college in Chicago, majoring in oboe and piano, and Troy was in the pastor's program studying for the ministry. We had both signed up to be counselors at a series of large youth rallies. Every Wednesday night for six weeks we attended training sessions in a quiet old church with tall, skinny, stained-glass windows along the sides. It was a large chunk of time out of my music schedule, especially since my junior year recital was coming up, but this was something I wanted to do. After we had been seeing each other for a while, I found out that counseling for this rally made up part of Troy's credits toward his degree. I don't know why this changed my opinion of him; it shouldn't have, but it did. But at the time, before I knew this, I admired his dedication, his willingness to give of his time to help teens make a commitment to Christ.

Troy had a highly developed sense of right and wrong, and I liked this. Often during the sessions he would challenge the leader on points of doctrine, calling his attention to chapter and verse. After the third training session he invited me out for coffee. We talked. He told me God was calling him to a ministry of "righting wrongs." This pleased me. I come from a family where this is a priority. My father, a public school principal, has been known to don work clothes and devote a month of Saturdays to help build houses for underprivileged families. Every Wednesday my mother, a schoolteacher, heads up a hot lunch program for children of low income families in her school. My older brother is a medical doctor who has volunteered in refugee camps all over the world. My parents have led neighborhood Bible studies in their home for years, so I grew up with strangers knocking on the doors at all hours.

Troy talked a lot about America's moral bankruptcy. He wrote long letters to senators and congressmen and devised elaborate petitions calling for the end of this or that, or the addition of this or that. Sometimes I didn't agree with his petitions and told him so, but he never wavered. I admired this, that no one, not even his fiancée, could change his single-mindedness.

When he asked me to marry him, to be his "partner in ministry," his "helpmeet," I said yes. He would be a famous evangelist, and I would be the wife at home who kept his clothes clean and softened all the rough edges.

His first job was as an assistant pastor in a large church in Ohio. We went, newly married and hopelessly green. After four frustrating months, we left. The senior pastor didn't understand Troy's vision. "I've tried, Sadie," Troy told me. "I've tried everything. I've tried reasoning with him, I've tried praying. Nothing works. He has no understanding of the issues, Sadie. None whatsoever."

"Things are black and white with Troy," I told my old roommate Clarice after this happened. "There's no gray with him. You have to admire someone like that."

Then he got on at a tiny church in Illinois as a youth pastor, not his first choice, but it would be a stepping stone, he said. I headed up the music program and loved it there. I could have stayed at that church forever! I had friends, young married women who came over for coffee and conversation. I played the piano, directed the choir, and small as we were, even got a youth orchestra going and put on a musical. But we didn't stay there very long, either. Troy had a conflict with the deacons' board that never did get resolved.

His serious dark side, his broodiness and mystery took on romantic proportions in my imagination. I would equate it with

Christ chasing the money changers out of the temple, or those Old Testament prophets wandering the countryside pronouncing judgments. I told Troy he was born about three thousand years too late, and that he needed to be walking around in animal skins. We both laughed at this.

I sometimes blame myself for not being there for him. I was sick with my first pregnancy, too sick to notice the problems Troy was having at church. I ended up losing our first child, a son, born two months premature with an undeveloped nonfunctioning heart. I named him Robin and held him to me after he was born, tracing my fingers around his face, memorizing it. Troy never held him, never saw him, never wanted to see him, and came into my room only after the nurse had taken my baby away. As soon as I was well, we packed up to move.

Knowing Troy's background has helped me to understand his darkness. He was an only child who grew up with a quiet father who largely ignored him and a grandmother who incessantly criticized him. Nothing he ever did met her approval. For any infraction, she marched him down to the basement and spanked him with a wooden paddle until he screamed. If he didn't cry, she'd keep spanking until he did. Then spank him more for crying. (I don't think so much spanking is good; maybe a little, but not the amount Troy would like. I have watched him beat Gavin with the back of a hairbrush on his bare bottom until the brush broke right in half, and I haven't seen that it's done much good.)

Troy's mother left the family when Troy was Gavin's age to join some cult group in California. She didn't come to his graduation from seminary. She didn't come to the wedding. Occasionally Troy gets a card. I have never met her. I grew up in a normal Christian home with public schoolteacher parents and one older brother, and to have a hippie mother was exciting to me, in a perverse sort of way.

When Troy used to tell me about his family he would blink back tears and cling to me, as if hanging on for life. He would tell me that he had never met anyone like me before, someone so accepting, so calm. I would be his shelter, the calm in his stormy life. I would be the rock he could cling to, the box he could hide inside of.

We moved into a small apartment near my parents and Troy tried various jobs. For a while he sold insurance, but he never made any money in that, despite all the promises by the company. The people in church dreaded to see him coming, I think, and finally the pastor had to have a talk with him about trying to sell insurance in the church foyer to unsuspecting visitors. To supplement the income he was not making, he got a second job working midnight to seven at a grocery store unloading pallets from the incoming trucks. He was let go after two weeks for shoving his boss during an argument. "I'm under a lot of stress," he told me. "I didn't mean it. I tried to tell him that, but he just wouldn't listen." The private music lessons I gave kept us afloat.

I was pregnant again and prayed that God would lead us to a good job, one that Troy would enjoy. I also prayed for a healthy baby. Every day I prayed for a healthy baby. Through an advertisement in a national newspaper, Troy heard about a sales job at SmartSystems; "a little computer company with a big edge" is how they advertised themselves. It was located in the coastal town of Coffins Reach, Maine, a place neither of us had ever heard of, a state neither of us had ever been to. This would be a chance to start over where no one knew us. We could be a normal Christian couple. How I longed for that!

The first night in our new house, this house, he knelt in front of me on the couch and took my hands in his and pressed them against his face.

"There's something I need to tell you, Sadie. Something I've been wanting to tell you for a while now, but I have been so afraid you'd be disappointed." He paused and looked down at our entwined fingers. "I know how much you wanted to be a pastor's wife, how much that meant to you, but I've sort of come to the conclusion that I'm not cut out for the ministry. The thing is, I think I'm going to like my new job. I think I can do well in it. I'm going to really try. I've learned a lot from my mistakes, and I want to make a clean go of it here, give you a house, a place to raise our baby. Our children." He put his hands on my belly. "I want a big family, Sadie. When I grew up there was just me. I never had a mother. Not really. I want us to have a dozen children. I want you to forgive me for all the stupid things I've ever done in my life. I need help controlling my anger. I know I do. I need you to help me. You don't know how much I need you."

He helped me up then, both of us laughing at how awkward and big I was, and we walked out of the house, down the street, and onto the beach.

He had knelt down, picked up a shell, handed it to me as a promise. Of course, I will help you. How could I not? This was my husband. And I had stood before God and our friends and family and pledged my faithfulness to him. For as long as we both shall live.

Chapter Four

The phone was ringing. I placed the shell back inside the shattered box, quickly picked up Simon's baby carrier by the plastic handle, shooed Gavin down the rickety stairs in front of me, and raced to the bedroom.

It was Phyllis Carter with an update for the prayer chain.

"Wait a minute," I said. "I've just got to find a pen." I scrabbled in Troy's end table. "Gavin," I whispered, "go downstairs and turn on the TV for a minute. Mommy'll be right there."

He slapped Simon on his way out and Simon let out a yell. "Gavin, why'd you do that?" I snapped. I picked Simon up. "Just a minute," I kept saying into the phone. "Gavin, what do you have in your hands?" He was clicking something against his thumb. When I saw that it was a reed for my oboe I said, "Gavin, give that to Mommy!" But he was already down the stairs. "Just a minute," I said into the phone again.

The drawer in Troy's bedside table was a maze of socks, paper stubs, a pair of old sunglasses, pens, and about a million dust bunnies. I found a pen and an old Visa receipt. The pen didn't work. I shook it, clicked it, tried it again, then threw it back in and picked up a stub of a pencil.

"Okay, I'm ready. Sorry. What is it? Did they find her? Oh, I hope she's all right."

"Oh no, I wish it were something like that. No, the request is to keep praying that they will find her, of course, and then also, to pray for the parents, Greg and Judith Buckley. They are really taking it hard, and Greg's parents are concerned."

I wrote as best I could, thick heavy letters with bits of lead embedding themselves into the flimsy Visa slip. I hoped this wasn't something Troy needed.

Down in the kitchen I remembered where the prayer list was, made the phone call, read off the request; and this time, I remembered to pray. Just as I was saying amen, the kitchen screen door slammed. The twins threw their lunch boxes on the table.

"What are you doing home this time of day?" I asked.

"No school this afternoon," PJ said.

"What do you mean no school this afternoon?"

"No school," Tabby said.

"Teacher's meeting," PJ said.

"Teacher's meeting; what teacher's meeting?"

Mary Beth walked in holding the hand of a small dark-haired girl.

"Mommy, you forgot. You *forgot*. And all the kids laughed at me. I was the only one who brought a lunch box. Everyone laughed at me. Even Mrs. Barry."

Gavin had scooted under the table and was warily regarding the strange girl.

"Mom-EEEEE, I brought you a note. You didn't even read it, and everyone laughed at me."

"No, they didn't." The dark-haired girl spoke for the first time and her voice startled me. It was husky and boyish. "Mrs. Barry didn't laugh."

Mary Beth turned to her. "Yes, she did. You weren't even there, Emma. Right away, she said what did I need my lunch box today for because we didn't have any school in the afternoon. And so I was the only one. The only one, Emma."

"Yeah, but she didn't laugh."

"You weren't *there*, Emma."

"Aren't you going to introduce me to your new friend?" I said.

"Mommy, you weren't even listening. This is Emma."

"Hi, Emma."

"Mommy, don't you remember?" said Mary Beth. "Daddy SAID she could come here. Daddy said you could baby-sit her. Can't you even remember one thing?" She was practically in tears.

"Mary Beth, no, I don't remember. I'm sorry. I don't remember." Simon was balanced on my hip as I scrabbled through the pile of papers on the counter. "I don't remember a note. There's no note here."

The twins leaned against the refrigerator, their arms slung around each other's shoulders, and giggled. I could barely tell them apart today. They were perfect rhymes of each other in their matching outfits. Putting Mary Beth's old clothes into their drawers was fruitless, I realized. They would only dress identically.

"Could we have lunch?" asked the twin on the right.

"Kraft dinner," said the twin on the left.

"We want Kraft dinner," said the other one.

"You have the lunches in your lunch boxes," I said.

"We can't eat those," said left twin.

"That's school food."

"We want home food."

"Your lunch box lunches are fine," I said.

"We can't eat school food at home."

"It's not allowed."

My stomach was hurting. "Would all of you like Kraft dinner, then? Should I make Kraft dinner? Is that what I should do? Throw out your lunches and make Kraft dinner?"

A chorus of yays.

I turned away from them. "Fine. I'll make two boxes. I'll call you when it's ready."

The four girls exited, but on the way out I heard Emma whisper, "Your mommy's grouchy."

Chapter Five

E mma's father showed up in my kitchen around five, and when I saw him standing there in front of me I dropped my wooden spoon on the counter, and it clunked onto the floor. I retrieved it and put it in the sink.

"I didn't mean to startle you. I'm Emma's father."

"Oh!"

"Your son let me in."

"Oh."

"I'm terribly sorry. That was unmannerly of me to just barge in like this."

"It's okay."

"No, it's not. And I, of all people, should know better. I'm sorry."

"There's no need, really."

I'd been grating four kinds of cheese into a Pyrex measuring cup for macaroni and cheese casserole while I studied the nutrition pyramid Troy had magnetized to the fridge some months ago. I tried my best most of the time to make well-rounded meals—something from each food group—but there were days when Simon was fitful, and of course, I had to keep a constant eye on Gavin.

So when Emma's father came, I was up to my elbows in cheese. Cheese was on the counter, my shirt, and I'm sure in my hair. I had put Simon's baby seat on the counter so when he fussed I could hand him hunks of cheese to keep him quiet. His little face was masked in smears of orange.

"I hope she wasn't any trouble," Emma's father said. "I really appreciate your offering. That was so nice."

I wiped my cheesy hands on a nearby dishrag, finger-combed my hair away from my face, and swallowed, conscious of my appearance: big, baggy, baby-stained T-shirt, cheesy hair. "It's no problem," I said. "What's one more?" I put my hand to my mouth. "Oh, I didn't mean it like that. They played outside all afternoon. The only time I saw them was when they came in for more cookies and drinks."

"That's good. Emma can be obstinate at times." He was a small man, like his daughter, slight of build with shiny dark hair.

"She was good."

"It was so nice of you and your husband to offer. Being in a new community and a new church is difficult."

"You're new?"

"Your husband didn't tell you?"

"Not about being new, no."

"We just moved here from Arizona. I'm Ham Franklin."

"Ham?"

He grinned. "As in radio. Or Virginia. Actually it's short for Hamilton. We just moved here. Emma and I. My wife, Emma's mother, passed away a little over a year ago."

"Oh, I'm sorry to hear that." There was a silence. "Is it quite different here from Arizona?"

He smiled. "Oh yes, quite different."

He told me he was a police officer. He had been on the city police force in Phoenix, but when his wife died, he decided that he and his daughter needed a complete change. Through an acquaintance in the department, he applied for a job with the Maine state police, but it was harder than he thought; fitting in here, getting Emma settled in school, finding a church. I looked at him, trying hard to imagine him meeting up with bad guys in alleys. He was about my height, but I probably outweighed him by fifty pounds.

"I have a regular sitter, a woman on our street who works mornings and doesn't get home until two. It usually works out perfectly, but with this meeting I didn't know what I was going to do. Last Sunday when your husband so kindly offered I just about got down on my knees in gratitude. Your husband was so friendly, just such a nice person."

"He's a real gem." I was wiping the counter back and forth, back and forth, sweeping cheese crumbs into the sink.

He peered at me and it made me feel all at once nervous. "The girls are out back," I said to the sink. "In the playhouse. Troy built it for the children. He's very good with his hands. With building things. He's good at that. He just didn't get around to finishing the roof yet. That's why it's only half on. He'll get to it, though. This summer."

When he left, I wiped cheese from Simon's face with the dishrag, cleaned his nose, and tied a clean bib on him. Then I threw both dishrag and Simon's old bib on the floor next to the washing machine, which is in the back hall beside the kitchen. I dumped the sauce on the macaroni, stirred it, sprinkled bread crumbs across the top, and stuck it in the oven. A green vegetable. According to the nutritional pyramid, I needed a green vegetable. I grabbed a can of green beans from the cupboard. That and some sliced tomatoes. For looks mainly. None of my family would eat sliced tomatoes, but Troy would appreciate that I tried. Meat! What was I thinking? I removed a package of hotdogs from the freezer and threw it into the microwave. Simon was beginning his hunger whimpers now.

"Shh, shh, Simon, Mommy's almost done. And it's almost suppertime for you, too, isn't it?"

"I didn't see them." Emma's father was back.

"Did you look in the playhouse?"

"I looked everywhere."

"Behind the garage?"

He nodded.

I called up the stairs. "PJ, Tabby, can you come for just a minute and look after Simon." I could hear myself breathing.

"Could they be in the field?" he offered.

"Mary Beth isn't allowed in the field. That's one of the rules. PJ, Tabby, I need you *now.*" I bent down and spoke to Gavin under the table. "You be good to your brother while I'm gone. I want no hitting or throwing things. None. PJ and Tabby are in charge."

"Why do they always have to be the boss?"

"Because they're older. I don't need you arguing with me now, Gavin. You be good, hear?" I sat a crying Simon in his playpen.

Emma's father and I walked the length and breadth of the backyard, calling, searching, but they weren't in the backyard. They weren't in the field. They weren't in the playhouse. They weren't on the street. I could hear Simon's hunger cry in the kitchen.

"My baby is crying," I said. "I need to feed him."

"You go back. I'll go door to door. It would also help to have the phone numbers of some of Mary Beth's friends. Maybe a neighbor has seen those two."

"I'll get that."

In the kitchen, the twins were stuffing pieces of cheese into Simon's open wailing mouth. I picked him up.

"What are we having?" asked the twins.

"Macaroni and cheese and hotdogs."

"Goody."

I took Simon into the living room, sat down on the rocking chair, and began to nurse him. My breath was coming out too fast, as if my lungs were not able to draw in enough air, as if Simon were sucking the oxygen right out of me along with milk. It occurred to me suddenly that I had no idea where Gavin was.

"PJ, Tabby, is Gavin in there?" I called.

A grunt from the kitchen.

"Be good, 'kay, Gavin? Don't get into anything."

He grunted again.

"Mommy, he's bugging us."

"PJ, Tabby, I'm feeding Simon now. Can you guys just try to get along?"

"GAVIN!" I heard shrieking.

"Gavin! Come here! Right now!" I called.

He goose-stepped his way into the living room and flipped the TV on and sat down in front of it. Simon nursed on. And I prayed. Had they found Ally? Not according to the prayer chain. I imagined that yesterday, just about this time, this same scenario was being played out in her world, in her neighborhood, in her home. I clutched at Simon's sleeper with my fingers. I forced myself to continue to breathe.

A little while later I heard voices and the screen door slamming. Ham and Mary Beth and Emma. And Troy.

"We found them," Troy called into the living room.

"Where were they?"

"My workshop. Inside." I couldn't read his voice.

"Oh. Your workshop."

Troy towered in the doorway. "Where were you when the girls were out there? There are tools out there, Sadie. Power tools."

"I didn't know they were there. I was taking care of Simon. And Gavin. Making supper. I just thought they were playing. In the playhouse. I'm sorry."

"You need to be more aware of your surroundings, Sadie." He left me and went back into the kitchen.

"It was fun in there." I could hear Emma's husky boy-voice and her father's low murmur.

"How many times," I heard Troy say, "have I told you that my workshop is off limits? You deliberately disobeyed my orders."

"But Emma wanted to see inside," Mary Beth said.

"And how did you get inside?"

"I know where the key is. Emma wanted me to."

"Emma," I could hear Ham say, "you shouldn't have talked Mary Beth into doing something she wasn't allowed to."

"No," said Troy. "I hold my daughter 100 percent responsible. She knows the rules in this house. She deliberately disobeyed and she is the one who will face the consequences."

Mary Beth started to cry. I continued to nurse Simon. She was ordered to her room, and Emma went with her. My stomach started to hurt.

Then I heard murmurmings, whisperings of the two men. "All of what's happened," I heard Ham quietly say, "has everyone on edge. It's understandable. When I came for Emma, Sadie really had her hands full. No harm done."

"That's no excuse. I apologize for my wife."

Ham and Emma stayed for supper, and I was glad.

Chapter Six

Troy wasn't like this when we first moved here. He was gentle and helpful and made all the meals for months when I was pregnant and sick with Mary Beth. Because of my first baby, I was monitored, sonogrammed, palpated, examined, and questioned almost weekly. Despite the awful morning sickness, everything pointed to a healthy baby. Troy would try to invent meals that I could keep down. He would add extra egg noodles to cans of chicken noodle soup, or hamburger to cream of mushroom soup and then ladle it onto slices of whole wheat toast. He would spread peanut butter thinly onto plain crackers for dessert.

Mary Beth was born full term, healthy but scrawny with a full head of hair and an enormous appetite. I wanted to name her Hannah, after the Old Testament woman, but we ended up naming her Mary Beth after a favorite great-aunt of Troy's.

"Aunt Mary Beth was the only kind person of all of my relatives," he told me.

"Mary Beth she shall be then," I said.

My mother took a week off school and came and stayed with us. She did the laundry, helped Troy prepare the meals, and generally kept things running smoothly. After supper I'd go to bed, and Troy and my mother would sit at the kitchen table drinking coffee. I would wake throughout the evening and hear their soft murmurs of conversation, the coffee mugs clunking, the occasional laugh. I've always wondered what they could find to talk about so late into the night.

I played the piano for my baby every day hoping to instill in her the same love of music that I have. She would sit in her plastic seat and wave her arms and legs in time, and my mother and Troy would comment that she was either going to be a dancer or the next conductor of the philharmonic.

My world was complete. I had a wonderful baby daughter, a husband who had matured from a volatile, idealistic wannabe minister to a salesman with a growing number of clients who respected him.

If there was anything that made me unhappy that first year, it was that Troy was on the road a lot and I was lonely. We weren't well established in a church yet, so we didn't have a lot of support there. Mary Beth, however, was a happy baby who slept through the night at six weeks. When she was five months old, I was pregnant again and so sick that most days I could not rise up off my bed. My mother came and stayed with me for two months in the summer when the twins were born.

She and Troy did not sit up and talk like they had the year before. Troy seemed distant toward her, leaving the room when she would walk in and excusing himself from the supper table as soon as possible to retreat to his workshop. He seemed edgy around her and despite the help she was to me, I was glad when she left. I was tired of the looks, the half looks, the snide comments on both sides. Just the two of them in the same room was enough to give me a stomachache.

I thought that once she left, we would settle back into the same comfortable routine. But we didn't. I was so busy and so tired that there were days, literally whole days, when I did not find the time to comb my hair.

I barely noticed it at first, so caught up was I in diapers and feedings and the antics of a one-year-old, plus infant twins, but Troy was changing. He would talk about that idiot of a customer who'd messed up the Augusta order beyond salvation, that moron in a blue suit, that nitwit in high heels. I would laugh with him when he described these people to me: the buffoon in the frilly blouse who didn't even know how to turn on her computer, the jerk with the crooked toupee who cheated him out of his commission, the imbecile with the white socks and black loafers. I would laugh and laugh, but there was something troubling about it, too.

Chapter Seven

When after three more days Ally had still not been found, Troy invited our pastor and his wife, the other deacons and their wives, plus Ham to our house for an evening of intercessory prayer. It's not that prayer hadn't been offered for her already; I knew that pockets of pray-ers of all faiths and concerns had assembled themselves in churches, in homes, on the school grounds all over Coffins Reach.

The evening before, Ally's parents had made an impassioned plea on the six o'clock news. The face of Ally's mother stayed with me far into the night. Tall, graceful Judith Buckley looked older than I had imagined her to be. She spoke without the Maine accent that I had come to know so well. I watched her hands fluttering in her lap as she faced the camera, her voice quavering.

"Please, if you know where my daughter is, please, please let her come home…"

I pressed Simon closer to me and checked off in my mind where my children were. The twins were in their room, Mary Beth was whining over her homework in the kitchen, and Gavin was under the piano bench cutting up old magazines with scissors.

"We're going to do something," Troy said, leaning forward on his easy chair and placing his palms on his knees. "We're going to pray."

"Yes, we should pray," I said, still looking at the face of Judith on the screen.

"I mean in a meeting, a specifically scheduled prayer meeting."

He rose. "I'm going to make a few calls. Maybe tomorrow night. Here at the house."

"At our house?" I looked around at the clutter.

"Praying for the safe return of a small child is far more important than a clean house."

He was right, of course.

I wasn't able to attend most of the prayer meeting, but from my perch on the top of the stairs where I cuddled Simon, I listened. When I heard someone pray, I prayed in my heart. Please let them find Ally. Please keep my children safe. Please keep us all safe. Tears were tracking down my cheeks. We need to be safe. Please. Please. Please, God.

"MOMMY." Mary Beth had walked up behind me carrying a school book.

I wiped the tears away from my cheeks. "Shh, Mary Beth, they're praying downstairs. Keep your voice down."

"I can't DO this one, Mommy. I can't DO it." She dropped the book on my lap. Simon squawked.

"Mary Beth, can't you see I'm busy with your brother?"

"You're always holding him. You never help me." I looked at her skinny arms and the two red marks where Troy had picked her up from the kitchen table earlier because she hadn't finished her peas.

Daddy, you're hurting me. You're hurting me!

And if you cry now, I'll really give you something to cry about.

From the top of the stairs I could hear Troy's deep voice. "God, we beseech you to bring her back to us safe and sound. You know where she is, Lord. Please calm and comfort her grieving parents."

"I help you every single night, Mary Beth." I looked at my daughter who stood before me shifting her weight from one leg to the other, staring at me through unsmiling eyes and rubbing her arm with her palm.

"Does your arm hurt much now?" I asked.

She dropped her hand as if it burned, looked as if she was going to say something, then didn't.

I rose. "Okay, Mary Beth, let me check on Gavin and the twins, and I'll come to your room and we'll work on your homework."

The twins were sitting on PJ's bed reading Archie comics, two blond heads close together.

"Don't you remember me telling you to clean up this mess?" I jostled Simon on my hip. "Don't you remember me telling you that?"

"We need cookies for tomorrow," said Tabby brightly, jumping off the bed.

"What cookies?"

"For the play," said PJ. "Our class is putting on the play for the old people and we're supposed to bring cookies."

"You want me to make cookies tonight? And you haven't lifted one finger to clean this pigsty?"

Two blond heads grinned up at me. "We always forget to bring cookies," said one.

"And now it's our turn," said the other.

"Okay. I'll make cookies…"

"Two dozen."

"That's how many we're supposed to have."

"I'll make two dozen cookies if you clean up this place. And do you have homework?"

"We already did it," said PJ.

"Let me see it," I said.

"We did it—"

"—at school."

"Clean up your room then. I want your dirty clothes in the hamper, your clean clothes and your toys put away."

In the boys' room, Gavin was dismantling the baby room monitor with one of Troy's screwdrivers.

"Gavin!"

"Mommy," he said sheepishly, part of the innards of the thing in his hand.

I closed my eyes briefly, then said quietly, more to myself, "Do you have any idea, any idea whatsoever, young man, what your father will do when he sees what you've done?" I placed Simon on his back in his crib and attempted to squish the wires into the back of the monitor. "Where did you get Daddy's good screwdriver anyway?"

"Mary Beth got it. She got the key."

With Troy's screwdriver I managed to get the back on. Then I shoved the screwdriver into Simon's top dresser drawer.

Gavin climbed under Simon's crib and was staring up at me.

"Gavin, can't you leave anything alone? Can't you be good just for one minute? For one minute of your life? I want you to get into your bed right this minute. And stay out of Simon's things. He's going to go to sleep, and I need you to be quiet. Daddy's having a prayer meeting downstairs."

"I'm a slimy worm. I'll hide in the ground."

I bent down and reached for him. My fingers held onto the cloth of his pajama tops. He winced away from me. "LEAVE ME ALONE."

"Mommy, are you ever coming?" Mary Beth said from the doorway.

"In a minute, Mary Beth."

"No!" Gavin said it louder and squeezed out of my grasp.

"Mary Beth, please go back to your room now." She left. "Gavin, if you're good tonight and don't disturb Daddy's prayer meeting, tomorrow I'll buy you a new game for your Game Boy."

"Two," he said.

"Okay, I'll buy two. If you get under your covers right now and no more arguing."

"I want the light on."

"Fine. You can have your light on." I turned on his *Star Wars* lamp, and on the way out switched the overhead light off. On the way to Mary Beth's room, I leaned for a few minutes against the wall to quell a rising nausea.

For the next half hour I quizzed Mary Beth on her spelling words. Downstairs the meeting was breaking up. I could hear voices.

"I have to go downstairs now and help Daddy," I said. "Time for bed."

"But Mommy…"

"No buts. Time for bed. I have to go down and make coffee for our guests."

In the kitchen Troy was spooning coffee in the Mr. Coffee.

"I can do that," I said. "Let me."

"It's no problem, hon." He grinned at me.

"I made some brownies for tonight. I'll get them."

"You didn't have to," he said, touching my hair. "You work too hard around here."

"I just want to do my best."

We carried the coffee and a tray of brownies into the living room and set them on the upended trunk that served as our coffee table.

Karen, one of the deacons' wives, wondered aloud if there was something we all should be doing for the Buckley family. Something tangible. Love with skin on, said Merilee, another of the wives.

"Ham," one of the deacons said. "You're probably more aware of the situation there than anyone. Do you know of anything we could be doing?"

"I'm probably not the best one to answer that. I haven't talked to the parents in a couple of days."

"Cheryl and I have been there," Pastor Ken said. "Greg's parents, Bud and Irma, are there a lot, too."

"Could we be helping out with anything? Food maybe?" asked another.

"Would that be needed?" someone else asked.

"The neighbors up on Coles Hill have been good this past week. But the generous spirit in which food is given is always appreciated. And bringing in food always provides an opportunity to visit, and it shows we care."

Betty Frost and Merilee Johnson organized a food pool. Merilee and I would be on second shift, which meant I would be making dinner in two days (provided Ally was still gone) and drive it over to the Buckleys' with Merilee. Since Merilee and Phil's second car was in the shop, and Phil had to be out of town on business, Troy volunteered our van. He said he'd see about getting a ride to work that day to save me from having to bundle up the kids and drive him to work and home again.

Later that night, after everyone had gone, I got out the flour and shortening and the chocolate chips.

"What are you doing?" Troy asked.

"Making cookies."

"We don't need cookies," he said gently.

"It's not for us. It's for PJ and Tabby's class. For a play they're in at the nursing home."

"And I suppose they just told you about it tonight? I'll go up and have a word with those two…" His voice was rising.

I put my hand on his arm. "I just remembered it this evening. All that talk about food for the Buckleys reminded me that it was my turn to make cookies. It's my fault. I forget a lot of things."

He kissed me on top of my head and walked into the living room and flicked on the television. I closed myself into the kitchen, placed a classical praise and worship tape, one of my favorites, into my portable cassette player, and stirred in the chocolate chips.

Chapter Eight

My mother called me the next day when I was spooning mashed potatoes on top of ground meat for two shepherd's pies and watching Gavin eat tomato soup at the table. I held the phone under my chin while I worked.

"We keep hearing about it on the radio," said my mother. "Are you okay? How are the children?"

"We're fine," I said, daubing cheese on the top. "The little girl that's missing now—Ally—her grandparents go to our church. So, we're doing food for the parents. I'm making a shepherd's pie to take over."

"Do they have any idea? Are the police any closer to finding that monster?"

"No one's sure that this one is related to the first one."

"But the body was found on the beach there, wasn't it? And now another little girl's missing? That's a bit too much of a coincidence, I'd say."

"Mary Beth's friend's father is a cop. But he hasn't said much."

"Will you promise to be careful?"

"We are. The bus stops right in front of our house. And the kindergarten driver comes right into our driveway."

She asked about the kids, then. They're fine. Gavin's going through a stage. Nothing more. And Simon is a bit under the weather, but with all the rain we've had it's no wonder. And Troy. He's fine, having a few little problems at work now. Nothing he can't handle. Things are looking up, in fact. You heard about the takeover? And spring's coming. That's always cause for celebration on the Maine coast. We're fine, Mother, just fine. Spring is coming to Maine, and it won't be any time at all before we're all taking picnics on the beach and watching the boats. We love to do that, you know. Crocuses are finished and the daffodils are up and blooming, and two little girls have disappeared, one was found dead, and everything is perfect and fine in this little life of mine.

When I hung up I washed my hands in the sink and thought about my mother. Good people, my parents. If they knew. If they had any idea. Everything so perfect and fine…

Merilee phoned. Would I mind terribly picking up the rolls and her dessert? She was sorry but she wasn't going to be able to make it over with me. She had two sick kids and a sick husband at home, and she was feeling none too well herself. The stomach flu. Horrible diarrhea. Had anyone in my family caught it? It was going around. So many of the kids at the Christian school were down with it, they were thinking of closing for a day or two. She was too sick to make anything new, but she had buns and a zucchini loaf in her freezer, and she'd get them out and defrost them. I told her it would be no problem and that no one in my family was sick.

"But your kids go to public school, right?"

"Except for Gavin," I said.

When I hung up I realized that I needed to wake Simon from his nap. I need to nurse him about three quarters of an hour before we go out in the car, otherwise he gets car sick.

While the shepherd's pies were in the oven, I nursed a sleepy, disinterested Simon, knowing full well that on the trip over to the Buckleys' he would be hungry. Never fails.

A sudden wave of nausea forced me to close my eyes and lean my head against the back of the chair. It can't be. It's just nerves, the missing girl, the stress of Troy's work problems. Maybe it's that flu that Merilee was talking about. But I knew better. I'd been feeling this nausea for weeks prior to Ally's disappearance, and weeks prior to the death of the other girl. And I know well the nausea that accompanies my pregnancies. I should. I've been pregnant seven times. Four live births, two miscarriages between Gavin and Simon, and of course Robin. The last time I was in for a checkup, my obstetrician recommended getting my tubes tied. She said I am at risk for more miscarriages and more problems if I get pregnant again. Did I want any more children? It was my decision, she said, my choice. I had looked down at my goosefleshed hands on the white examining sheet. I couldn't tell her that Troy would never hear of something like that.

The nausea passed, and I continued nursing Simon.

I wasn't pregnant. I couldn't be, because by now I'd be throwing up. That's what happens to me. And that wasn't happening. Everything so perfect and fine in this little life of mine.

Forty-five minutes later, after Gavin was picked up for kindergarten, I took the shepherd's pies from the oven, placed one on top of the stove and wrapped the other one in layers of newspapers (being careful that I didn't wrap it in any articles about Ally or the other girl). I strapped Simon in his car seat, covered the front of him with a towel in case he got sick, placed the boxed casserole on the floor of the front seat of the van and drove to Merilee's. It wasn't until I had her plastic grocery bag full of still-frozen rolls and zucchini loaf leaning precariously on the passenger seat, that I realized I would be going to the Buckley home all by myself. My stomach started to flutter. Merilee is outgoing and knows all the right things to say. What was I possibly going to say to this Judith person who was so much older and elegant? Even her name sounded elegant. Rich people are named Judith and Meredith and Simone. Not ordinary names like Sadie and Barbara. What possible comfort could I offer? I turned the van into the road leading up to Coles Hill. The homes up here are high above the town, with just about every house offering an uninterrupted view of the sea.

When I finally found the address and drove down the driveway to her house, my T-shirt was damp with sweat and sticking to my back. Simon was asleep, his head lolling to the side, mouth open, but thankfully not sick. I parked in front of a two-car garage and rang the doorbell. Chimes sounded from the inside. I waited. Maybe no one was home. If I was lucky, everyone would be out, and I could scribble a brief note about how sorry I was to have missed them, and leave the box of food right here on the steps.

But in a few minutes the door was answered by Judith herself, with her neatly cut blond hair, straight around her head like a Dutchboy's. She wore camel-colored slacks and a matching sweater.

"Yes?" she said quietly. Her eyes were red.

"I'm Sadie Thornton and I've brought some supper for you. Plus some rolls and a zucchini loaf. I think our pastor phoned you, at least I hope he did. To tell you I was coming. I also brought some cookies. Left over from my daughters' school." I bit my lip, wishing I could take back the last sentence.

"Would you like to come in?" Her voice was barely above a whisper.

"Oh no, I don't want to disturb you."

"You wouldn't disturb me. I would love the company."

"My baby's sleeping in the car." I was backing away from her.

"Why don't you get your baby?"

"Oh, I don't know."

"Please. I'm all alone right now. I find it so hard to be alone."

"Are you sure?"

"Perfectly."

"Well, okay then, I'll go get Simon."

"Simon! What a lovely name."

When I returned holding the handle of his plastic baby seat, the diaper bag slung over my shoulder, she said, "What did you say your name was?"

"Sadie. And you're Judith?"

"Yes, I'm Judith. Greg's at the police station right now. I didn't want to go. Not again."

"You have a beautiful home." The Buckley house was a sprawl-ing dark wood ranch house with a deck that wrapped around at least the three sides I could see. She placed the cardboard box on the kitchen counter without opening it, the rolls and loaf and plas-tic bag of cookies on top. I should have made something more exotic: steaks, or baked fish, lobster chowder. Things I never make. Troy hates seafood. We live on the coast and the only kind of fish Troy will eat is fish sticks. Simon was whimpering in his sleep, mov-ing his lips, and I rocked the baby seat. She motioned to a peach-colored sofa in a spacious living room that overlooked the town. But I stood for a moment and looked out the bay window. In the dis-tance the sea was a pale blue line on the horizon, barely distin-guishable from the sky.

If this room were mine, I would have a dark mahogany grand piano right over there by the French doors. Right next to it would be one of those old fashioned wooden music stands, and next to that, a stand for my oboe. On the wall over there would be wooden bookshelves for my music.

Judith walked to the window and stood for several minutes looking out, facing away from me. The house was quiet, but more than that, it was stilled. I heard no electrical hum. I heard no clocks. It was as if the heartbeat had stopped and was now an empty shell, a corpse.

"You have a lovely view," I said. "The ocean is beautiful."

"I don't like the sea." She hugged her arms around herself. "I stand here and look out, and I think, what a cruel God who made something so violent, so uncontrolled."

"The sea?"

She turned to me. "No, a man who takes children." She paused and turned away from me again. "I stand here and look out and I think, somewhere out there is my daughter. I keep thinking that if I look hard enough, I'll see her. If I stand here long enough, I'll find her. All it takes is my concentration."

I sat down on the sofa and lifted Simon out of his carrier and played with the buttons on his shirt. "People are still looking. Everyone's concerned. You should know that…"

After several minutes she came over and sat across from me. "Would you care for something to drink?" On the coffee table was a bottle of wine and a tall stem glass. "I'm drinking wine. Would you care for a glass?"

"Wine? Oh, um, no thanks. No. I'm nursing my baby."

"Wine's supposed to be good for nursing mothers. No one's told you that?"

"Oh, I didn't know that. I don't drink anything like that in any case. No." I stopped. "I'm sorry. I didn't mean it to sound like that."

She rose. "Well, I could make coffee. Maybe that would be a good thing. Maybe I should. You'll drink coffee?"

"Coffee would be nice," I said. "But don't go to any trouble."

"It's no trouble."

From the living room I could hear coffee beans being ground, and soon I could smell them. I looked at the paintings on the wall, peaceful scenes of grain fields and barns, a few cows, some horses. I found myself drawn to them.

When she returned I said, "I like your pictures. They remind me of home."

"Where's home for you?"

"Indiana."

She looked at me sadly. "You're a long way from home. Both of us are. I grew up in Saskatchewan. That's in Canada."

"You miss it?"

"I miss the peacefulness of it there. The quiet. Not these storms. Not these waves."

"I miss my home, too."

"Those—" she pointed—"are of Saskatchewan. They were painted by a Canadian artist of some renown, an old friend of mine. Greg hates them. He'd prefer lighthouses and fishing boats."

Simon started to fuss and I held him to my shoulder and patted his back. "He's just getting over a cold," I said. "I thought he was coming down with something, but he seems to have gotten over it…" I bit my lip, stopped myself from talking. How could I go on about my sick child when hers was missing?

"I can hear it in his lungs. I'm a nurse." She smoothed her hair away from her face. It wasn't completely blond; I could see strands of gray throughout. "My little Ally sounded like that when she was a baby. It developed into asthma. I worry about that. She has an inhaler that she carries with her. I worry that she's lost it." She brought up an unsteady hand and touched her cheek. "I blame myself. I can blame no other. I was working late that day. We had an emergency at work and I called and left a message with the school. I'm usually right here when she's home."

"Everyone's looking for her. They'll find her."

"I don't know. I don't know if they are anymore. They don't seem very hopeful, the police. They use all the hopeful words, but I can sense something else, something they don't want to tell us."

"We've all been praying so hard about this."

"How many children do you have, Sadie?"

Her question startled me. "Five."

She bowed her head, looked down at the hands in her lap and said quietly, "You are indeed blessed. Ally is our only child. I didn't have her until I was thirty-five. We tried and tried. She is my blessed little baby. And now God has taken her away from me."

"I'm so sorry," I said. Simon was wide awake now, eyes open. He was reaching for my face, my lips, my hair clips.

"Can I hold him?" she said.

"You'd like to?"

"I would like nothing better."

"He just ate a little while ago. I'm afraid he'll spit up."

"That doesn't bother me. Why don't you give him to me and then bring the coffee things in. The coffee should be ready now.

Cream's in the fridge. Unless you take milk. That's there, too. There should be a tray on the counter."

I placed Simon in her lap, expecting him to screech. Instead, he smiled up at her.

"He seems to like you," I said.

"Babies can usually tell if you're comfortable with them or not."

"He normally doesn't respond to strangers."

"What a sweet baby you are," she said, looking down at him. "So like my blessed little Ally."

Her kitchen was large and roomy. And clean. That was the first thing I noticed about it. The cleanness of it almost hurt my eyes. Above the sink an immense window overlooked the ocean.

She called in. "What should I do with the casserole? Does it need cooking or just heating up?"

"Just heating up." I took the shepherd's pie out of the box and placed it on the stove. "It's just a shepherd's pie. It's really nothing fancy. I hope it's all right."

"I'm sure it will be fine."

I turned toward the fridge and stopped. On the door a large, childish painting was held crookedly in place with plastic fruit magnets. The entire page was taken up by a gray stone house, every stone painted meticulously and outlined in black. A hedge-lined path led to the front door, and smoke ascended in a straight line from a chimney. Along the front, bright red, oddly shaped fruit dangled from trees too green to be a part of any real world. The whole page was thickly painted in bright poster paints, and when I touched the paper it crackled. Across the bottom in green paint the artist had written her name—Ally Buckley. The painting, though childish, had a surreal quality to it. And I could picture ten-year-old Ally, tongue out the side of her mouth, concentrating on getting every leaf, every stone just right. I was about to compliment the painting, but changed my mind. In the living room Judith was talking to Simon. I could hear his gurgles of contentment.

I opened the fridge, located the cream, poured some into a little pottery pitcher on the counter, and took the tray with our coffees into the living room.

When we had settled Judith said, "Have you lived here long, Sadie?"

"Nine years."

"We've been here just a year," she said. "A little over. This was going to be our happy place in the country. Safe little community. And Greg works right here in town; he doesn't even have to commute. This was going to be a good place to raise our only daughter. A good place to start over."

"Yes." I knew what she meant.

"We came back here to be closer to Greg's parents. Greg grew up here. We met out west where Greg was working. Then when this job came up, he applied. It's nice to be closer to them. For Ally's sake. Sometimes Ally even goes to church with them…" She brushed a wisp of Simon's hair away from his forehead. He was sleeping again, his mouth working. "Did you know that my mother-in-law went back to her job today? My mother-in-law teaches tole painting to women who come to her house. They all sit out in her big solarium and paint little daisies on trivets. That's what she's doing now. There are all these groups of ladies painting flowers on wooden boxes, and Ally is still gone."

I took a sip of my coffee. I didn't know what to say to her. Because I don't spend a lot of time with adults, I never seem to be able to come up with the right adult phrases. I don't even get to the adult Sunday school class most weeks because of Gavin's tantrums. When I do go, I sit quietly beside my husband. Whenever I think of saying something, I go over the words in my head, and by the time I have them all ready, the discussion has moved on to something else. Occasionally, someone will turn to me and say, "We haven't heard from Sadie in a long time; what do you think?" That makes me more nervous than if I had thought of saying something in the first place. When that happens I usually mumble something into my lap. I felt like that now.

"What do the police say?" was what finally came out of my mouth.

"Nothing." She frowned. "They're following up on leads. They've called off the dogs."

"The dogs?"

"They use dogs to find missing people sometimes."

"Oh. I thought that was only on television." Stupid. What a stupid thing to say. I finally said, "Do you know Hamilton Franklin?"

"No, who's he?"

"He's a police officer that goes to the same church. His daughter is friends with my oldest girl. You maybe could ask for him, or something. He seems like the type that might help."

"Would you be so kind as to write his name down for me? There's a pad and pen by the phone over there."

I wrote it down for her.

"She's the only daughter I'm ever going to have. They have told us…" Her voice broke. She coughed, went on. "That the longer it goes, the less chance there is of finding her…alive."

"Everyone's praying. We even had a meeting the other night at our house. My husband organized it. He's a deacon in the church."

"That was nice of him," she said, running a finger across Simon's brow. "But I'm not so sure it will work." She looked at me. "Do you believe in prayer?"

"Prayer is the one thing we can do. It's the one thing that will work."

"Does God answer your prayers?"

"All the time. Yes."

She sighed. "I worry about her now." And then she told me about Ally's sickness, about Ally's birth, how she had to take time out of her work, and how many months of maternity leave she got at the hospital. "I wanted to stay at home with her, but I do enjoy my work so much." The whole time she talked she smoothed Simon's hair or fiddled with the snaps on his terry sleeper. "Now, tell me about your children. I can't help it. I have a thing for children."

So I did. I told her about Mary Beth's good spelling marks and the antics of my twins and Gavin's unceasing energy and about my husband who is so good with his hands and built a playhouse for the kids and these wonderful lawn chairs just by copying a picture from a magazine and how he is building brand-new kitchen cabinets.

She held Simon with one hand, and with the other drank her second cup of coffee. She told me that moving here was at first upsetting to Ally, especially since the nanny wouldn't move with them, but Ally had adjusted. Kids do, you know.

I told her that it was the same with me, that I liked it here, but sometimes felt lonely.

"Lonely." She waved her hand. "They say that if your grandfather isn't buried behind the church, you're a stranger."

I smiled. "That's how I feel sometimes. Even in church...well, especially in church where everybody is related to everybody."

"You'd think it would be easier for me, Greg being from here and all. But it's not. That makes no difference to them."

Later, at the door, I told Judith I would pray for her every single day. Then she did a surprising thing. She hugged me. Tightly. I could smell her perfume and it made me think of my mother.

"Thank you so much for coming, Sadie. I really mean it. And if you don't think I'm too forward, if you ever need a baby-sitter for Simon, would you call me? I would love to look after him. I really mean that."

"You don't know what you're offering."

"He reminds me of my Ally. So sick all the time. But just someone in need of so much special care and love. And please call me again?"

"I will. I promise I will."

Chapter Nine

It always amazes me that things can go pretty much back to
normal after a disaster has occurred. You read about earth-
quakes, tornadoes, bombings, shootings, and then a week or
so later no mention is made, not a whisper in the papers. Life, it
seems, is back to normal; the bloodstains mopped and bleached
away, the houses rebuilt, the children back to school, the backyards
cleaned up.

Ally had been gone for three weeks now and there was hardly a
word about it in the local papers anymore. My children didn't talk
about it. Troy hadn't mentioned it, nor had he offered to host
another prayer meeting. It was like the waters had filled up to cover
and smooth over that missing place.

I hadn't spoken to Judith since that day two weeks ago when I
took supper to her. I thought about her a lot, though. Every day I
thought of calling her, but somehow I never got around to it.

"I should call Judith this week. I shouldn't forget. At least to get
my casserole back," I said to Troy on the way home from church one
Sunday. The pastor had prayed for the Buckley family from the pul-
pit. He didn't pray that they would find Ally; he prayed merely that
the "Buckley family would find peace and comfort during their time
of sorrow." As if Ally were already dead.

"Judith?" he asked me.

"You know. Ally's mother."

"Why would you want to call her?"

"I took food to her that one time."

"Sadie, so many people visited her, I doubt she'd even remember who you are."

I shrugged. "We had a lot in common. We talked for a long time. She seemed lonely. Plus, she asked me to call her."

"If I were you, I'd stay out of that whole messy business."

I looked away from him and out the window. Messy business. But what if it were one of my children? Would prayer and my faith be enough? And when everybody else forgot, or called it messy business, would I still remember? And for how long?

I wanted to call her, I really did, but with each day that ended without calling her, it seemed more unlikely that I would the next. I had waited too long.

I looked down at the stack of books balanced on my lap: my Bible, Mary Beth's colorful children's Bible, plus a bunch from the church library. I squared the edges of them and thought about Ally, a little girl who painted great garish swirls of color.

"I was with Ham yesterday," Troy was saying. "The police are letting up on their search for that girl anyway."

"They're not going to look for her anymore?"

"They're thinking the parents might have had something to do with it. Both parents have been in for questioning. That was in the papers."

"But Judith would never do anything like that!"

"Judith? You're calling her Judith? You talk like you know her."

"MOMMY!"

"Mary Beth, don't *yell* so. What is it?"

"Simon spit up," she said in a tiny voice.

"Can you wipe his face, please? There's a roll of paper towels on the floor."

"They're too dirty, Mommy. They're all slimy and gross."

"We're hungry," said the twins in unison. "Can we have Kraft dinner?"

"We'll be home soon. Just wait."

"Yeah, but what're we having?"

"Pizza. Little frozen pizzas."

"That's the best we can come up with?" Troy said. "You got any cookbooks in that stack?"

I put my hand on top of the books. At the top were a couple of mysteries for Mary Beth and the twins. Underneath this was Mary Beth's Bible, and underneath that, a new hardcover novel for me, a book on time management for Christian women, plus one on losing weight. I'd read through that one carefully. Maybe all I need is to buckle down, start making lists, learn to manage my time better, watch what I eat, pray more, have devotions every morning. Under them was my own Bible and a new picture book for Gavin. He probably won't look at it, but I keep trying. I pulled the novel out of the stack and turned it over. It was the fifth in the Idaho Pioneers series, and I was anxious to get into it. There are times when I long to live in those easier, kinder days.

"That is such a waste of time," said Troy.

I looked up. "What is?"

"All those books you insist on reading."

I tucked the Idaho Pioneers back in the stack.

"If you spent as much time with your real family as you did with all those imaginary ones, we'd be a lot better off."

I bent my head down so that the sides of my hair covered my face. I usually read at night while Troy watches television. Sometimes, if the book is really good, I'll hold the pages down with saltshakers while I cut up vegetables for supper. Troy was laughing now, and I peered at him from underneath my hair. It was a mirthless laugh, a sound I hated. A sound I feared.

"Okay, that one. That one on losing weight? You *do* have my permission to read that one. That is one you *can* read. With my blessings." He was still laughing.

I looked out the window at the houses passing by, white ones with fences and gardens, green ones with vinyl siding, brick ones. I don't cry much anymore when he says these things. I used to. I have this whole other life now that he knows nothing about. I am an Idaho pioneer. I wear a long calico dress and a bonnet. A blue one with dark ribbons. I am standing beside a wagon train, looking into the distance, a contented smile on my face. If I imagine hard enough, I can be there. When I lie in my bed at night, and when I can't sleep, and when I can't even pray, these dramas work themselves out in my thinking. I am an Idaho pioneer and I have a tall, handsome husband that I am deeply in love with. We are on a wagon train west to a new life. Oh, we struggle with our problems all right, we have our hard times, but we work through them. With God at our side there's nothing we can't face. It's a place where a man loves me for me. It's a place where a man listens to me, and tells me I'm pretty just the way I am and how I don't need to lose weight, even after five babies. It's a place where no one ever lashes out at me. A place where I am safe and sheltered. A place where I am smart and important and say clever things to people. A place where I have long, serious discussions with my husband and my best friends. A place where we laugh together, cry together, read the Bible together, and pray together.

It is a place where I am good enough.

Chapter Ten

Judith Buckley called me that afternoon. I had finished putting the lunch dishes in the dishwasher and was scrubbing the kitchen counters with a mucky dishrag that probably should have been thrown into the clothes hamper three days ago, when the phone rang. I remembered Judith's clean pottery canisters lined up evenly along the back of her counter, the way they matched the tiles behind the sink. I remembered the counters, eggshell blue with tiny yellow and green daisies. I thought of the way her serving utensils hung shiny from an overhead rack, the counters free of children's books and papers and bills and old bank statements, the gritfree window ledge behind her stainless double sink. The window over my sink looked out over our backyard, but the ledge was grimy with grease and dust. Every time I scrubbed it, more paint flecked off. I would be getting down to the bare wood soon.

Troy was in the living room leaning back in his easy chair watching a baseball game, a can of ginger ale beside him. Mary Beth was at the kitchen table, telling me about a boy in school who always made fun of her; the twins were in the playhouse outside; Gavin was under the table with his Game Boy; Simon was asleep in the playpen in the kitchen; and the phone rang.

"Sadie?"

"Yes?"

"This is Judith. Judith Buckley."

"Oh, *hi.* I was going to call you." I tried to make my voice as sympathetic as possible. "I've just been so busy here, I meant to phone you. How are you?" How could I not have called her?

"Not very good. I suppose you've read the papers?"

I thought of our pastor's carefully worded prayer. "I haven't."

"Well, then you're the only one. They're crucifying us."

"That's so unfair."

"I'm sitting here shaking. Literally shaking. And I was wondering if you might be able to come over?"

"Now?" Too late I realized that my voice had risen sharply at the end.

"I'm alone here today. Greg has gone to see a lawyer. I just can't face that. I'm all alone."

For a moment I envied her. I wondered what it would be like to be alone in a house on a Sunday afternoon. "Oh, Judith, I would love to, but I can't right now. I've got all my kids and husband." I wiped my hands on the sides of my T-shirt.

There was silence. Finally she said, "I'm sorry. It was forward of me to ask. Your name was the first that came to my mind when I thought of this long afternoon ahead. That visit we had was so nice. You seem like a kindred spirit."

"I could come tomorrow."

"Tomorrow would be nice."

When I hung up, Troy, hair ruffled, Sunday shirt untucked on one side, entered the kitchen. "Who was on the phone? I'm expecting a call from Ham."

"It was Judith."

"Judith? What did she want?"

"She wanted me to come over today."

"Now?"

"Yes."

"She wanted you to just pick up and come over on a Sunday afternoon? Just like that?"

"She's all alone."

He took off his glasses and rubbed his eyes.

I took a deep breath. "She asked me to come tomorrow. So could I drive you to work so I could have the van?" I felt like crossing my fingers behind my back.

He sighed heavily and squinted and pressed his fingers to his forehead. "I wish you'd give that woman and her problems a wide berth. We've already talked about this, Sadie."

"It will just be for tomorrow."

He shook his head and snorted. "Okay, you can drive me to work. It wouldn't look right for you to go back on your promise. But I don't want this to become a habit."

"It won't, it really won't. It's not too much trouble, is it? For me to drive you?"

"Sadie, what do you expect me to say? I said it was fine, didn't I? Don't belabor the point." He was rooting through one of the counter drawers, throwing things on the counter. "Where the heck is the Tylenol? I've got the mother of all headaches."

"Upstairs. In the medicine cabinet."

He closed his eyes. "Sometimes I get so darn tired of living in such a pigsty. Look at these cabinets. I'm building these nice kitchen cabinets for you, and what happens? They're cluttered with junk."

"I was cleaning, Troy. I was trying to. Look at the counters. I was working on them." Mary Beth was bent over her spelling, loudly sucking on the sides of her hair.

"Can you at least get me some Tylenol or some Advil, Sadie? If it's not too much to ask."

"Yes. I will. I'm sorry."

I ran up the stairs and when I returned, Troy was back in his living room chair, a fresh can of Canada Dry on the arm of his La-Z-Boy. I handed him two Tylenol. "I hope this helps," I said.

I went back to the kitchen. I am an Idaho pioneer applying stove black to our stove, layering it on with careful, even strokes, back and forth, back and forth until it gleams. Later I'm going to make sourdough bread, then there's butter to churn. Outside, my husband is milking the cows. Later on, we'll hitch up the wagon and drive to church. When I ride beside my husband in the wagon, I keep my gloved hand on his knee. After church there's an ice-cream social. I have an apple pie all made and ready...

"MOMMY! You're not even listening to me!"

I turned, wet dishrag in my hand. Mary Beth was sitting at the table, tears streaking her pale cheeks. "I was talking and talking and you weren't even listening."

That night after Troy got home from the evening service, and after the kids were somewhat settled into their beds, he asked me to forgive him. When I came in from the bathroom he was sitting on the side of the bed, his elbows on his knees, his head in his hands. He looked endearing and little boyish in the red-and-green plaid boxer shorts I'd gotten him for Christmas, his hair all mussed around his ears and graying in spots.

"I'm a lousy person," he said to me as I laid stacks of clean underwear into drawers. "I don't know why you stay with me. I'm 99 percent lousy and maybe 1 percent good. If that."

"That's not true."

"It is true."

"No, you shouldn't say that."

"Sadie, look at me. Look at me, Sadie."

I turned.

"Tell me what you see."

I put my hand to my throat.

"What do you see? Be honest."

"I see you."

"And who am I? I'm a nobody. I'm barely hanging on to a job I hate. Can't even provide a big enough house for my family. Can't do anything right."

"Oh, Troy." I sat beside him, a pile of folded socks in my lap.

"I'm no good as a father, no good as a husband. I should never have laughed in the car about your weight. You're beautiful just the way you are. I don't know why I say half the stuff I do. I don't know what comes over me. It's like I can't control myself. It's not me saying those things to you. You've got to believe me when I say that it's not me."

I put my arms around him and could feel his heartbeat through my nightgown. "I believe you, Troy. I believe you."

"You're the best thing in my life right now. You're the only good thing. And…" He coughed. I held him tightly. "I don't know what I'd do if I lost you."

"You're not going to lose me."

"It's just that when I hear Judith wanting you to come over, I think that you'll start spending more time with your friends than with me, and I couldn't stand that. I couldn't stand to be second in your affections."

"I don't have any friends," I said. "Just you."

"I get so afraid…" His voice cracked. "That you'll leave me. That one of these days you'll realize what you married, and you'll take the children and get the heck out. I couldn't bear that."

"Oh, Troy, I would never do that."

"Do you promise me? Do you really promise me?" Tears glistened in the corners of his brown eyes. There was frailty there, and vulnerability.

"Troy, I promise you that I will never, *ever* leave you."

"I love you, Sadie."

Later that night, after we made love, I lay in bed for a long time turned away from him, staring at the shadowed wall.

Chapter Eleven

I'm not the kind of person people generally go to with their problems. I guess I've always been a loner, content to work on my music for long hours. Even as a child I could spend the entire day with a book. That's not to say I had *no* friends. In college, my friends were other music students, and after working through our scales and recital pieces long hours in tiny windowless practice rooms, we'd all head out for pizza and Cokes to talk about music. Piano teachers told me I had great promise. When he found out I was leaving college a year short of my degree, my oboe instructor, Professor Petersen, took me aside and told me how disappointed he was. I told him that marriage and a home and family meant more to me than a career in music. He seemed to accept that and wrote me a glowing letter of recommendation when I left.

"You play more than the notes," he told me. "You play the music. Keep in touch, Sadie. You have a gift. You have *the* gift. I expect great things from you."

I just thought of something funny. No one in our church even knows I play the piano. It's partly my fault, I guess. I don't think I've ever mentioned it to anyone. If I was quiet as a girl, I've become even quieter as an adult. I think it's because people can't see beyond my children. They don't see me; they see a quiet, chubby, tired young mother with too many children.

A few times I went to a moms and tots group at church, but one day Gavin hit a little girl over the head with a metal truck so hard that she had to have two stitches. We sopped up the blood with dish towels from the kitchen, and the mother of the little girl drove her over to emergency. Later that night, the mother called to tell me her daughter was fine now, so fine that she was running around outside without a care in the world. It wasn't my fault, she said, her voice breezy and matter-of-fact. These things happen, and she hoped I'd still come to the group. I never did. And no one from the group ever phoned to ask me why.

But now there is someone who actually wants me to come over, someone who actually called me, out of all the people she could have called, she called me on a Sunday when she was lonely.

I planned to leave for Judith's the minute Gavin was picked up for kindergarten. In the morning I did three loads of laundry, vacuumed the living room, threw all the toys into the toy box and planned supper, even writing it all down in the meal planner Troy got me for Christmas. At the table, Gavin slurped his tomato soup and growled at his tuna fish sandwich until the van driver for the Christian school came down the driveway. The driver is a large jolly man who calls Gavin "little big guy" and always waves at me through the window. I waved back today and handed Gavin his lunch box and shooed him out the door.

Twenty minutes later, I was knocking at Judith's door.

"Sadie, I'm so glad you came. Come in. And I'm glad you brought your baby."

"The fact of the matter is that I don't really have anyone to leave him with."

"The offer still holds. If you ever need a sitter I would be happy to look after him, just call me. Oh here, give him to me."

Judith was wearing a sweatshirt and baggy gray sweatpants tied up at the waist with string. I hadn't noticed before how painfully thin she was. In the living room I saw her nest of blankets on the couch, and beside it on the table, half a bottle of wine. The drapes were drawn, and the room's only light fell unwillingly from the floor lamp beside the couch. It was hot in there and uninviting. Not like the last time.

"It's the one thing I miss about pediatrics. The babies."

I was looking at the empty wine bottles beside her blankets. She followed my gaze.

She waved her hand. "You must think I'm a lush. I'm not, I can assure you. The most I ever have is a glass or two with meals every now and again. Greg collects wine, all vintages, all years. He's quite furious with me lately because I keep drinking his precious stock he's been saving for special occasions. And I say, what are you saving it for anyway? Do you think there will ever be another special occasion? Do you think we will ever have another cause for celebration?"

She sat down and I sat down next to her. Simon was gurgling in her lap.

"I meant to call you," I said. "But I get so busy with things. My kids—"

"We had to take lie detector tests. They said it was just routine." She was stroking pieces of Simon's hair between her thumb and forefinger. "You wouldn't believe that about me, would you?" She leaned toward me. Her short, straight blond hair fell in oily tendrils around her cheeks. There was a musky, humid odor about her. About the whole house. The room suddenly seemed airless, stifling, as if the house, dead since Ally left, was now rotting. I couldn't breathe. I moved away from her slightly.

"Would you like me to open a window?" I asked.

"Are you overly warm? Go ahead if you think it's warm. Simon, are you too warm? It's getting warmer these days. Spring is coming. Ally and I always enjoyed the warm weather."

I pulled the drape cords and opened the patio door wide. A spring breeze filled the room with cleanness. She hugged Simon and he grinned.

She looked into her empty wine glass. "I'm not eating very well these days."

"I could have brought something for you to eat. I meant to."

"I couldn't eat anyway. Nothing I eat stays down."

I smiled. "I know the feeling."

"I've got to get myself pulled together. I just don't know how. Bud and Irma get after me—Judith, wash your hair, take a shower, go for a walk. Greg's a wreck, too. But he's holding up a little bit better. He has less at stake than I do. He's even back to work. When this first happened, all the neighbors brought over food, and everyone was so kind. But now everybody's gone back to their jobs, and I can't even go out. I can't stand to have people look at me. I can't stand to have them talking about me, thinking things about me, saying, there's the woman whose child disappeared. There's the one. Do you see that woman over there in the cereal aisle? She's the one."

"It wasn't your fault." I sat beside her on the couch. "No one thinks it's your fault."

"Tell that to everybody who's gossiped about me in the last month." She pulled a stray thread on Simon's sleeper and he gurgled and smiled. "You need some new clothes, little man."

"It's a hand-me-down. It was new for the twins. He has another one just like it at home."

For some reason she found that enormously funny and began to chuckle.

"That's what happens when you have twins." I was giggling now, too. "You get two of everything."

She stopped laughing as quickly as she began and put the back of her hand to her mouth, bit it. Then just as quickly, she and Simon were bent into my arms and she was crying. We stayed that way for a while.

"I'm sorry," I said. "This is hard. It must be so hard…"

She reached for a Kleenex from a box on the table beside her and blew her nose.

"Are you sure you don't want anything to eat?" I said. "Can I fix some lunch?"

"Lunch. People still eat lunch. At regular hours. Somehow that doesn't seem right."

"I know."

"Maybe some tea."

"I'll get it."

"Iced tea. There's some in the fridge. Greg made it before he left this morning."

The picture on the fridge was gone. I almost called out to ask her, and then I understood. No mother needs that kind of reminder every time she goes into her kitchen. I imagined her lovingly placing it between sheets of tissue paper and putting these sheets…where? In Ally's bedroom? In her own bedroom? In the attic? What do you do with a room when a child disappears? Do you change the bed linens, clean up the toys, and do the laundry? Or do you leave it the way it was, toys strewn across the floor, dirty clothes piled with clean?

I poured two iced teas into tall glasses. On the counter a plate of sandwiches was covered by plastic wrap. I uncovered them and just as quickly put the cover back on. Edges of the bread were blue with mold and the cheese gave off an odor.

I put her iced tea down beside her and took a crying Simon and sat down in the chair across from her.

"He's hungry," I said. "That's all it is. It's not you."

The wine bottle beside her was now nearly empty, and her eyes were wide and too bright. She was talking rapidly and with exaggerated gestures about Greg and how she couldn't understand why he was going back to work. "How could he possibly? He feels he has to be there. I call and call him, but he won't come home. I think it's absolutely ridiculous, and he knows it. So what if there's lots to do. I just don't understand why he has to go, how he can go. While Ally is still gone…"

I drank my tea and mostly listened. That's what I did a lot with Judith, listened. I prayed a little bit, too, that God would give me the right words to say.

"I've told him, you're the boss; why do you have to go there every day? Can't you do things from home? But the problem is, he wants to make a good impression. I suppose that's admirable, but his problem is that right now he has to lay off people. So that's why he has to be there. I should have more understanding of his point of view, for his predicament. But I just can't, you know? Now we've got lawyers and police to deal with and still no Ally. I just wish I knew what happened to her. Where *is* she?"

"I've been praying," I told her. "Every day. God's angels are watching over her." I wasn't entirely sure this was true, but since it popped into my head I thought maybe God had told me to say it.

"Angels. I wish I could believe that. I'd like to be able to believe that."

"God is watching over Ally. I know that is true."

She reached across and touched my arm. Her fingers were warm. "You're a good person, Sadie. So sincere. You have an innocent faith. But mine's been tested. I look at your life and I think you are so fortunate to be able to believe in God the way you do. I look at you and say, there's a person who has it all—wonderful family, lots of children, a husband who loves her and builds chairs out of magazines for her—"

"I'm not that fortunate," I said.

Chapter Twelve

*T*here were four phone messages from the Christian school when I got home. Something had happened to Gavin. I was sure of it! Gavin had been lying in the hospital all afternoon while I was out visiting a friend. I should have been home.

I handed Simon an arrowroot cookie and hit the speed dial for the Christian school, but by mistake I pressed the speed dial for the public school where the girls went, then had to explain myself before hanging up and getting it right. My call was transferred to the principal, who said, "Mrs. Thornton, we've had a problem with Gavin."

"What kind of a problem? What happened? Is he okay?"

"Would you and your husband be able to come in later this afternoon?"

"Is he gone? Is he missing? Is he missing, too?"

"Missing?"

"Like the little girl. You know." My stomach hurt.

"Oh no, Mrs. Thornton, it's nothing like that. What we'd like at this point is a face-to-face meeting. Can I expect the two of you here, say, around three-thirty or four today?"

"What?"

She spoke more slowly this time. "We would like to speak with both you and your husband this afternoon."

"Today? But Troy works at least until six, and the girls'll, they'll be home any minute."

There was silence. "Can you come? By yourself. And bring Gavin with you when he gets home."

"But..."

"I'd like you to come. This can't wait."

"But I don't have anyone to leave the girls with. Can you just tell me what this is about?" I felt close to tears. Simon was whimpering. I handed him another arrowroot.

"I had hoped to sit down and talk with you both before a final decision is made."

I felt as if I couldn't breathe, couldn't talk. As if there wasn't enough air around me.

"Mrs. Thornton?"

"Final decision about what?"

"About Gavin continuing as a student in Coffins Reach Christian."

There was a wet hand on the back of my neck, which began tracing its way down my spine. I was going to throw up. I swallowed several times.

"Mrs. Thornton?"

"What? What did you say?"

"There was an incident today that makes it impossible for us to allow him to continue here."

She is talking to some other mother, I thought. She has me mixed up with someone else. Simon was crying and grabbing at the snaps on his sleeper. I moved the phone into the living room, as far as the cord would allow, and sat on the floor. She was still speaking and I was still trying to make sense of her words. "We have been dealing with Gavin's increasing hostility, his tantrums and disruption as best we could. He is a lovely little boy when he wants to be, and I think a very creative child, also very intelligent, artistic. But an incident today has left us with no choice but to take him out of the school. We feel he needs special help that we aren't equipped to deal with."

"You mean for next year, right? You're saying he can't come back for first grade?"

"Mrs. Thornton, his expulsion begins immediately. At this point we must be concerned about the safety of the other students."

I held my breath, incapable of speaking.

"Mrs. Thornton?"

"I don't understand."

"Today there was an incident with a hamster. As soon as it occurred we tried to call either you or your husband, but there was no answer at either location. We were going to ask you to come and get him at once. We have kept him in the time out area until we could reach you. But Nick, our van driver, bless his heart, seems to have a special friendship with your son, and offered to spend the rest of the day with him and then take him home."

"What do you mean a hamster?"

"Gavin killed a hamster."

I said nothing.

"Okay, I'll do my best to explain what happened. It seems the kindergartners have a hamster in their class. They take turns feeding and caring for it. They named it Moses. I'm not entirely sure of all the specifics, but apparently Gavin was assigned to the group to feed Moses today, and this is when the argument between the two children broke out. And the poor hamster was in the middle of it."

"What about the other child?"

"The other child?"

"You said there was another child. So it wasn't all Gavin's fault."

"The other boy shouldn't have provoked Gavin, that is true. But Gavin was holding the hamster, and when the boy asked for the hamster back, Gavin threw it against the blackboard."

"Oh." The word was like a cry. I put my hand to my mouth, tasted bile.

Gavin throws things. He always throws things. But he doesn't mean anything by it. It's just a bad habit. Troy throws things, too. Troy throws telephones and telephone books and his briefcase and videos, all sorts of things. But he doesn't mean anything.

"The other children were very upset. We just cannot have Gavin in this school anymore."

"He didn't mean it," I said. "He gets like that sometimes. He loves his class. We're so thankful, Troy and I are, for the grounding all our kids got in the Christian school. We had all our kids in kindergarten there. Troy feels it gives them a good start. We'd have them there for all the grades, but we just can't afford it, that's the only reason. If you could just give him another chance."

"Mrs. Thornton, there have been other incidents. We've been increasingly concerned about him. We love him dearly, and his teacher, Gloria Albert, is remarkable, but he cannot continue here. The other students need attention. This is a Christian school, not a reform school. He needs special help."

"What should we do then?"

There was a long silence. "There's public school for next year, but frankly I'm not sure he's ready for that. I'd like to talk with you and your husband about options. There's a wonderful child psychologist we'd like to recommend. He's in Bangor, but well worth the drive. He's also a Christian. I've known other families that've been to him with excellent results."

"But they cost money." My voice was whiny, unfamiliar even to myself.

"Money well worth investing, I should think."

"I don't understand. I don't know what to do. What am I supposed to do?" The room was spinning. I felt faint.

Long after the phone conversation, long after the girls had come home, I was still saying, "I don't understand."

Later, I said to Gavin, "Why did you do it?"

"I wanted to see the insides," he said. And then he crawled under the piano bench with a plastic Fisher-Price person.

"I have to tell your father about this!" I yelled at him. "There's just no way around it. Do you understand? I *have* to tell your father!"

But he was lying face down under the piano bench, bonging the foot pedals with the toy. "Gavin, don't *do* that. You'll dent Mommy's piano. What's the matter with you anyway?"

I had to tell Troy, of course I had to. I couldn't hide something as major as that. I waited until we had eaten our Shake 'n Bake chicken, then I herded the children to their bedrooms. We were standing in the supper-cluttered kitchen when I told Troy that his son had been expelled from school for throwing a hamster against the blackboard.

"He didn't mean anything by it," I kept saying. "It was an accident." But I could see Troy's eyes go red.

I held Simon to me and locked us together in the downstairs bathroom. I sat on the floor and curled both of us up like a little ball and leaned against the sink. We waited there, crouched, both of us crying.

It went on and on—Troy's ragings, the high-pitched wailing of my eldest son. I did throw up, then. I sat Simon on the bath mat and I threw up into the toilet, the flushing masking the sounds above. I kept flushing and flushing.

Later, much later, I went to bed. I lay on my side facing the wall. My head was clogged and my eyes were puffy from crying and I had to breathe uncomfortably through my mouth as I lay there, a balled-up Kleenex in my hand, my hand close to my face. I thought of getting up then, just getting up and packing all of my children into the van and driving away.

I tried to mimic the steady breathing of sleep when Troy came to bed. But still he reached for me. I did not move. He has such an insatiable appetite when all I am is tired. So very, very tired. Every part of me. So tired. Please, just let me sleep. Just let me sleep.

Chapter Thirteen

The music came to me for the first time that night, a strange, haunting, hopeful thing that woke me up and made me lie on my back and listen. It was the clear sound of the oboe I heard first. Then strings, the low sound of cellos. Or was it merely the sound of the bell buoys, the whistles, the fog horns—a ship in trouble? I got out of bed carefully and went to the window. My house was quiet, my children asleep, as I stood beside the fluttering sheers, my eyes gummed with tears and sleep. No, this was music. Definitely music. It seemed to be coming from the beach. Or out on the point. There was the piano, a melody in counterpoint. The sound of a harp? For a long time I stood there and basked in the music, my nightgown fluttering around my knees.

It was not music I recognized, so I tried to memorize it, humming it inside my head, so I wouldn't wake Troy. I began picturing how it would look as notes on a sheet of music score, the instruments coming in at various points. I began playing the oboe part on an imaginary instrument; I flexed my fingers for the piano. I stood there listening, imagining, until I heard Simon's soft whimper across the hall.

Both of my sons were awake. Gavin was sitting on his bed, looking at me through wide eyes. I lifted Simon from his crib, changed his diaper, then held him on the rocking chair as I nursed him. Gavin crept out of bed and came to my lap, his thumb in his mouth. He was warm and sweaty and smelled of that musky little boy smell.

"Do you hear the music?" I whispered.

He looked up at me, his thumb in his mouth.

"Isn't it pretty?" I said.

I saw the red marks on his cheek and I stroked his damp hair. It's going to be all right, Gavin, I wanted to tell him. Daddy doesn't mean anything by it. He sometimes gets that way, and we just have to be more careful with what we say and do. "I love you very much, Gavin," I finally said, but by this time he was asleep in my arms.

I lay with my head against the back of the rocking chair, my sons in my lap, until I could no longer hear the music.

In the morning I asked Troy, "Did you hear music last night?"

There were gray bags under his eyes. "Were those kids across the way having another one of their parties? I'll speak to Ham about that today."

"No, not rock music. Classical music. Well, not classical really, Celtic sounding. Soft. Like a hymn. Strings. I recognized a harp, an oboe."

"You were dreaming."

"Maybe."

But I remembered part of the melody line and kept humming it to myself so I wouldn't forget it. A few times I looked at my piano, but I didn't go to it. I can't explain it, but I haven't played the piano since Gavin was an infant. I remember the day I quit. Gavin was a baby and I was so caught up in my melodies that I hadn't heard him crying. Troy had come up behind me, taken my hands in his and lifted them off the keys. "Gavin is crying," he said. "You're a mother now, not a musician. You'd do well to remember that."

We keep the piano for the children, now. I would like my children to take lessons, but none of them have shown much interest.

Underneath a pile of papers in the kitchen I found an old school notebook of Mary Beth's with more than half the pages blank. I quickly drew in staffs and roughed out the notes that I remembered. I used to be able to do that. People who don't know any better call it perfect pitch, but it's not. And it's not something magical or even all that difficult. What I do is find middle C in my head, then work from there. It took me a while, but I roughed out two lines of melody.

I closed Mary Beth's notebook and put it inside the piano bench underneath some old music books.

In the evening Troy told me he would not spend one penny on counseling for Gavin. "We are not driving to Bangor every week to throw money at a shrink when all he needs is more discipline."

"But this is a *Christian* psychologist," I said. "Someone who could help us."

"Gavin's not the one with the problem. That's not the way I see it. It's his mother who lets him run freely through this house with no discipline."

"But what if he has ADD or ADC or something? I saw a television program about that once. It could be something that's fixable. Why can't we even try? They have these medications now—"

"Nobody these days wants to call a spade a spade. They don't want to call it lack of discipline, so they make up fancy names for it, give it fancy initials. And suddenly it's some sort of fancy disease."

We never did see the school principal. The next day Nick stopped by with the stuff from Gavin's desk. When Gavin saw him at the door, he started racing around the living room making car noises, until I had to tell him to slow down or he'd get dizzy.

"He sure has the energy, don't he? Hey, little big guy, you want to hear a joke?"

For twenty minutes, Nick and Gavin sat on the couch laughing at knock-knock jokes. I watched them from the kitchen while I got supper on.

Chapter Fourteen

Emma and Ham have been around the house a lot lately, and that both surprises and pleases me. Just about every other day Troy tells me they had lunch, or that Ham dropped by at work and the two of them went for coffee. I don't fully understand the friendship between them, but I'm happy about it. There's a part of me that believes this is the beginning of God answering my prayers that Troy would have a close male friend. He's respected enough in church, but no one goes out of their way to invite us over. But that could be me and not Troy, anyway.

Sometimes in the novels I read, the female character has a bosom buddy she talks to for long hours. They sit with their legs over the side while the wagon train rambles through the sagebrush. They talk about husbands and children and share secrets and problems and recipes. They congratulate each other on successes, they listen to each other's tears. When one has a problem, the other is always there to listen and to pray with. I don't have anyone like that. And I have so many secrets. I have a marriage full of secrets I've never shared with anyone.

Ham is coming and bringing supper tonight, and so I was kneading dough for homemade rolls when Judith called to tell me Ally had been seen in a van in Ellsworth with a man wearing a blue suit.

"Really! That's great news! Did they find her? Did they actually find her?"

"Not yet, but it's close. Someone actually saw her. And that's important. That gives the police something to go on."

"When did they see her?"

"A couple days after she disappeared, actually. I guess someone saw *Crimestoppers* and remembered something."

When she hung up I prayed while I shaped the rolls for supper. The rolls were perfect. Troy would be pleased, I was sure. Good news all around.

Ham, Emma, and Troy walked in together that evening, Ham carrying a Dutch oven full of his spicy Arizona stew, which I placed on the stove and turned the burner on low.

"I heard someone saw Ally," I said. "Is that true?"

"Where did you hear that?" asked Troy.

"Judith called me."

Troy opened the fridge and grabbed two Cokes. "And you believe what she says?" He handed one to Ham.

"She sounded pretty excited. Is it true?" I looked at Ham.

"Actually we're following that lead," said Ham. "It's the first real break we've had."

"So someone actually saw her?"

Ham opened his Coke. "Thought they saw her. Big difference. We have a hotline set up, an eight hundred number. We've had it up for a month now and we've been getting hundreds of calls. It's been on *Crimestoppers* twice. The problem is that in a case like this, all the crazies come out of the woodwork and start admitting to things they never did."

"You mean people actually phone in and say they kidnapped someone when they really didn't?"

"Happens all the time. You wouldn't believe."

"But this one? You're more confident about this one?" I asked.

"So far, yes."

"Judith will be so happy."

Troy said, "My wife's got this idea she's Judith's new best friend."

I stirred the stew with a wooden spoon.

"Judith could probably use a friend now," said Ham.

"When's supper?" asked the twins from the doorway.

"Yeah, when's supper?" asked Mary Beth and Emma.

"Soon," I said. "When the rolls are done. Go wash up."

Ham's eyes had a way of wrinkling at the corners. "I hope you guys like this. Emma and I call it spicy supreme."

"Smells good," said Troy. "Those rolls look wonderful, Sadie." He hugged me from behind.

Emma thought having a separate dish for each food item was quite charming, and insisted on it for herself. I complied. Even Mary Beth, after looking at me and then warily at her father, decided that she, too, wanted little bowls for all her food.

During supper I watched them place the potatoes from the stew into one little bowl and the carrots into another and the chunks of meat into yet another. I saw Troy eye them. He said nothing.

Meanwhile Ham was sopping up the broth with the rolls and exclaiming over them.

"My wife's the best bread baker in all of Coffins Reach," Troy said.

Ham looked at me and raised his roll in a toast. "You actually made these? From scratch?"

"She actually did."

"I feel quite bakerlike when I can manage those brown and serve ones," Ham said.

Then PJ asked Emma what it was like to have a cactus in her yard.

"Just normal," said Emma.

"No, really, how was it?"

"I don't know."

"Can you climb them?" Surprisingly this came from Gavin.

"Yeah, if you want to get your bum full of stingers."

"Emma!" said Ham.

I laughed.

The twins laughed, their faces close together.

Gavin said, "If you put a worm on it, it would stab out the insides and they would drip down."

"Gavin," I said. "Not at the table."

"Gavin got kicked out of school," I heard one of the twins whisper. They giggled and looked at him.

"SHUT UP!" Gavin said, stabbing a potato with his fork.

"PJ, Tabby," Troy said gently, "we're not going to talk about that anymore, remember?"

"But he did," whispered PJ.

It was late that night, after our nice dinner with the fresh rolls and the spicy stew and pleasant conversation with Emma and Ham, that Troy hit me so hard with a library book that it cut into my skin and blood ran down my leg.

After Ham and Emma left, Troy complained of a headache and fell asleep in his chair in front of the television news.

I got the children ready for bed, the twins bathed, Mary Beth's homework done, Gavin's teeth brushed, and finally, late in the evening, was nursing Simon on a chair in our bedroom, my new library book open on my lap.

"What's the matter with you? You can't even acknowledge me when I talk to you, are you that stupid?"

I looked up, startled. Troy was standing in the doorway. I hadn't seen him enter.

"I'm calling and calling. All the way up the stairs I'm calling and I'm standing right here and you don't even look up."

"I didn't hear you." I closed the novel and placed it face down on my lap, and then he cursed at me with a string of foul words that left me gasping. "Troy," I said. "Please."

"Oh, don't *please* me…"

The corner of his eye was jerking up in that tic he sometimes gets. I stared at it. "It's bad enough the idiots I work with, I have to come home and find them in my own house. Always with all the answers. All the books. All the answers. Everybody has all the answers."

My body became very still. Simon's breathing was wheezy. I rubbed his back and looked down at my novel. The author's picture smiled up at me from the back cover, her coiffed blond hair, her earrings. And I wondered, does her husband throw loaves of bread across the kitchen? Has he ever dropped, on purpose, a full cup of coffee on the floor, and then expected her to clean it up? Has her husband ever shaken her shoulders so hard that her head hurt for hours afterward? Has her son ever killed a hamster?

He came across the room then, and grabbed the book from my lap, the author's face squeezed between his forefinger and thumb. With a quick motion he tore the dust jacket off and crunched it up.

"That's a church library book." My voice was so quiet I doubted he heard me.

"Garbage," he said. "That's why you're so fat and lazy, you just sit and read this garbage all day."

"I don't."

"If you did something decent with your life we wouldn't be in this mess." He lifted the book above his head.

"Troy..."

I held Simon close to me, my hands protecting the back of his head. Troy threw the book hard at me, and the edge of it hit me square in the shin of my right leg, and caught me in such a way that a thin line of blood bubbles sprouted there, a perfectly symmetrical line. In slow motion I watched the blood dribble onto the ruined cover. Troy left the room, and I bent my head and prayed.

All of this—Troy's outbursts, Gavin's problems, this new pregnancy—all of it is meant by God to purify me. And when I come through it, I will be like gold refined in the fire. You endured abuse, Lord. You endured more suffering than I have ever experienced. Besides, the Bible doesn't have any qualifiers. I heard somebody say that once, and I wrote it in my prayer journal. It says to submit to your husband, and it doesn't say submit only when you feel like it or when it's convenient. It means submit all the time, regardless. I try to do that, God. I was trying to do that tonight. But it's hard sometimes. Really hard. And sometimes when I think about leaving, dream about it, plan it all out in my mind, I know that's wrong, too. Forgive me, Lord, for even thinking those thoughts.

When I looked up from my prayer, and squeezed the tears out of my eyes, Mary Beth was standing in the doorway, looking at me, the sides of her hair in her mouth.

Chapter Fifteen

*I*n the morning, when it was just the boys and me, I laid the ruined book on the kitchen table. I uncrumpled the cover, squirted a little detergent onto a dishrag, and tried wiping the back, ever so gently. But all I managed to do was to smear the blood, turning the author's face a blotchy brown. I rubbed harder and the glossy cover started coming away in places.

"Oh, Simon, look at this. What a mess. Your mommy's just making it worse."

Simon was on a blanket on the kitchen floor, where he was up on all fours, grunting as he tried to move forward. He was doing what Troy calls baby push-ups. I was glad he wasn't crawling yet. Mary Beth crawled and walked early. So did Gavin. The twins were later (crawling and taking their first steps on exactly the same day), and now Simon was the latest of all. I couldn't be pregnant when my current baby wasn't even crawling yet.

When the phone rang I put the book on top of the fridge. It was Judith asking me to go on a picnic.

"A picnic?"

"Look outside; it's gorgeous. It's supposed to get even warmer. I haven't been outside in so long. I just feel like trying it."

"You're thinking today?"

"Why not?"

"Oh, I don't know."

"But look outside."

The sky was deep blue and cloudless, as if it had been poster painted by a patient and meticulous child. Someone who painted within the lines. Someone probably like Ally.

"I was thinking for lunch," she was saying. "I could make sandwiches for all of us. I'll even bring drinks. Coffee in a thermos. Or iced tea, if you prefer. Maybe even lemonade. Do you like lemonade?"

"I can't, Judith. It's hard to explain. I just can't."

"It's your husband, isn't it?"

"What!"

"He's coming home for lunch today?"

"Oh no. No, he's not. He never does. That's not it."

"What then?"

"I'm just not feeling all that well, that's all."

"The sun will do you good."

"Probably it will," I said.

"It would do me good, too. And spending some time with someone who's living a normal life, and not in some kind of hell. That would be good for me, too."

"I have both my boys home with me now. Gavin doesn't have any school anymore."

"School's over already?"

"For him. For his grade."

"Oh, then bring him along. What kind of sandwiches does he like?"

"Peanut butter. But I'll make them."

"You will not. This was my idea, so I shall do the preparing."

We agreed to meet at eleven-thirty down at the picnic area by the town wharf. Easy walking distance for me. We could watch the fishing boats from the picnic tables. I decided I might bring a blanket to sit on, maybe even a book to read.

"This will be fun," she said. "I have such a good feeling about today. I know the police are close. That man in the navy blue suit. And Ellsworth's not all that far…"

I felt my body go cold.

"Sadie, you there?"

I could barely speak. "I just thought of something."

After I hung up I made my way swiftly to our bedroom. That Visa receipt, the one I had written the prayer request on, the one I found in Troy's sock drawer. I had left it in there, hadn't I? Or had I taken it with me to the kitchen? I ran my hand under the bed, looked around behind the dresser, went through the clutter on the top of Troy's highboy, opened the drawer of his bedside table.

And stared.

His black socks were lined up neatly on the left, his white socks on the right. But where were the scraps of paper, the old tubes of Chapstick, the loose change, the shoelaces, the old sunglasses? There was nothing in here but neat rows of socks.

I closed the drawer and went downstairs to the kitchen, holding tightly to the railing as I did so, not trusting my balance, not trusting my feet to move in appropriate ways. Had I placed the receipt in the front of the church directory along with the prayer chain list? I found a couple of old bulletins from months ago, but no receipt.

I sat down at the kitchen table and stared at the cabinets Troy had made and thought about the four things that I knew for sure. First, the Visa receipt, the one I had written the prayer request on, was for a gas station in Ellsworth, Maine—I was sure of it. Second, Troy had a blue suit. Third, Troy had a van, and finally, in the last couple of weeks, Troy had felt the compelling need to clean out his sock drawer.

Chapter Sixteen

Something is screaming inside of me. I am sitting at the kitchen table staring down at a church bulletin lying there, as if that will tell me something. I pick it up and crumple it like the cover of the Idaho Pioneers, remembering how I stood fixed, on the spot, when I watched the two *Crimestoppers* reenactments. Something about it had seemed so familiar, I realize it now, the man in the van, the actor that played him. And the little girl that was Ally walking beside him wearing a red jacket and scuffed pink sneakers.

I cannot admit what I am thinking. I cannot say this out loud. I press my palms against my ears. No matter what Troy has become, no matter what his moods, no matter what he may have done to me, it is unthinkable. And what is Ally to him? There would be no reason. How can I even think it?

I stand up, shove the kitchen chair away. Crazy thoughts. I am thinking crazy thoughts. I will go on this picnic today. On this beautiful day with the poster painted sky, I will turn my face into a mask and take my sons down to the harbor and we will watch the boats and Judith and I will sit and talk like normal people.

At quarter after eleven, I packed up a couple of juice boxes and a small bag of cookies, some Cheerios in a little plastic bag, and we set off, Gavin on his bicycle and me pushing Simon in the tottery old stroller. It was a pleasant day and I shoved black thoughts into the back of my thinking. Even Gavin was content as his one remaining training wheel whined on the pavement.

"You're learning how to ride a two-wheeler, Gavin. Look at you."

We passed other mothers pushing strollers, in groups of twos and threes chattering among themselves. Halfway down the block, I could see the bay, silk blue at the end of the street.

"Look, Gavin; look at the water. See the boats?"

"I'm faster than you." And he started to take off down the steep sidewalk.

"Gavin, slow down. Stop at the corner. Wait for us." I raced to the corner and reached for his handlebars just before he careened into traffic.

"*Wait* for Mommy. Please wait for Mommy. Don't go running off. We're almost there. Stay with me."

Judith was sitting on the bench of a picnic table gazing at the water. She hated the sea; that's what she said. Yet she seemed transfixed by it now. I sat down across from her.

"It's a lovely day today, isn't it?" she said, still facing away from me.

"It is."

"Do you come here a lot?"

"I try to. I'd like to. It's just packing up everything. I have to make sure there's enough diapers and clean clothes, plus toys and food. Packing up to go on a picnic is a major procedure."

She smiled and turned to me, finally. "If I had children I would bring them here every day."

"I thought you hated the ocean."

"I like it when it's calm. Like today. I like placid things."

Gently I pushed the stroller back and forth, back and forth, even though Simon was perfectly content without my doing that. My hands just needed to be doing something. Gavin had thrown his bicycle down and was pulling yellow petals off a dandelion.

"I'm trying to think of myself as childless." She was plucking at some embroidery on a wide-brimmed white hat that lay in her lap. She looked older in the harsh brightness of the sun, her face seamed with threadlike wrinkles. "I've had a lot of…bad things happen to me. I've been in this dark night for too long." She looked up at me. "I don't know if I believe in God. Greg doesn't. He used to. When I married him I thought he was religious. I needed that in my life then. But then it was business, business, business. For him it's all get ahead and work and buy things."

Smarter people, people more in touch with themselves and God might lean forward, touch her arm, and say, "Do you want to talk about it?" I didn't. I looked at Simon and said, "I'm sorry to hear you don't believe in God."

"I believe in God," she said quietly, plucking at the threads. "I just don't think God believes in me anymore."

"I want LUNCH!" Gavin growled.

She looked at him. "Hey, Gavin, you hungry?" She smiled broadly, suddenly looking years younger. She spread out her arms. "Gavin, come here. Give your Aunt Judith a big hug."

Gavin ignored her.

"Gavin, say hello," I said.

"HELLO," he growled. "I'm a WORM."

"A worm, you say?" said Judith. "Well, does this worm want a peanut butter sandwich?"

"I want lunch! Lunch. Lunch. Lunch."

"Gavin, say please," I said.

Judith placed an old-fashioned picnic basket on the table and proceeded to unload it. Simon was asleep in his stroller, a sun hat tied underneath his chin. I moved him so he faced away from the sun. Overhead, cirrus clouds took on the shapes of dragons and dinosaurs and out on the horizon a low-slung black freighter moved slowly across the horizon.

"Look, Gavin." I pointed. "Look at the boat."

"NO." He was on his bicycle again. "I don't wanna look at boats. Want lunch. Want LUNCH."

Judith set three place settings around the picnic table. "I've brought plenty," she said. "Lots and lots of food. Peanut butter sandwiches. Baloney. Tuna. Even egg salad. I went to the store, Sadie. For the first time since... I needed to see if I could do it."

"How was it?"

"Not as bad as I expected. No one said anything to me, and I just ignored the few people who looked at me."

"You didn't have to go shopping. I told you I could have made sandwiches."

"No, I needed to do this. Needed to see if I could."

"You made enough sandwiches for an army!" I said.

She pondered the stack. "Well, maybe I did get carried away a bit, but I had fun doing it. One of the things I did with the children in pediatrics was to have tea parties with them. They loved that. I would make tea in the nurses' lounge and serve it to the children. Those who could drink it."

"I'm sure the children loved you. Simon adores you."

"It was sad working there, sometimes. Children shouldn't have to die. They shouldn't have to get so lost."

In the distance a ship sounded its horn, and at the table Gavin was growling at his sandwich. Simon was beginning to stir. I pushed his stroller back and forth. It squeaked.

"Oh, Simon, come here to Aunt Judith."

She lifted him out of the stroller and jostled him until he quieted. "I never understood what it felt like to lose a child. All those sad parents I would see, day after day, year after year in the hospital, while their children slowly died. Sometimes—" She looked away from me. "Sometimes I think I'm being punished. Paid back..."

"Paid back?" I asked quietly.

"Never mind. It doesn't matter now. Greg wants me to see a counselor."

"Maybe that would be a good idea, to talk all this over with someone. I hope you do that. Someone else you might want to talk with is our pastor. He'd be good."

Gavin started poking Simon with a stick, and Judith took it from him gently, and exchanged it for a cookie. I marveled that he listened to her. Her head was bent away from me and she played patty-cake with Simon's hands, lifting them with her own.

"Have you thought about going back to work?" I asked. "You seem like such a good nurse."

"I can't see me ever going back to work. Facing those people."

"Judith, you said you'd never go out shopping, but you did. Maybe in time you'll be able to go back to work, too."

She looked up at me suddenly. "Ally was a wonderful artist. Did you know that?"

"I saw her picture on your fridge. It was beautiful."

"All that waste." Her eyes were bright, intense. Quietly she said, "I just wish they'd find the body."

"Judith, don't—"

She held up her hand. "Please, Sadie, don't be like the others. When I mention 'find the body' they refuse to talk about it, try to shut me up. But it would help me to know for sure. I want to find a body. You're the only one I can say this to. Greg shuts me out when I say this."

"Oh, Judith."

We were quiet for a couple of minutes. I was wishing I knew what to say. Even "I'm praying for you" sounded phony, so I didn't say anything.

"You're a good listener," she said.

"Thank you."

She was twisting a piece of her hair between two fingers. "And Greg's gone back to work and I'm alone with my days."

"That would be hard."

"I know I should be more understanding. He's got his problems,

I've got mine. But you'd think head office would be easier on him, considering…"

"Does your husband work in Bangor?"

"He manages a company here in Coffins Reach."

"Well, that's handy at least."

"A little computer company with a big edge."

"What?" My hands were very still on my knees.

"That's how they advertise themselves: a little computer company with a big edge."

"SmartSystems."

"You know of it?"

I looked past her. "I've heard of it."

"He's the new manager there. The one that's supposed to oversee the layoffs and the takeover."

Down at the wharf a couple of fishermen in stained yellow rubber overalls were walking away from us.

Chapter Seventeen

Why didn't I tell her? There are any number of ways I could have worded it. It looks as if our husbands work in the same place. Isn't that a coincidence! Or, my husband works for SmartSystems too. He's a salesman there. Isn't it a small world! Or, are you kidding? My husband works there, too. Wow! And here we are.

But I didn't say any of those things. Because of what I suspected, or maybe half-suspected, I didn't say a thing. And now there would forever be this secret between us. For how could I tell her now? *Oh, yesterday, Judith? I forgot to mention that my husband works in the same place as yours.*

The first thing I noticed this morning—the morning after I discovered Troy's sock drawer, the morning after I found out that Troy works with Greg Buckley (probably *for* Greg Buckley)—was the heat. At first I thought it was me. Pregnancy makes me either too hot or too cold. The second thing I noticed was that I was alone in the bed. I sat up in a panic. Had I slept in? The children! They'd be late for school. I always get up before Troy. I like to get downstairs, get the coffee going and lunches made, breakfast on the table before anyone else is stirring. I glanced at the bedside clock. It was only five-thirty. We still had an hour before the alarm would sound. I got up, threw on my housecoat, and in the bathroom ran cold water on my face and brushed my teeth.

Downstairs, Troy was reading the paper and drinking a cup of instant coffee beside the kitchen window. Birds sang outside.

"You're up early," I said, closing the kitchen door.

"Couldn't sleep."

"You should have called me. You should have woken me up. I could have come and made proper coffee for you. Not that instant stuff."

"You were sleeping, hon, and I didn't want to disturb you. This is fine. Good, in fact. The first cup of the day always tastes the best, you know."

He was smiling. Maybe it would be a good day.

"It seems so warm today. Did you notice that? Here," I said filling the coffee drip with water. "Let me make you some proper coffee. And would you like some breakfast? I could do up some eggs."

He yawned and stretched his arms up over his head. He was still in his housecoat, a years-old plaid one with a rip under the arm. "That would be nice. We could have a nice breakfast together, just the two of us." He flattened the paper on the table. "And yes, you're right. It is hot. We've got a heat wave on the way. I was watching the weather a little while ago. The kids still sleeping?"

I nodded. "All of them. Even Simon."

"It must be the heat."

"Must be."

"They were up late last night."

"They don't like going to bed when it's still light out," I said.

"Something they'll have to get used to."

"I suppose. I'll sort of be glad when school's over for the summer and it's not this rush, rush, rush every morning. Getting the twins up is like moving heaven and earth." I cracked eggs into a bowl. I got out the cheese grater and found some not-too-bad-looking mushrooms in the fridge.

"So what's on tap for you today?" he asked looking up from his paper.

"The usual. Laundry. Maybe make some bread. I think Emma's coming over after school this afternoon. It's nice for Mary Beth to have a special friend. PJ and Tabby can be so mean to her at times."

"She needs to learn to stand on her own two feet."

"She reminds me of me so much. When I was that age." I poured the egg mixture into the frying pan. It sizzled, and I spread it out evenly with the spatula. He went back to the paper, and I glanced at him every so often while I cut thick pieces of bread and made sure the eggs didn't burn. I thought for a long time before I said, "I was thinking about something. I was thinking about Ellsworth. About a bakery there." I chose my words carefully. The toast popped up. Perfect. I buttered it, poured two orange juices and two fresh coffees.

"What bakery?" asked my husband.

I could hear the sounds of stirring up above us.

"I seem to remember some wonderful poppy seed buns. Have you been there recently? To Ellsworth, I mean?" I set down the plates of food on the table. He held my hand, said grace, and we ate in silence for a couple of minutes.

I took a forkful of eggs. "So, have you been there recently?"

"Where?"

"Ellsworth. I was talking about Ellsworth."

"I go there all the time. It's one of my stops. What's gotten into you this morning? Why are you looking at me like that?"

"I'm not looking at you like any way."

He went back to his eggs.

I cut pieces of my omelette with my fork. "I was just wondering when the last time you were there was."

"Why are you going on about this?"

"It was just a bakery, that's all. I was thinking about poppy seed buns for the next time Ham and Emma come over. That's all."

He grunted and went back to eating. "Sometimes you make no sense to me at all."

Upstairs Simon was whimpering. I heard a door slam. Shouts. I could feel Troy tense. In the distance through the open window, crows were arguing.

"Stupid birds," he said. "Like some of the idiots I work for. I'm surrounded by idiots."

Later, after he left, after I had scraped what he didn't eat into the garbage, I went into the downstairs bathroom and threw up. I rinsed my mouth, threw water on my face, combed my hair back with my fingers, and went upstairs to tend to the noise of my children.

Chapter Eighteen

I did the most stupid thing," I said to the church librarian on Sunday morning after church. "I put this book down on the floor to run and answer the phone, not realizing that I'd placed it right where Simon could reach it, and the minute I turn around, there he is, tearing the cover off, crinkling it up and eating it."

The librarian held the book in one hand and the cover in the other.

"I rushed over to stop him, but it was too late. I'm so terribly sorry." I held my breath. I was in the fifth grade. I was standing in front of the principal.

"Sometimes I can be so stupid. I mean, I know what Simon is capable of, and here I go leaving the book right on the floor. Right where he can get at it."

The librarian, whose name is Lillian, smiled up at me from her desk. "Stop it, dear. It happens. A little library tape will do the trick just fine." She turned it over in her hands. "Did you get to finish it? It's awfully good, isn't it?"

"I started it, but when I saw what I had done to the book, well, I just couldn't bring myself…"

"What *you* had done? You didn't do a thing, dear. Now, you just stop. You didn't do a thing, and babies, well, they just aren't to blame for things now, are they?"

"Well, yes, but…" I hoisted the diaper bag higher on to my shoulder. "And then, to make matters worse, in my haste to get the book away from him, I slammed my finger against the edge of a cupboard, cut it without realizing it. There I am dripping blood all over the book. Without even realizing."

The librarian put up her hand. "A little library tape and this will be just fine. Don't you worry about a thing."

"Then I tried to clean it up with a sponge, and all I did was wreck the back cover. Make it worse."

"Dear, that's all right."

"I'd like to replace it," I said.

"Oh, there's no need. Really. Don't you worry."

"I feel really terrible about the whole thing."

"If you want to, and only if you want to—there is no need really—you can buy the next book in the series. It's just out." She was taping the cover while she talked. "What we should be concerned about is your finger."

"My what?"

"Your finger."

"Oh. I'm fine. It's fine." I shoved my hands into the pockets of my long skirt, grateful that it had pockets.

"Wasn't that a lovely baby shower?"

"What?"

But it was not me she was talking to. Next to me, a woman named Millie Dennis was placing a couple of books on the corner of the table.

"It was, wasn't it?"

"Rhonda was just beaming."

"I would say so was Charles. And they had that baby in such an adorable little outfit."

"And the place was decorated so nicely. Everyone really went all out."

Millie laughed. "Well, you're only a little prejudiced. Being the proud grandmother and all."

"When I think of all they've been through, Millie," said Lillian. "For so long they've wanted a baby, and so many miscarriages. And now finally a lovely baby girl. How precious little children are."

"Thinking of that makes me think of poor Irma. She wasn't at the shower, I noticed."

"We all noticed. She's not handling this well at all. Not at all." Lillian was talking in a low conspiratorial tone, as she stamped the books and placed them in a pile. I was renewing the one on losing weight. I hadn't had time to copy down some of the recipes from the back yet.

"So sad. So unthinkable."

"To think something like that could happen here."

Lillian was wagging her head as she handed the books to me. "And Irma is a wreck. Have you seen her? Have you actually laid eyes on her? This has aged her ten years, I tell you. And her health isn't all that good to begin with. I shouldn't be saying this, but you know what they're saying now, don't you? What everybody's thinking now? That the parents are responsible. The mother."

Millie clucked her tongue. "Like that poor little girl that was in the news for so long. They even look like each other, don't you think?"

"What do we even know about her anyway? This Judith? I grew up with Greg—well, he's younger than me, of course, but I remember his first wife. Do you remember that wedding, Millie? It was so beautiful, and I mean we all knew Sylvia, she was one of us. And then when she died, she's barely cold and he's up and married someone from away, someone no one even knew! How much does anyone know about her?"

"Now Lil, Bud and Irma have accepted her. They've met her family. Irma said she was going to accept Judith as her own daughter, and Ally as her own granddaughter."

The librarian's glasses reflected the glint from the fluorescent overhead. "Well, I'm not so sure. They made a show of accepting her at first, because really, what else could they do? But I think they rue the day when Greg got hooked up with her. Her and that daughter of hers."

Millie bent her head forward. "I don't think it was the mother. First of all, what about that other girl? The one they found on the beach? I believe there's a connection between the two, both the same age, both little blond girls. There's so obviously a connection, and what would Judith have to do with the other girl? No, if you ask me it was someone else entirely. That man in Ellsworth. How does he fit into the picture?"

I was backing away from the conversation, shoving my library books into the depths of the diaper bag next to clean Pampers and Sunday school papers and bulletins, and backed square into a large black woman who was perusing books in the Christian Counseling section.

"Oh, I'm sorry." I braced myself. "I didn't see you."

She laughed and steadied me with her hands. "I'm just fine."

"Sometimes I'm such a klutz." I was near tears and didn't quite know why.

Her hands were warm on my shoulders. "I take up too much space as it is." Her laugh was hearty. "I'm Bernice Jacobs, by the way. I don't believe we've met."

"Sadie Thornton."

"Sadie." She was regarding me intently. "I'm so pleased to meet you. I'm fairly new in town, so I haven't met everyone. It's so nice to meet you, Sadie." She took both of my hands in hers.

Her shoulder-length black hair in tiny ringlets was held back by a colorful wide headband that matched her caftan. There was something about her face that reminded me of music: large brown eyes, wide smile, smooth blackness of her skin, marred only by a slightly crooked nose. Her hands felt smooth and warm on mine. Her touch was almost a caress.

"It's nice to meet you," I said. "I hope you like it here."

"Well, I hope I do, too."

And then Troy was towering in the doorway. With one hand he held Simon and the other was on Gavin's shoulder. Peeking out from behind was Mary Beth. "Do you know where the twins are?" he asked me. He was looking from Bernice to me and then back to her again.

She let go of my hands.

"I don't know," I said. "I was just bringing back some books."

"I bet they're out in the educational wing," said Lillian, looking up and pointing with her pencil. "I saw a bunch of the kids head that direction. And you—" the librarian grinned at Simon—"we're going to have to take away your library card now, aren't we? Can't have you destroying all the books in the place, can we? But maybe you just wanted to read it, didn't you? You tell your mommy and daddy you just wanted to read it."

Troy was frowning at me. I kept my gaze on the librarian's glasses.

"Oh, there's Jason now. Jason," Lillian called to a little yellow-haired boy in the hallway. "Jason, sweetie, have you seen PJ and Tabby?"

"They're in the gym. They got the basketballs out."

"They're not supposed to do that," Mary Beth said. "Not on Sunday. Not without permission."

"Oh, I'm sure no harm is done," said Bernice. "I'm sure Jesus Himself would've played basketball on a Sunday if given half a chance."

"That's not the point," Troy said.

"They always do things without permission," said Mary Beth.

Don, the head of the missions committee, came up behind Troy and put a hand on his shoulder. "Can I steal you for a moment, Troy? We've got to come up with a time for the next meeting."

Troy handed Simon to me.

"We've got the Fogartys on furlough from Japan, and Clyde and Marianne from that French mission in Canada. We've really got to get the ball rolling on this..." The words trailed off as the men left. I took my three children, and accompanied by Bernice, found the twins in the gym. Bernice put the basketballs away. I thanked her and left. At the van, I strapped everyone in their seats and waited for Troy.

Chapter Nineteen

*T*uesday night and the three of us were going out for supper: Troy and I and Ham, Ham's treat. Troy and I tried to tell him that he didn't have to, that we loved having him and Emma over. And that it's no trouble really to set a couple of extra places at the supper table, and like Troy says, you just add water to the soup and cut the bread a little thinner.

But no, Ham said he wanted to do something special for the two of us who have been so kind to him and his daughter. He had even taken care of the baby-sitters. He'd brought Emma to our house and hired two sisters, daughters of the secretary in the sheriff's office, to baby-sit all six kids. All I had to do was feed Simon before we left, and hope and pray that Gavin didn't go into a tantrum.

We don't often leave the kids with a sitter. One night a month we have our board members' and spouses' Bible study and dinner. I have been taking Simon to that, but we get a sitter for the others. I can count on one hand the nights we've been able to stay for the full meeting and Bible study. Still, we try. Or Troy does. I would just as soon stay home.

And as for Troy and me going out to dinner or a movie, just the two of us, that's just something we absolutely never do.

But here we were tonight on our way to the fanciest, most expensive restaurant in Coffins Reach. The Lighthouse View Restaurant is part of an exclusive and expensive bed-and-breakfast. I had carefully chosen a blue chambray summer dress with matching sweater that my mother had bought for me at L. L. Bean last summer. Halfway there I worried that I wasn't dressed up enough. In the next minute I worried that everybody else would be in jeans.

As it was, some people were in jeans and some in suits and ties. I was just about in the middle.

Troy and I had been quiet with each other the past two days. Judith had called three times, and I still hadn't told her that Troy also worked at SmartSystems. She told me the police were still trying to find the man in the van. I had said no more about it, but quietly searched the house for the receipt. I never found it. A few nights ago I woke up and wondered if I should go to Ham with my suspicions. I lay awake for a long time thinking about that and in the end decided I had no real evidence. But still, something nagged at me, like a stray thread I would pick at during odd times of the day.

The Lighthouse View was dim, with real candles at each table. It was also cool, despite the warmth of the evening. Ham had reserved a table next to a window which offered a spectacular view of the point, the lighthouse, and the water.

"This is so nice," I said.

"Nothing can really repay the kindness the two of you have shown to Emma and me, and this is just something special I wanted to do for the two of you. I have a feeling you don't get out very often."

"We don't," said Troy. "This is a rare treat."

"I just hope we can sit through the whole meal without a call to come home," I said.

Ham seated me where I had a clear view of the lighthouse. There was a bit of a park on that point, a place for public parking and a trail down to the rocks. Most of the trail was unsafe and there were small signs advising of this, but still people ventured beyond the safe areas. Occasionally you heard about someone falling and being killed. Especially when the wind and tide were high and the waves beat against the rocks. In the fall a ten-year-old girl had disappeared. Her crumpled body was found the next day at the bottom of the cliff. At first it was thought to be an accident. Later it was determined that she was raped and murdered.

A young man in a white shirt and black bow tie poured water for us and asked if we wanted anything else to drink. Troy and Ham asked for iced teas. Water was fine for me, I said.

A plaque on the wall beside our table gave a bit of history of the lighthouse. Constructed in 1829, the Coffins Head Light was a working lighthouse. For more than a hundred years it guided ships that came to unload goods and fish. In 1947 the light was moved to a smaller, skeleton tower where it remains today, and the older structure was decommissioned. The old tower and keeper's house beside it became the property of the town of Coffins Reach, and the house is used as a residence today, I read.

"Look at this," I said, touching the plaque. "Coffins Reach got its name from all the shipwrecks during the fog on the reef down there."

"A lot of dangerous eddies down there, too," said Ham.

The drinks came. We studied our menus. I had a sudden thought.

"Ham," I said, "maybe you know something about this. You know that sort of a gazebo thing over on the point? Beside the lighthouse?"

"I know the gazebo is in worse shape than the lighthouse, but what about it?"

"I thought I heard music about a week or so ago, and the more I think of it, the more I think it was coming from that direction. And I was wondering if any bands or orchestras were practicing out there on the point." I turned to Troy. "Remember that morning when I woke up and said I heard music? Well, the more I think about it the more I think it was coming from the point."

"Sadie thought an orchestra was down there on the point practicing in the middle of the night."

Ham was looking at me intently. He leaned forward and said

quietly, "You heard music, Sadie? From the point?"

"You were imagining it," Troy said.

The waiter came and took our orders. Troy wanted steak, rare; Ham ordered salmon; and I ordered broiled haddock. "I never get fish at home," I said. "Troy doesn't like it, so it's nice to take advantage of it when I'm out."

Troy rolled his eyes. "Sadie, Ham's really not interested in that."

"Oh, sure I am. As local state police officer I have to keep a careful record of everyone's likes and dislikes."

The three of us laughed. Then, for a few minutes, Ham expounded on the Atlantic culinary delights he had grown to love since moving here, fiddleheads and lobster being the two main ones.

When our salads came, Ham asked me about the music.

"It's hard to explain," I said. "It was just an impression I had. That's all. I thought it might have something to do with that old lighthouse. You're thinking I'm crazy."

Ham shook his head. "I don't think that."

"It was a stereo you heard," said Troy. "That's all it was. Or someone's television."

"I don't think so. I think I would've known that. It had a different sound, more like live music."

"And you heard music? You definitely heard music?" Ham was tapping his fork on the side of his salad plate.

"Yes, I'm positive."

"Do you remember the kind of music it was?"

"Classical. And very beautiful. I had never heard that composition before. At first I thought it was Debussy, but no, it wasn't."

"Sadie, haven't you taken this a bit too far?" Troy asked.

"You seem to know a lot about music," Ham said.

"Music used to be a hobby of hers," Troy said.

"It still is, sort of…" I said.

Troy snorted. "You haven't touched that piano in how many years, and you call it a hobby?"

I took a sip of my water.

Ham said, "There was something in the police report about music. I didn't pay too much attention to it at the time, though. But I seem to remember one of the witnesses saying they heard music of some sort down at the point where the lighthouse is. I think that was it. What Sadie is saying may be significant."

"Think about it, Ham. Even if Sadie did hear music, and even if it originated at the point, we're a good mile, mile and a half away. How would she hear it at our house?"

"I don't know, but it's worth checking out."

"It was someone with their stereo on," Troy said. "The windows were open that night. That's my opinion on it, and that's all I'm going to say."

"Have you heard the music since?"

"No, just the one time," I said. "But what about the lighthouse? That was where the little girl's body was found."

"The murderer wanted to make it look like an accident," Ham said, "but it didn't work. Bodies don't lie."

Troy lifted his iced tea. "I propose we change the topic of conversation for the rest of the evening."

"Fine," said Ham, "but I want to talk to you more about the music, Sadie."

Our meals came. We didn't talk about the lighthouse or the murder or the music for the rest of the evening. Instead, Ham talked about Arizona and his wife, Celia. Troy filled him in on our life up to this point. I listened, fascinated, as Troy rewrote the history surrounding our two failed churches.

There was one phone call for us when we got back to the house, and the baby-sitters had written down the name and number on a piece of paper by the phone. Troy picked it up and looked at it. From behind him I could read: "Mrs. Thornton, please call Bernice Jacobs." The name meant nothing to me at first. And then I remembered— Bernice Jacobs, the lady in the library.

Troy crumpled the paper and stuck it in his pocket.

"What is it?" I asked.

"Nothing, just more garbage from work. More fires to put out. It never ends."

Chapter Twenty

*I*n the middle of the night, after I had nursed Simon and got him settled, I went downstairs and in the closet I reached into Troy's jacket pocket and retrieved the crumpled note. I flattened it out, wrote Bernice Jacobs's phone number on the back of an old bulletin, shoved it far into one of the junk drawers, and then crumpled the original note and stuck it back into Troy's pocket.

Then I went back upstairs and climbed into bed beside my deeply sleeping husband and thought about Bernice Jacobs and wondered why she was calling me, and why Troy was keeping this from me.

In the morning when it was just me and the boys, I retrieved the number from the drawer and called her.

"Sadie Thornton! Well, I am so glad you called me back."

So absolutely surprised was I that the words, "You are?" were out of my mouth before I could draw them back.

"Of course I am. When we bumped into each other I thought, I should call this person."

"Oh."

"The reason I called was that just yesterday I was sorting through some children's clothing. I work for an organization where we get lots of donated children's clothing. And, well, it seems that right now we have more than we can use. I was going to take a bundle down to the Salvation Army, and then I thought of you. And I wondered if you could use some of these clothes. All of them are quite nice, many are brand new."

And that is how the two of us came to be in my kitchen that morning sorting through two black garbage bags full of clothing. She was wearing an orange caftan and her hair was held back with a thick orange band. "Your house is absolutely charming," she said when she entered. "What beautiful wainscoting around the doors."

"It's so small, though," I said. "It's hard to find a place for everything, especially with seven of us living here. I feel like I'm constantly apologizing to people for having to step over things."

"I grew up with ten brothers. I was the only girl. All of us in a house smaller than this."

"Really?"

"Really."

"Where was that? Where did you grow up?"

I grabbed two mugs from the drain board and poured coffees.

"Trinidad is where I'm from."

"Really? Wow."

"Where did you grow up, Sadie?"

"Nothing so exciting—a city in Indiana called Michigan City."

She asked me about my family and I told her.

"How come you live in Maine now?" I asked. "It's got to be a lot different than Trinidad."

"I married a man who got a job teaching at the university. So, that's how I ended up here. It's a nice place." She paused. "I hope some of these clothes will fit your family."

"Oh, I'm sure they will. You don't know how much I rely on hand-me-downs. Outfitting five kids gets to be so expensive."

"I know," she said. "I raised three sons. I could never understand how some parents could afford all new clothing for their children year after year."

Our cups of coffee sat on the kitchen table beside the piles of clothing. On the floor Simon was doing baby push-ups, and Gavin was under the piano bench in the living room.

This was like Christmas for me. She even had some women's

clothing in my size, a peach and white sweater with matching wool skirt. I took the items into our downstairs bathroom and tried them on.

"So, there's someone out there as big and fat as me!" I said showing off the new outfit, twirling in the kitchen.

Bernice chuckled. "Don't ever say you're fat, child. If you're fat then I should sign up to be the fat lady in the circus."

I stopped and stared at her. "But you look beautiful. The way you have your hair, and those colors. Regal. Like a queen."

Now she was laughing loudly. "Regal. Now there's a word. But, honestly, why do women think they have to be thin sticks to be beautiful?" She put her hand on my arm. "We are both beautiful, Sadie. Oh, look at this lovely sweater." She held up a boy's sweater. "Will this fit your little boy, do you suppose?"

It was a red and blue, hand-knit, striped sweater. "It's lovely. But it might be too small for Gavin. Gavin," I called, "would you come here a minute? I want to try something on you."

He growled his way into the kitchen, and I held it up against his back.

"Don't like it," he said.

"Well, it's a good thing," said Bernice, "because it looks a bit too small for you, little man."

He swung his arm wildly. "DON'T call me that!"

I looked down hard at Gavin. Bernice held out her hand to him. "Okay, I'm sorry. I never will again."

But he turned and ran from her. I heard a crash from the living room, and when I raced in, he had picked up a video and was threatening to throw it at the television. I raced toward him, grabbed it, and held him.

"Gavin, no."

He squirmed and shrieked.

"We have company now, Gavin. Please."

"I HATE you and I hate EVERYBODY."

"Go to your room. Right now. Right now!" My voice was hoarse and my throat hurt, as it always did, when we ended up screeching at each other. He slapped at me with his hand, and I grabbed him and took him, thrashing and yelling, to his room, where I placed him firmly on his bed and left him there. I would let him scream it out upstairs, and later I would assess the damages—broken toys, ripped bedding. Oddly, he never hurt himself when he went into these rages. I was grateful for that.

Halfway down the stairs I slumped against the railing. My hands were shaking and my stomach hurt. Upstairs Gavin was still scream-ing, *I hate you!* With the ends of my fingers I wiped the tears from under my eyes. I stood there for several seconds, breathing deeply, trying to muster up the courage to go downstairs.

Back in the kitchen I said breezily, "He's very energetic."

Bernice was at the table. Simon was in her big arms. "Well, no more than my boys used to be."

"Really?" I sat down and folded the sweater, the sweater that started it all, and placed it back into the garbage bag.

"Kids tend to misbehave more when there are strangers around," she said. "You should have seen my Judah, a terror if there ever was one. But he grew up okay. Despite everything." She looked down at Simon when she said this. "God's grace covers a multitude of family challenges."

"How old are your children now?" I asked.

"Grown up. All grown up. Let me see." She counted on her fin-gers. "Peter is thirty-two, Jefferson is thirty, and Judah is twenty-six." She paused and shifted Simon on her lap. "You're right in the middle of it now, Sadie," she said gently.

I nodded. I couldn't say more. I intended to; I felt she might be an ally—but I couldn't. I knew if I opened my mouth to say one word I would burst into tears and there would be no stopping me.

"With me the problem was compounded by the fact that *my* husband was head elder..." Bernice was talking. "We were expected to have the perfect family. It was difficult for me most of the time. To be perfect. To stay perfect. To keep up the facade."

I nodded, incapable of speaking. Simon grinned at me. He reached out his arms to me, and Bernice handed him to me. She didn't wear a wedding ring, I noticed.

"It always seems to fall to the mother," she was saying. "To keep the children behaved. It's part of being a mother. The work of it, feeling that there is no life beyond children and babies."

I held my son close, burying my face in his baby smelling hair. I ran my fingers over his faded blue T-shirt. I had the idea she was talking about more than Gavin's temper tantrums, but I didn't know what to say. I looked at her and nodded.

"And I know how difficult it must be with Troy on the board and with certain responsibilities in the church…"

"Do you know Troy? My husband?"

She shook her head. "Not really. I met him for the first time that day in the library. The day you and I bumped into each other."

"Do you…" I stopped, looked down at Simon. "Do you know, um, anything about the girl that disappeared? That Ally?"

She looked at me. "No, I don't. Why do you ask?"

"Nothing." I opened my mouth and clamped it shut again.

Bernice looked at me, reached into her purse, and pulled out a card. Then she pressed it into my hand. "I'm going to give this to you, Sadie. I want you to keep it, and if you need to talk, just to talk, I want you to call me."

I stared at her, puzzled. I looked down at the card. Bernice Jacobs and a number. That was all there was. When she left, I hid the business card inside a jumbo box of Bounce up in the laundry cupboard.

Chapter Twenty-one

So Troy didn't know Bernice. Despite the crumpled-up paper, Troy had nothing specifically against Bernice. Troy wasn't trying to hide anything from me. Bernice had nothing to do with Ally or Ally's disappearance. There wasn't anything specifically wrong with Bernice, it was just Bernice in general. I should have known. I should be used to Troy's jealousies by now, but it always bewilders me.

Clarice and I wrote letters back and forth for a few years after Troy and I were married, until he demanded that I stop.

"We're married," Troy had said. "We're one. We're supposed to be each other's best friend. We shouldn't need other people. Our friends should be friends to both of us, not just your friends or my friends."

So I stopped writing to her. Now, we just exchange Christmas cards, which I sign: Love from Troy, Sadie, Mary Beth, PJ, Tabby, Gavin, and Simon.

All of us together, one.

I tried to break it off with Troy once. We had been dating for about six months. He was graduating in June and wanted to get married a week later. It was all he talked about. We would take long walks and I would listen as he went on about wedding plans, about cakes and food and honeymoons, about where we would live, about what he would do, about how many children we would have.

When we started dating, I was smitten, struck with love, unable to eat, hardly able to breathe. He was handsome. He was smart. He was spiritual and he was going to be a minister. He had ideals. And he needed *me!*

But by six months, I felt suffocated. My only other boyfriend had been a missionary kid named Ben who grew up in South America, so I didn't have a lot of experience. And I still had another year to finish my degree. I enjoyed study. I enjoyed my music. I especially enjoyed writing music and was looking forward to my last year when I would be taking some advanced composition courses.

That's when I began to feel that Troy was jealous of my music. It made no sense to me, but how could I explain the number of times he would show up, just when I had booked a practice room, with some earth-shattering problem that I had to listen to and pray with him about?

So instead of telling him I was working on theory or a composition, I began lying, telling him I had to study for Christian ed or write a paper for Psalms or Romans. Oddly, that was all right with him.

When I was able to convince him that I needed to practice, he would drag a metal chair into the little practice room and sit and watch me while I played, his chair legs creaking back and forth. Troy told me he didn't like having me out of his sight, not for one second. And every time I looked up from the piano, there he would be, staring at me with those small, dark intense eyes of his.

"Troy," I would say to him, "you don't have to keep looking at me."

"But I like looking at you."

So I would go back to my piano or my oboe, and I would feel guilty because I was thinking about the music and not about him.

"Sadie," he said to me late one afternoon after I had finished practicing, "you and I are meant for each other. I prayed for a woman like you, and God answered my prayer. Even our meeting was ordained of God. Don't you sense it?"

I folded my hands on top of the music book in my lap. "Troy, I was thinking. I don't want to hurt you, but I was wondering, maybe we shouldn't see each other for a couple of weeks. So I can study. I've got midterms and a ton of papers due. And then there's my music. I guess what I'm saying is that I love you. Or I think I love you, sometimes, but there are times when I don't even know if I know what love is. Maybe I just need a couple of weeks to study. I need some time off."

"You sound like you're talking about a job. Like you need some time off from a job. Like I'm a job."

"That's not what I mean. It's just to study. For both of us. Your grades must be falling, too. And I'm not feeling well. It's like I'm sick all the time." I didn't look at him when I said, "I would like us to take a couple of weeks away from each other. Pray about our relationship, think things through, and then come back and see how we feel about each other. I'm just tired, Troy. Look at me. I'm going to be up until two this morning as it is. I should practice another two hours, and then I have a paper on Romans due tomorrow that I haven't even started yet."

"Why are you even worrying about school and papers when we're going to get married in June?"

"But I want to do my best. That's how I am."

"You could drop out now, Sadie, and nothing would be lost. In fact, in a way I wish you would. Then you could be by my side without any distractions of your own, to help me."

"To help you?"

He nodded smiling widely. "A helpmeet."

"Troy…" I stopped. "What if I want to go to school next year? What if I want to finish my degree? Isn't that important, too?"

He was shaking his head. "I don't think you can handle any more school, Sadie. Look what it's doing to you now. I don't think you're cut out for the rigors of study."

"Troy, I need a break from you." I said it quickly and quietly. "I have to be strong in this. I have to tell you how I feel. I'm asking you…well, no, I'm not asking, I'm telling. Two weeks. Come back in two weeks."

"No."

"No? What do you mean, no?"

"Just what I said. No. I won't let you go for two weeks."

"Troy…"

"One week," he said. "One week is all I'll give you. I'll see you here in this practice room in one week."

He got up and walked out.

Chapter Twenty-two

We are recommending that PJ and Tabby be placed in different classes next year." Troy and I were sitting on wooden chairs in an airless office. Facing us, the principal was making a tent of her hands on the desk, fingertips together. Our children were at home with one half of the sister baby-sitting team Ham had hired for our night out. The sisters were as tough and as capable as Ham had indicated.

Troy sniffed at the air and said, "It's perfectly all right with us."

"Your daughters won't like it, however."

"Well." He sniffed some more. "It's time they grew up."

"Why can't they stay together?" I asked. "They're very close."

"That's precisely the problem." The principal put on her glasses and rifled through some papers on her desk. "They're doing fine academically. Both of them are. Above average. I wanted to show you some test papers. They are not problem children in the least."

Troy said thank you and that we both worked hard at raising good children. He patted my hand when he said this. I looked at my husband, a man I had known for a dozen years, and suddenly I did not know him. He looked like a stranger to me, with his pursed lips, those intense eyes, and for a moment I recoiled as if struck.

"Academically they are no problem at all. Our concern is," she was saying, "that they are more and more isolating themselves from the other children. Do they play with your other children? How are they with Mary Beth at home?" She took her glasses off. They hung from a chain around her neck.

"Things at home are fine," said Troy. "They get along fine with the family. They always include Mary Beth in their play."

I stared at him.

"That just doesn't seem to be the way it is here. They often exclude their older sister. Tease her. Make fun of her. It's almost like…" She put her glasses on and rifled through more papers. "They don't acknowledge anyone but themselves. Ah, here we are. Take a look at these results." She handed us a sheet of paper. Troy took it, read it, and showed it to me. The lines and numbers on a graph meant nothing to me. I handed it back to her.

She took her glasses off again. "We'd like to try separating them next year. We had the school psychologist look at them, and she's of the same opinion, that gradually we need to get them weaned away from each other. They're awfully dependent on each other."

"If you think that's the best solution, we're willing to try it," said Troy.

But that's the way twins are, I wanted to protest. Instead, I said, "I don't know. They'll be so hurt by it. They have this secret…I don't know, this private way of communicating with each other. They always have. I've read about it. With identical twins." I was fingering a loose thread on my denim skirt. "They'll be so disappointed."

I once had this dream that their real mother came for them. They had been switched at birth. Their real mother was a bouncy young thing with white-blond hair who skipped rope with them and understood everything they were saying and laughed at all their jokes, and I said, Well, I guess I knew it all along.

On the way home, Troy said, "You contradicted me back there. You have contradicted me in front of Ham, and now in front of our children's principal."

I opened my mouth but didn't say anything.

"A wife who contradicts me in public? How do you think that makes me look?"

I made patterns on my skirt with my forefinger and stared out the window. "Ham?" I said. "How did I contradict you in front of Ham?"

"Going on about some ridiculous music the way you did the other night."

"But he asked the questions."

"Are you with me in this or not? Answer me, Sadie."

"With you in what?"

"In separating the twins."

I scrunched up a handful of skirt fabric, scrunched it until my knuckles were white. Then I let it go. "Can't we at least talk about it?"

"You heard what she said. It's the best thing if the twins are separated. I even think we should separate them at home. Put Mary Beth into the room with either Tabby or PJ and put one of the twins in Mary Beth's room."

My twins had separate beds, and more often than not, when I would wake them in the morning, they would be sleeping in one bed, arms entwined.

"Oh Troy, no, we can't do that. We can separate them in school, but not at home. Mary Beth's old enough that she likes her own space."

"It's about time those twins grew up."

"It'll hurt them so much."

"That's the problem with you, Sadie. You have selective hearing. You read all those fancy psychology books but only follow the advice that suits you. Here you have a professional stating the facts as she sees them, and you refuse to listen—"

"Can you stop?"

"Stop?"

"The car. Can you stop? Right now!"

"Why, for heaven sakes?"

"I'm going to be sick. I need you to stop right NOW."

He sighed loudly and pulled up onto the shoulder. I opened my door, leaned out, and threw up, glad this was a wooded area instead of a boulevard or someone's manicured front lawn. When I was finished, I wiped my mouth on a crumple of paper towels I found on the floor.

"Sadie, for heaven sake, close your door. Let's go. Let's get out of here."

I leaned my head against the back of the seat and held the paper towels to my face all the way home. They smelled of grease and shoe dirt. Troy turned on the radio to a light rock station.

When we got home Gavin was sitting under the piano bench in the living room watching VeggieTales, and the twins and Mary Beth were upstairs. The baby-sitter was rocking Simon in the living room. Troy drove her home, and carrying Simon on one hip, I dumped some instant mashed potato flakes in water while hamburgers defrosted in the microwave.

Upstairs, Mary Beth and the twins were arguing loudly while I patted the hamburgers in the bottom of a frying pan. The smell of the frying meat nauseated me and I had to sit down a few times. I must be coming down with something. I wasn't pregnant. I was just coming down with something.

Into the microwave went a glass container of frozen corn. I wasn't going to even attempt a salad. Not with the way I was feeling. I hate making salads, all that cutting, and then no one eats them anyway. The kids just pick at them.

Troy was sitting in the living room in front of the evening news. Police were still looking for the man who had been seen with Ally, but as the trail grew colder, police were holding out little hope the child was still alive. Through the open door I also learned that Ally's father, Greg Buckley, was front and center in the takeover of SmartSystems by Federated, a Georgia-based company and call center specializing in debt consolidation. "Police do not believe that the disappearance of Ally Buckley has anything to do with the buyout—" Troy switched quickly to another channel.

But I stood in the doorway, the mixing spoon in my hand,

Simon on my hip and said, "What's this about a what—a call center? What is it, Troy?"

"Nothing. Just work stuff. Nothing to be concerned about."

"But what is it?"

"Just some changes at work."

"But Greg Buckley?"

Troy turned to me. "Sadie, this is just about the last thing I feel like talking about right now, okay?"

"You'll be able to keep your job, won't you?"

"Of course. It doesn't even concern me. You don't know a thing and you're jumping to conclusions."

He gave me a dismissive wave of his hand and went back to his television. I went back to the kitchen. Greg Buckley was the manager of SmartSystems. Greg Buckley had moved into Coffins Reach a year ago. Greg Buckley was responsible for a takeover. Greg Buckley's daughter goes missing.

I went to the bathroom off the kitchen and threw up again even though my stomach was empty. When I got back to the stove, the hamburgers had burned on one side.

Chapter Twenty-three

I almost ran after Troy that day he left my practice room more than a dozen years ago. When he walked out, my hands went back to the piano keys, but they were strange hands that moved up and down, hitting all the wrong keys.

A week without Troy. I tried to swallow but couldn't. I closed my music book, slid out from the piano, and went to the door. I half expected him to be there, standing there, waiting for me, telling me he couldn't bear to be without me. And I would say, I'm sorry, Troy. I didn't mean it. Don't go.

He wasn't there.

He didn't show up in my practice room at the end of that week, and I was frantic. Every five minutes I was at the door, looking out, scanning the groups of students, but Troy didn't come.

During the miserable days that followed, I saw him occasionally from a distance, at the other side of the cafeteria, across hallways. I would glance in his direction, and he would always look away from me.

"I think I love him," I told Clarice. "Because I wouldn't miss him so much if I didn't. I can't stop thinking about him, what I did to him."

During that week I wrote long letters to him that I didn't send. I scribbled our initials entwined by hearts on scraps of paper that I threw out. I sat by the phone waiting.

Clarice told me finally, "Why don't you call him? Maybe he's waiting for you to call him."

In the end I didn't have to. He called me. And two weeks to the day that I told him I needed space, we were eating dinner in an expensive restaurant in Chicago where he presented me with flowers, a diamond ring, a poem he actually wrote himself, and declarations of love. We were married in June. I never went back to school.

Chapter Twenty-four

"I had a terrible dream," Judith told me on the phone the next morning.

"Oh, Judith."

"Greg left me and I was all alone."

"That won't happen." I ran my forefinger along the edging of the kitchen cupboard. At the very back of the counter, the head of a nail protruded. I reached at it with the tine of a fork, loosened it, and brought it out. Troy had made these cupboards; well, half of them anyway. He'd gotten half of them installed, and then became convinced that the fellow down at Ochs hardware was cheating him on the price of nails. At Ochs hardware you could still buy nails out of bins where they were weighed in little paper bags. He argued with the guy that his scales were inaccurate and then came home and threw the nails all over the kitchen. I had to clean them up. Occasionally, I still find one.

Judith was talking. "He was saying I'm a bad person. That I don't deserve him or a daughter."

"It was just a dream." The singsongs of Gavin's video intruded into the kitchen. I reached over and swung the door closed. Simon was awake and doing baby push-ups in his playpen.

"Would you be able to come over this afternoon, Sadie? I really need to talk to someone."

"I would love to, but I don't have the van today."

"Could you take a cab?"

"A cab?"

127

"I'll pay for it, of course."

"Oh, I don't know. I can't impose that way."

"It's not imposing."

"Well…" Troy was in the northern part of the state today and wouldn't be home until six or seven. There was plenty of time. He would never have to know.

"How does twelve-thirty sound?"

"Twelve-thirty sounds okay."

At precisely twelve-thirty, a taxi pulled up and I climbed in the back with the boys. When we arrived at Judith's, the driver turned expecting payment. I looked up at the house, all closed up, windows shut in the warmth of midday. "The person in that house is supposed to pay for this," I ventured.

"I don't know anything about that," the driver said.

"She was the one who called you."

"No one told me anything."

"Okay then, just a minute." I began fishing in my wallet. Troy had given me my week's grocery allowance this morning. I was hoping to use any extra for a pair of summer sandals for Mary Beth.

He took the money without a word, and I unloaded Simon and Gavin and we walked up the path to the house. I rang the doorbell.

No answer.

I tried the bell again. Still nothing. The taxi driver was long gone, and I was beginning to be afraid. I knocked loudly. When there was still no answer, I tried the door. It was unlocked. I opened it a crack and peered into the stale darkness.

"Judith?" I called softly.

I opened the door wider. It was cooler in there and dark. "Judith?"

I stepped inside and called her name again. Still no answer. The house smelled sour and shut up and for several seconds I stood there, holding Gavin's hand and carrying Simon in the other. I felt panicked, bewildered, and alone. Suddenly, Gavin tore away from me and chased through the house and out the back door and on to her deck. I followed him. On the deck Judith was rocking in a chair, back and forth in the heat, a cotton throw across her shoulders.

"Judith?" I called softly. "Are you okay?" I was standing in front of her. "Are you okay?"

She shook her head, ever so faintly, her chair still moving back and forth. She snugged the shawl around her. "I'm thinking today. And thinking is dangerous." She paused. "The nights are the worst. That's when I think. That's when it all comes out."

I sat in a lounge chair across from her with Simon on my lap. The air was dense, the sun was hot, and my shirt stuck against my back. Down below was the bay, slow moving today and the color of iron. We were quiet for a while. Judith's eyes were closed and she had leaned her head against the back of the chair. She reminded me then of a very old woman out for her morning air, cold in the heat of the day. Her chair creaked back and forth. The only sound. Even Gavin was quiet.

"I know what you mean," I finally said. "About the nights being the worst."

She opened her eyes. "It's when all the terrible thoughts start coming. Is she dead? Is her body out there somewhere? What were her last minutes on this earth like? Did she suffer? Whose face did she see in those dying moments…" Her voice trailed off. "Sometimes I feel I can't bear it."

After a while I said, "Can I do anything for you?"

"A cup of tea would be nice. Hot tea on a cold day like today would be nice."

"I'll go make some." Gavin followed me into the kitchen where I gave him a cookie from a plate on the counter. I placed a blanket on the floor and lay Simon down. Then I filled the kettle, put it on the stove, and lit the burner. I found tea bags in a cupboard and got a tray with teacups and cookies ready, a tea bag for each cup. Earl Grey. Judith had her tea sent to her from Canada, she had told me once. When the tea was ready I took it out to her.

"You are a good person, Sadie." She touched my arm. "Already I feel better. Just having someone here."

I sat down with Simon on my lap.

"When I called you," she said, "I knew I needed to spend time with someone normal, to see that there are still normal people around with normal families where normal things happen to them—"

"You keep saying that."

She smiled. "It's true. I think there's a part of me that's slightly jealous of you. Loving husband. Lots of kids. I always wanted a big family. We tried and tried, and finally Ally was born." She reached out her hands then for Simon, and I handed him to her. She hugged him to her face.

"Please don't be jealous of me," I said, looking into my tea.

"But you seem so sweet. Like nothing bad would ever happen to you."

I almost told her something I have never told another person in my life—that Troy hits me. That my life is not so normal. I almost told her that Troy also works at SmartSystems and that Greg is probably his boss, the boss he seems to despise. I would have. The words were right there. Instead, I told her I was pregnant, and that I didn't know how I was going to cope.

"Is your husband pleased?"

"He doesn't know."

"You mean you haven't told him?" She looked at me surprised.

"I wanted to be sure."

"You're not sure 100 percent then?"

I shook my head. "It's hard to tell with me. My cycle has gotten so screwed up, with nursing and all. This may sound funny, but I've been pregnant for most of the last almost twelve years of my marriage. I've had lots of miscarriages and difficult pregnancies. So, no, I'm not positive. But I've got the nausea. And the throwing up."

"You haven't taken a test?"

"I haven't been to the doctor, no."

"I'm not talking about going to the doctor, I'm talking about a test you can buy. Do you know they can practically tell if you're only one day pregnant? The tests are truly amazing. I've taken so many of them, I could write a book. And I only have one child. Life is unfair at times, isn't it? You are blessed, Sadie. You are so blessed."

"That's not exactly the word I would use. Five children is a lot. Six will be even harder."

She leaned forward. "Well, on those days, friend, you can drop off Gavin and Simon with me."

"You might regret saying that." I smiled.

"I don't think so."

"And you might be going back to work soon."

She didn't say anything for a while. "They called me this morning to see if I would. They're busy over there. I just didn't have an answer. It's like life is just supposed to go on, and I've taken enough time to grieve, now I'm supposed to buck up and get with it."

"That must be so hard."

When it was time for me to leave I said, "Well, I guess I should call a cab."

"Oh, you didn't drive your van over?"

"No, I had to take a cab here."

She put her hands straight above her head. "Where's my head? Here I was so taken with talking that I completely forgot. You need money for the cab."

"No, that's okay. I have some."

She went to her wallet and then came back and pressed a fifty-dollar bill in my hands. "You take this. It should cover it. Keep the change."

I stared at the bill in my hand. "It's only two cab rides."

"Keep it. Use it for cab fare here again."

"I'll give you the change next time I see you. I promise I will."

"And I will refuse to take it. You keep it, Sadie. Spend it on those beautiful children of yours. Or use it to buy a pregnancy test. And Sadie, I can't thank you enough for coming. It meant so much for me to have you here."

I put the money in my wallet and phoned for a cab.

Chapter Twenty-five

When I got home Emma and Mary Beth were sitting at the kitchen table drinking coffee mugs full of chocolate milk. All over the table there were sprinkles of cocoa powder and white puddles of milk where Mary Beth had attempted to pour.

"Oh, Mary Beth, Emma, I'm so sorry I'm late. I had to take a cab and one didn't come for a long time…"

"I know where the key is," Mary Beth said. "Emma came over 'cause you said we could run through the sprinkler." She was pouring more milk and only some of it was landing in the cup.

"Mary Beth," said Emma, "you're spilling."

"I KNOW, Emma! You're making me spill."

"Let me do it," I said, reaching for the milk carton.

"I can do it, Mommy."

"I know you can. You're a big girl, but even big girls need help sometimes."

I wiped the milky mess from the table with a smelly dishrag, then threw it on top of the overflowing laundry pile beside the washing machine. There were at least three loads of laundry that would have to be done before supper. "It's so warm," I said. "That's a good idea, running through the sprinkler. Where're PJ and Tabby?"

"Outside. And this isn't fair, Mommy. We said we were going to run through the sprinkler? And right away they had to. They took our idea."

"We have two sprinklers and two hoses so there's room for all of you outside. Does Emma have her suit with her?"

"She's going to wear my old one. But Mommy, we want the sprinkler that goes back and forth, not the one that goes around. Can you tell them that?"

"We'll take turns by the kitchen timer."

"I want to, too," said Gavin.

"Okay, but you have to be good," I said. "No teasing or fighting. And no running off. Stay in the backyard. I have a lot to do before Daddy comes home." I glanced at the calendar and with a kind of horror I remembered that this was the night of the monthly deacons' and wives' potluck and Bible study. How could I have forgotten? I was supposed to bring a salad, just about my least favorite thing to make.

Tonight's supper was going to be at the spacious home of Jim and Betty Frost. The Frosts were in just about everything in church. Their three adult children also attended with their various grand-children. Betty had, at one time in her church life, headed up the social committee, the missions committee, the Sunday school, the hospitality committee, and the welcoming and hospital visitation committee, and Jim was chairman of the board and had been on the board for as long as we had lived here.

The twins appeared in the doorway, clad in identical bathing suits from two years ago that tugged up on their elongated bodies. When had they sprung up like that?

"What are you wearing those for?" I said.

"Because…" said PJ.

"Our bathing suits from last year don't match," Tabby said.

"And these match," PJ said.

"Well, what's wrong with that? They look nice on you. And they're close enough, they're just different colors."

"But we have to match…"

"Exactly."

"That's the rule."

When the five of them, including Gavin, were outside running through sprinklers, I put a load of laundry in, folded some from the dryer, and shuffled around in the bottom of the refrigerator for salad ingredients. I found a head of lettuce in not too bad a shape (just get rid of a few outer leaves), half a tomato, some carrots, a few radishes. It would be a boring salad. Nothing like some of the other wives made with spinach leaves and little sections of oranges, or various kinds of lettuce leaves and lobster meat, or real Caesar salads made from scratch in wooden bowls from secret ingredients.

And then there was the question of what to wear. If it were cooler I'd wear the peach sweater and skirt Bernice had brought over. But it was warm so I'd wear my L. L. Bean dress. It was comfortable and suited me. I usually felt pretty good in it until I stood next to someone like Betty Frost. I could picture her tonight in some silky pantsuit and lots of glittery jewelry. And those golden slippers she always wore.

Two and a half hours later I was holding my boring salad on my lap in an old chipped glass bowl we sometimes used for popcorn while Troy drove. We were late. Troy had been detained in the north, and he was in a foul mood. When he talked it was with a growl that reminded me of Gavin.

The Frost home was comfortably air-conditioned and the dining room table was set with fine china. Betty handed us glass cups of punch as we entered. I had to sit on the couch in such a way that my skirt covered my shin, which was turning shades of blue.

There were five other couples plus Pastor Ken and Cheryl. I was the only one who brought a baby, even though Maxine and Art's first baby is a month younger than Simon. They left her with Art's mother. The huge dining room table was laid with trays of shelled lobster, scalloped potatoes, and fiddleheads. And when Betty called us in, I noticed she had transferred my salad into a silver bowl with tongs. She had also added a sprinkling of croutons and had poured my store-bought salad dressings into little matching silver pitchers.

Ken said grace and the food was passed. Maxine sat next to me and asked about Simon, comparing his development with Kristen's. When do they walk? Kristen is crawling already, but when do they walk? When do they start talking? On the floor beside me, Simon was whimpering softly in his baby carrier. I handed him a crust of bread.

"Is he okay down there?" Betty was smiling at me, her large glasses glinting in the lights of the chandelier.

"He'll be fine," I said.

"Does he need something underneath him?"

"Underneath him?"

"To catch the crumbs. Babies, adorable as they are, can quite devastate a floor. My goodness, what a cutie he is though." She plopped her linen napkin on the table and pushed back her chair. She returned a few minutes later with a plastic sheet printed with cartoon characters. She lifted Simon and his baby seat and spread the sheet on the floor. "This is what grandma uses for all her grand-kids. I love it when they come over, but, oh my, they can demolish a floor. But we'll just use grandma's old trick here. We just put this plastic sheet right underneath and here we go. Now, we're all set, aren't we? He must be crawling by now?"

"Not quite. He's almost got it. He does these baby push—"

"Would anyone care for more pickles? Merilee, you? Phil? How about some?" asked Betty sitting down again.

"Oh, no thanks, Betty. I'm fine."

"Karen, how are you doing? More of anything?"

"I'm fine, Betty. This is wonderful, as usual."

During supper, quiet instrumental praise music wafted through the room. It reminded me at first of the music I had heard. But my music was more mellow, more minor. Less bright, somehow, a little more off-key. Sadder.

"Sadie, are you with us?" Troy's hand was on my shoulder. "Garth asked you a question."

"Oh. I'm sorry. I was listening to the music."

"It's beautiful, isn't it?" said Betty. "Our son works at the Christian radio station and he's always giving us CDs. Some we like, some we don't; right, Jim? I like this one because it has so many of the old hymns. You don't hear a lot of the old hymns nowadays."

"I like them, too." Then I turned to Garth. "I'm sorry, I didn't hear you."

"I was just wondering if you were stuck up, that's all." He was grinning.

"Stuck up?"

"I thought I saw you this afternoon in the backseat of a cab. I honked and waved at you, but you didn't even acknowledge me."

Troy was listening to this with great interest. I put my hand to my mouth and stared at him. I looked down at my food. Karen saved me by asking something about the twins.

Then someone at the end of the table asked Troy about the Federated takeover. Troy was talking in his work voice, his important voice, and I learned things I hadn't known before.

"It's called credit card consolidation. You buy their card for a small start-up fee and then you use it exclusively," he said.

"There's no percentage in that," said Garth.

Troy smirked. "You're absolutely right there."

"But what's that got to do with computers?"

"Precious little. That's why so many of us are upset."

"Is your job safe?" someone else asked.

"Oh, it should be. I've done a lot of good work for that company. I'm pretty respected there."

Cheryl said, "They're going to build a new facility, I hear."

"You hear right. They'll use the present SmartSystems for the admin offices only."

"But I hear it's going to be right on top of that marshland, and there are all those ducks and things," said Karen. "Isn't anyone saying anything about that?"

Troy grinned. "You can't stop progress, you know. It'll bring too many jobs to this area for people to be too concerned."

Later, we took our coffees into the living room where the remainder of the evening would be spent in Bible study and prayer. Betty, however, was smilingly brimming with information about "a new project."

She was sitting at the edge of her chair, her hands folded on her knees, looking at Ken. Ken smiled and said, "Betty has something she wants to talk to us as a group about. Go ahead, Betty, you have the floor."

"Thank you, Ken. Well, I've talked with Ken about this, Jim and I have, and we think it's something we should perhaps consider as a church. It's a real outreach ministry...Jim, do you want to say anything before I begin?"

"No, Betty, this is your baby."

"Okay, then. This is something I'm quite excited about. Well, I'll begin at the beginning. About two weeks ago I met and talked with—well Jim and I both did—with Bernice Jacobs from church." A few heads nodded and smiled. "Well, she's just moved here from Orono and has taken on the directorship of the Safe Harbor House for Women. And in case any of you don't know what that is, it's a safe house for battered women. Well, the former director left, and I just think it's so exciting that a Christian is in charge of it now. And I just think we should give her as much support as we can. Our church, I mean. What she's interested in is getting a twenty-four-hour help line where women who are being abused can call and find help. And what she wants from us is to train volunteers to work on the help line."

"Is this a real problem here in Coffins Reach?" asked Art. "I mean, I can see Bangor, maybe, but Coffins Reach is such a little community. Everyone knows everyone."

"Well, Bernice says that according to the statistics, it's a big problem here, which is why the safe house is located here. The center also needs money and blankets and cookware, dishes, clothes for all ages. Just about anything. Personally, I've got a couple of old sets of dishes that I'm willing to donate. Bernice suggested a garage sale to raise money."

"I thought they had a lot of clothes. Extra clothes, I mean," I said. Troy eyed me quizzically. I had never told him that Bernice had given me clothing.

"On the contrary," said Betty. "They're begging, quite literally begging for good used or new clothing."

"A garage sale might not go over with some of the older members of the congregation," said Garth. "Not many of them would want any sort of a church-sponsored garage sale. Plus, there are those who feel that extra money should go to missions, rather than women."

"But this *is* a mission field, Garth," said Betty. "Right in our own backyard. If we do get involved, think of the outreach we could have, we could get these women involved in a church. Something that would help all of them. One of the things Bernice wants is to update the brochures—they're rather ratty looking now—and get them in to various places, doctors' offices, that sort of thing."

"I'm trying to place Bernice," Garth said. "Is she the one who always wears that getup?"

Betty laughed. "They're called clothes. And you have to agree they're quite charming on a woman of Bernice's stature."

"Well, what's the consensus?" asked Ken. "Is this a ministry we want to be involved in?"

"I'm not sure," said Garth. "It doesn't directly relate to the ministries of our church. I'd have to give it some thoughtful prayer. And where's the accountability?"

"But think of the outreach. These poor women."

The group talked about this for half an hour and in the end decided that we would support it. We would announce Bernice's training session in the bulletin, and allow her to speak to the church as a whole, but we wouldn't give Safe Harbor House any *budgeted* money. A special fund would be set up where individual donations could be made through the church, however. My husband volunteered to help any way he could, and it was decided that he and Betty would cochair the committee.

I held my hands tightly clasped in my lap the whole time.

I didn't say anything during the Bible study that followed either. Troy kept looking at me. I think he wishes I were more like Karen or Merilee or even Betty, for that matter.

When it came time for prayer requests, Garth said, "Any requests? Sadie, we haven't heard from you in a while…"

I opened my eyes wide. "Uh, I don't know. Maybe just that we should continue to pray for the Buckleys that Ally will be found."

"That's one family that has had its share of problems," Garth said.

I looked around me. "We should pray for Judith. I know her a little bit. I don't think she's back at work yet, although she's been talking about going back. We should pray that the hospital is lenient and allows her to come back when she's ready. Maybe we could pray for that. That she won't lose her job or anything…" My voice trailed off at the end when I realized everyone was giving me and each other strange looks. Cheryl looked at Ken, and I felt a coldness I couldn't explain.

"Sadie," said Ken, "Judith doesn't work at the hospital. She hasn't for a long time."

"Yes, she does. She told me she was a nurse in the pediatrics department."

The men looked at each other. The wives looked down at their laps. I looked first at Ken and then at Troy. No one said anything for a while. Ken finally broke the silence. "No, she doesn't, Sadie. There were some problems there, and she was let go a year ago."

Chapter Twenty-six

When Ham called at nine in the morning and asked whether Troy was at home, I became momentarily flustered. "No, Ham, he's at work. I just dropped him off there. If you call him there, you'll probably get him."

"Actually, Sadie, it's you I wanted to talk to. I wanted to make sure you had some time and space in which to talk."

I smoothed my hair back with shaky hands. "About what?"

"I want to ask you about what we were talking about at dinner the other night. The music."

"The music?"

"I'd like to come over if I could."

"But it's probably like Troy said, someone's stereo."

"I don't think so." He paused. "I've spent the past couple of days going over the Amanda Johnson case. When you told me about the music it rang a bell, but I didn't realize how much of a bell until I started delving into it all again. I don't know if the music you heard was at all connected to the music that our witness heard, but it seemed too much of a coincidence. And since, as you say, music is, or used to be, a hobby of yours, I wonder if you might be able to help me. I don't know any people who know very much about music."

"Well, I don't know if I can help. What would I have to do?"

"I'd like to come over and talk with you about this."

"I was just on my way out shopping."

"This won't take long."

Ham and another officer, a young deputy he introduced as Julie Baker, arrived at my door fifteen minutes later. We sat at the kitchen table while Gavin watched television and Simon did push-ups on the kitchen floor. I looked at Julie's incredibly yellow curly hair and wondered idly if it was a wig.

She was looking at Simon. "Strong little guy," she said.

Simon was up on his toes, grunting as he attempted to move forward.

"He is," I said.

"I have a little nephew about that size. Really active."

"They are at that age."

"Into everything."

Across the table, Ham said, "There's a house a few hundred feet from the lighthouse. Actually there are some other summer homes there, but this one seems to be the only one occupied year round. We've just come from there. They were very reluctant to talk to us. They acted real strange. But what we did find out was that the woman was awakened around 2 A.M. to what sounded like an orchestra or a band playing down on the point. She described the music as classical, but soft. Very pleasant to listen to, she said. Actually her story is much like your own. She got up in the middle of the night, stood by the window, and listened. Eventually she went outside and stood on the porch. She said she thought the music came from a boat.

"When the music ended, about an hour later, she went back inside and to bed. And then the next morning Amanda Johnson's body was found on the point."

"What has the music got to do with anything?" I asked.

"I don't know. Nothing maybe."

Simon had moved about a body length forward and his head was now crunched up against a cabinet. He was crawling with straight legs and on tiptoes. I drew him back onto the blanket and he squawked as if to say, I got that far. Let me go! Julie looked at him and grinned.

"The sergeant," Ham said, "thinks I'm chasing down wild geese, and Julie here thinks I'm a little too close to believing in *The X-Files* or *The Twilight Zone*. But I have another question, and bear with me on this one. The husband of our witness said that during the night he woke up to see his wife standing by the window swaying. He said he watched her for a few minutes, then went back to sleep. He has no recollection of music. None whatsoever. He never heard it." He looked at me. "Sadie, did anyone else in your family hear what you heard?"

I shook my head. "Troy slept right through." I paused. "Wait a minute. I went into the boys' room, and both Simon and Gavin came and sat on my lap. The music was plain as day in there. I remember telling Gavin to listen to it."

"And did he? Did Gavin hear it?"

"I think so. But maybe I just assumed so. Gavin," I called, "can you come here a minute? Mommy needs you for a minute."

There was not a breath of movement. He was sitting on the floor, his legs bent underneath and behind him, in that way only children can manage, while vegetables danced on the television.

"Gavin!" I called more loudly. No answer. I went to him and knelt beside him. "Gavin, can we put your video on pause for a minute? Mommy has to ask you something really, really important."

Gavin looked at me, looked up at the two uniformed police officers, and nodded.

"Hey there, guy," said Ham.

"You gots a gun," said Gavin.

"I do indeed."

"Gavin," I said, "I want you to think about something really, really important. Remember a long time ago when Daddy spanked you that night? And in the middle of the night I was feeding Simon and you came and sat on my lap? Gavin, do you remember that night?"

He put his thumb in his mouth and nodded.

"Do you remember the music that was on?"

He stared at me.

"The music, Gavin, do you remember music?"

He shook his head.

"Remember when Mommy said to listen to the pretty music? Gavin, do you remember that?"

"Don't 'member."

"Don't you remember the music?"

"Don't 'member, don't 'MEMBER."

He grabbed the remote out of my hand. I stood up.

Ham said, "I don't think we're going to get too much here. He was probably asleep, or half asleep." Back in the kitchen he said, "And I don't know how important it really is to begin with. Might not be significant at all."

We sat down again, and Julie said, "So, Ham, let me get this straight. Music was playing the night Amanda Johnson was murdered, and then music was playing again two months later…"

"When another girl, approximately the same age, disappeared."

"But we know that girl's body was not found on the point," Julie said.

"Even though we looked."

I was looking from one face to the other as they talked, trying to comprehend.

"And our witness didn't hear the music the night Sadie did, and she only heard it the once."

"If we could hear what it sounded like—whether or not that's important, we have no way of knowing," said Ham. "Sadie, do you remember what it sounded like? Do you remember any snatches of melody? Was it a familiar tune?"

I got up and retrieved Mary Beth's school scribbler from the piano bench, tore out the last page, and handed it to him. He stared at it uncomprehending. "What's this?"

"The music. The melody line at least. I wrote it down. Or what

I could remember the next morning. It was such a haunting melody I didn't want to forget it."

"You did this?"

I nodded.

"Just out of thin air? You can write down music that you hear? People can do this?"

"I can. Sort of."

"I would say that music is slightly more than a hobby for you."

"I'm about a semester and a half away from a degree in composition."

"Composition?"

"Music composition. Composing music. Writing songs, in other words."

He held the sheets and stared at me, then eyed the piano. "Would you?"

I shook my head and looked at the floor. "It's a personal thing. I can't. I just can't. Don't ask."

He looked at me for a long moment before he said, "I'm going to need to take this with me. But I'll make sure you get it back. I'll probably make photocopies. I can get one of those to you right away."

"It's okay. I don't know why I did it. But it was such a haunting melody. I can't explain it."

"I can't either," he said. "I can't explain any of it."

Chapter Twenty-seven

ater that morning, I got Gavin and Simon ready for grocery shopping. After groceries I would drive up the highway to the Christian bookstore. I still had the change from Judith's fifty dollars in my wallet.

At the Shop 'N' Save, I strapped Simon into the cart, Gavin grabbed one of the little grocery carts they have for kids, and we started up and down the aisles, filling our baskets with cereal, milk, pasta, cheese, hot dogs. I looked down the toiletries aisle but couldn't find any pregnancy tests. There was a Rite Aid on the way to the Christian bookstore. I'd stop there.

Simon fell asleep in the car almost as soon as I started driving again, he who never sleeps in cars. Twenty minutes later I pulled into the parking lot of the Rite Aid. Gavin was strapped into the backseat beside Simon quietly looking through a picture book from the church library, and Simon was still asleep, his head lolling to the side. I parked in the shade. I whispered to Gavin, "Don't wake up your brother, I'm only going to be a minute. Be good." He smiled up at me cherubically. At the door I looked back. All was quiet. Just one minute.

The pregnancy tests were expensive, but I would scrimp on something else. I found the cheapest one, took it to the counter, and held it against my body as I stood in line. At the counter a woman with an entire basket of toiletry items was arguing over the sale price of nail polish. Next, a man stepped up, and the cashier began looking in vain for photographs which he swore were supposed to be ready by today and that he needed by tonight. I tried looking out-side, but could not see to the van. I shifted my weight from foot to foot. Please be good, I said. Please, God, make them be okay. I was only going to be a minute. And the minute had turned easily into ten. Still, it couldn't be much longer now, could it?

The door opened. A man approached the counter. "Does anyone in here belong to a van out there? There seems to be some trouble…"

I dropped the pregnancy test on a row of gum packets and fled.

Simon was twisted in his car seat, redfaced and screaming, flail-ing his arms and legs. Gavin was jumping up and down on the front seat and growling. I inserted the key into the lock, and no sooner had I done that than Gavin pressed the lock closed again.

"Gavin! Let me in!"

Laughter. Just laughter.

"Let me in, Gavin! Right now! Let Mommy in!"

He pressed his little face up against the window, a grotesque gar-goyle in the glass. "No," he said. "No, no, no, no, no. NO! NO!"

"Gavin!" I tried the lock again, but he managed to thwart me. Simon was wailing louder now. A crowd was beginning to gather. Tears of anger, embarrassment, frustration threatened to spill.

"Gavin, please let me in! Please!"

Voices surrounded me:

"I can't believe a mother leaving her children in an unattended car…"

"Someone should report this to Social Services…"

"Gavin, please!" I was frantic to get in, frantic to get out, frantic to get away from the voices. I kept dropping the keys on the ground. Simon had nearly twisted around sideways, and I hoped dearly that the straps on his seat held.

"Gavin! Let me IN!"

But from within Gavin was screaming, "No! No! I hate you! I hate you! Bad Mommy!" He was screaming, shaking his head, his face red.

I felt a hand on mine and looked up into the face of a tall young man with tiny round glasses. "Give me your keys," he said quietly, gently. "Give me your keys and I'll unlock the passenger side. You continue to pretend to unlock your side."

Around me the voices continued:

"What that kid needs is a good swat across his backside…"

"No discipline. That's the problem with parents nowadays…"

"I've got a little nephew who gets into these tantrums," the young man was saying. "I know how to handle him. I'm about the only one who can. I've done it a million times with Eric. What's his name?"

"Gavin. His name is Gavin."

"Gavin, right." He cocked his finger and thumb at me and went around to the passenger side.

"Gavin, let me in," I said, pretending to insert a key. Gavin rushed toward me. On the passenger side, the young man opened the door. When Gavin realized what had happened, he rushed toward the man in a fury of flailing arms and legs. The young man held the screaming, thrashing, cursing Gavin for some minutes, while I looked on. The man didn't let go. I went around to Simon.

I don't know how long we were there, but eventually the soft whispers, the tight holding on, the stroking of his back, quieted Gavin. Then the young man placed Gavin on the front passenger seat and strapped the seat belt across him. He was still talking non-stop to him, whispers and smiles and strokes on his shoulder. I craned to hear what he was saying but could not.

He turned and left. By this time the crowd had also dispersed.

"Wait," I called running after him. He turned.

"Thank you," I said. Tears blurred my vision.

"It was nothing."

When I started the van, Simon was whimpering softly, and Gavin was quietly reading his picture book. I drove to a roadside turnout and picnic area where I nursed Simon, while Gavin sat in

the passenger seat calmly looking at his book. It was a glorious day
and ahead of us, the bay sparkled. A sailboat moved along the horizon, its sail full with wind.

"Look at the boat, Gavin," I finally said. "Look how pretty."

We sat that way for a while, the three of us.

At first I thought it was the sound of a far-off boat, or the sad
moan of a foghorn. And then I realized. The music? I rolled down
my window. Yes, it was louder, and definitely *the* music. *My* music.
Simon had finished nursing and I sat him up on my lap. I reached
under the front seat where I knew were a bunch of old church bulletins and Sunday school papers.

"Gavin, do you hear that? Do you hear it now?"

He looked at me.

"Do you hear the music?"

"What, Mommy?"

"The music. Do you hear the music? Do you?"

He shook his head.

"Listen, Gavin, off in the distance. You have to listen carefully."

He smiled.

"Let's go outside for a while."

I got the old stroller out of the van and placed Simon in it. On
the back of a bulletin, I quickly drew a series of staffs and then
rewrote the melody line.

Then there was a variation on the melody. I sat at the picnic
table and wrote furiously. There was the oboe solo, the one I heard,
and the strings coming in at the end. A new sound. The sound of a
flute. No, a recorder.

"Do you hear it now, Gavin? It's louder now. Tell me that you
hear it."

But he was racing around the table making car noises.

There was a path of sorts that led from the picnic area down to
the beach. I got a couple of blank sides of bulletins, stuffed them in
the diaper bag and said, "Gavin, let's go down to the beach."

He raced ahead of me on the path, and I pushed the stroller as fast as I could to keep up with him. The path to the beach wound over roots and pebbles and rocks and various species of overgrowth. In the distance seagulls sounded like the bleating of sheep. I could hear the insistent sound of the sea, but it was the music that I listened to, the music that I followed, the music that seemed a part of the air itself.

"They must be down on the beach, those people playing the music." The underbrush, pale green with spring, was spongy under our feet. "I want to find out where they are. Do you hear them, Gavin? Tell me, do you hear them or not?"

At one point I stopped and clamped my hands over my ears, and it diminished the sound. The music was real! Nearer the water's edge the music was loudest of all, yet I saw no one. I lifted the stroller over stones and rocks and bits of shell and pieces of driftwood. I stood still for a minute. What was that instrument on those high notes? A human voice? But no human voice could make that sound. Not that high. Not that clear.

And then it dawned on me where I was. I was on the other side of the point, the other side of the lighthouse. I had never been on this side of the lighthouse before.

I sat on a rock and wrote music across the back of the bulletin, while Gavin threw pebbles into the water and stomped in the tide pools.

In the distance, from the direction of the point, someone was walking toward us holding the leashes of at least three dogs. At first I thought it was a woman, but closer I could see it was a young girl, someone not a lot older than Mary Beth. She was clad in a too-big-for-her faded pink sweater, wide dark pants, and old canvas shoes that flapped on her feet. I waved as she got closer. She was even younger than I had originally thought. Maybe more like the twins' age, quite young to be out walking on a beach with three huge dogs. Her dark blond hair was blown in wisps all around her head.

"You've got some nice dogs there," I said to her.

"Thank you."

"Gavin, come look at the dogs," I called, but his back was to us. "Are you taking them for a walk or are they taking you for a walk?" I laughed.

She looked at me very seriously and said, "I'm taking them for a walk. They need air. They need exercise."

The one nearest the stroller stuck his nose near Simon. Simon didn't budge, didn't even wrinkle up his nose, even though he usually sneezed his face away from animals.

"Simon, get away from there!" The girl pulled on her leash. "Where are your manners? Simon sometimes forgets his manners. I'm awfully sorry."

"Your dog's name is Simon?"

"Yes. These are Simon, Jody, and Dorry."

"Well, isn't that funny. My baby's name is Simon."

"His name is Simon?"

"Yes, it is. Isn't that a coincidence?"

"Well, it is if you believe in coincidences. Which I don't happen to. I've never seen you on the beach before."

"We've never been on this beach before."

"Most people go to the beach at Coffins Reach or up the beach toward Bucksport. This stretch of beach no one seems to know about. It could be the current. There's a pretty bad one out there. I'd watch that little kid of yours."

"Gavin," I called, "keep away from the edge. She says there's a current."

The music was still clear and loud.

"I came down because I heard the music."

"They all come down here eventually," she said importantly.

"Do you know where it's coming from? The music?"

"Well, there's all kinds of theories." She held on to the leashes, and cupped her right elbow into her left palm and tapped her cheek with the fingers of her right hand. "Well, the one that seems to get the most credence is that someone left their radio on. The second most believed theory is that it's ghosts. And then there are those who favor angels."

"Angels?"

"But I personally don't hold to that theory because nowhere in the Bible does it say that angels sing. That definitely is a misreading."

"I didn't know that."

"Well, it's true." Her three dogs sat obediently at her side.

"Do you live nearby?"

She picked up a piece of driftwood and pointed toward the lighthouse. The dogs thought she was going to throw the stick and stood at the ready. "Up there," she said. "With my granddad."

"You live in the lighthouse?"

"With my granddad." Her fair hair blowing across her face reminded me of a painting I'd seen somewhere.

"I thought the lighthouse was abandoned."

"That too is a misconception. A misreading. I live in the keeper's house. Don't lose your papers there," she said.

I had stuffed the papers in the back of Simon's stroller, and the wind was blowing some of them loose. I stuffed them back into the diaper bag. "I was trying to write down the music."

"You'll never get it all down." She was walking away from me, her dogs pulling her forward. "It's unfathomable."

I stared at her until she was a speck in the distance. "Well, she was a strange one, wasn't she, Simon?"

On the way home I stopped at the Christian bookstore and picked up the new Idaho Pioneers from a display at the end of a bookshelf. "Your children are so obedient," said the saleslady. "Boy, mine? You can't take them anywhere!"

Chapter Twenty-eight

roy was standing beside the curb in front of SmartSystems, his briefcase in hand, when I pulled up. I looked at my watch; I was early, yet he was standing there already. He looked more forlorn than angry when I stopped the van. I got out and went around to the passenger seat so Troy could drive. He prefers to drive.

In the back, Gavin was playing with his Game Boy. In the far backseat sat Mary Beth and the twins.

A few moments later Troy said, "Sadie, I had a rough day. First of all a meeting, and then another meeting. And who shows up looking angrier than stink, but you-know-who. But I didn't say anything. I was trying to keep my cool. Then this client demanded all sorts of stuff, trying to blame me when it was head office that screwed up, and of course, they believed him. But it's this whole takeover thing. No one knows whether they're coming or going." He looked over at me. "I tried calling you. I just needed someone to talk to, but I kept getting the machine. And I didn't want to leave a message."

"I was out. Getting groceries. I didn't go far. Ham and Emma are coming for supper and I wanted to pick up a few things."

"I just needed someone to talk to. So, by then I didn't know what to make of the situation, so I called Ham, just to get him to maybe pray for me or something. I don't want to retrain to work in a call center, phoning people, asking them to use our credit card. I just can't see myself doing that. Supporting my family doing that.

They don't think us salesmen warrant any consideration. I wanted to know what you thought about the whole situation because it affects us…"

I was staring at him. I was looking at his mouth, at the words forming there, his teeth behind the lips, talking to me, every so often a glimpse of red tongue. He was *talking* to me. Talking to me as if I were an equal, a friend, like I imagined other married couples talked to each other. Sharing things. Asking for my opinion, as if what I had to say might be important. And he had called home, not to check up on me but to ask my opinion! I felt my eyes tear. I sniffled and looked at his mouth, still talking, still smiling at me. Oh Troy, oh, Troy! I'm so sorry I wasn't there for you today.

"…so, I'm asking you what you think."

I looked at him and could think of nothing to say.

"So, what do you think? How would you react to that?"

"How would I react." I said the words slowly.

"Yeah? What do you think I should do?

"Uh."

His face darkened. "You haven't been listening to me."

"Yes, I have."

"No, you haven't."

"I have, Troy."

"Okay, then tell me what I was talking about."

"Your boss. You don't know what to do about your boss. And the client blaming you. And the takeover." I put the back of my hand to my mouth. It was trembling.

"That was five minutes ago."

"There was a meeting, and your boss was blaming you."

He slammed his fist on the steering wheel. "This is it! This is *exactly* the problem. This is exactly what I'm talking about! I try to have an adult conversation with you when all you are is a child. I'd get a better response from Simon. Sometimes I wonder why I bother. Somebody please tell me why I bother."

"No, please, please tell me again. I'll listen this time. I promise. Don't treat me like a child."

"If you behaved like an adult I'd treat you like an adult. Boy, I try with you, Sadie, I really do. But you make it so impossible. Sometimes I don't even know you."

I kept my eyes averted from him the rest of the way home.

Troy was in a dark mood during supper, even though Ham and Emma were there. Ham had brought two large pizzas he had made himself, and even those were not good enough for Troy. He said we needed more protein in our supper and that everyone would be better served if Ham and I engaged in more preplanning for the meals. Never before had Troy criticized Ham, and this astonished me. Across the table, Ham winked at me.

After supper, Ham started scraping plates and loading the dishwasher. He didn't stop even when Troy, frowning, motioned toward the lawn chairs outside with two tall iced teas.

"And you're too busy, too, to give me the time of day?"

"Let me just help load the dishes," Ham said. "Then I'll join you."

"Oh, don't bother." Troy walked out. "If it's too much trouble."

"He's having some problems at work," I said to Ham. "That's all it is. It's that whole call center thing. It has everybody who works there on edge."

Later on, I watched Ham and Troy out on the lawn chairs Troy had made. Troy rested his head against the back of the lawn chair, his eyes closed, and Ham leaned forward, his elbows on his knees, talking.

Not until Ham and Emma left did it occur to me that I never told Ham about the music I had heard that day, nor about the girl on the beach.

Chapter Twenty-nine

Where were you today? Where did you go?"

I was lying on my back on our bed where Troy had thrown me.

"I don't know what you mean."

"I don't know what you mean. I don't know what you mean." His voice whined in a parody of my own. "You know. When I called home all those dozens of times and the phone rang and rang."

"I already told you. I was out, getting groceries. For supper. You knew that. For Ham and Emma." My voice was choked and strained; I could hardly get the words out.

"That's what you said, but I called two hours later and there was still no answer."

"On the way home we stopped at the beach. I took the boys for a walk. It was a beautiful day."

"Oh, and suddenly you remember that right now. How convenient."

"I stopped to feed Simon at a picnic area, and then I heard the music—"

"Oh, you and that music. Ham says one thing about music and that's a convenient excuse for everything. And that cab ride the other day. Since when can we afford cab rides all over town?"

"What?"

"What? What?" he mimicked. "As if you didn't know. It takes Garth to tell me where my wife goes."

I felt my face get hot. "Judith paid for that cab. She needed me to come over. She was having a really rough day and—"

"But when I'm having *my* rough day, well, that's not important, is it?"

"I didn't know you were having a rough day. I'm sorry, Troy."

"Yeah, well sorry just doesn't cut it anymore, I'm afraid."

Then he cursed at me, a string of foul words that made me cringe. I turned and faced away from him. I hate it when Troy curses like that. He reached across the bed, grabbed both of my shoulders and lifted me up.

"You're lying," Troy said. "And do you know how I know you're lying? I checked the speedometer. You went seventy-five miles today, Sadie. Seventy-five miles? The grocery store is only two miles away. That's why you didn't give me the time of day in the van this afternoon. You had a guilty conscience. You didn't think I would figure it out, but I'm smarter than that. Speedometers don't lie. Would you mind telling me where you went, and why you needed to go seventy-five miles?"

"Shopping and the beach. That was all. I swear."

"Look at me, Sadie. Do you think I'm that stupid?"

"Okay, then I had to go to the Christian bookstore to buy a book to replace the one that got ripped. It's way up the highway twenty-five miles. And then on the beach I met this girl who was telling me about the music. There was music. I swear there was."

"You lying slut!"

He let go of me, and I scrambled away from him and crouched against the headboard. I dabbed a corner of a pillow to my eyes.

"Who were you meeting? Who were you meeting behind my back? That's what I want to know!"

I opened my eyes and stared at him.

"You did meet someone."

"No. I promise you. I didn't see anyone. I didn't even visit Judith, if that's what you mean."

"I'm not talking about Judith. I'm talking about a man. I see the way you look at men." He grabbed the pillow away from me, held my wrist in a vise grip.

"Troy, there's no one else. I told you, we went for groceries, then I drove to the Christian bookstore, and then on the way home we stopped and went for a walk on the beach. Gavin and Simon and I…" I was crying now, frantic that the children not hear, frantic that the neighbors not hear, that no one hear. I was conscious that the window was open, the white sheers fluttering in the evening breeze, neighbors walking by below our window.

"I know you're lying. Who is he?" He cursed some more, called me a whore, a slut, and more.

"There's no one." I crouched as far away from him as I could.

"You are such a liar. Look, you can't even keep a straight face when you lie."

"Troy, the children…"

"Yeah, let's talk about the children, Sadie. I just wonder how many of them are really mine."

I opened my mouth absolutely unable to speak.

"Your lying, slutting ways, the way you strut around church. I've seen you, little whore. None of them look like me. That hasn't escaped my observation. Thought you could keep it from me…"

"Troy, you're talking crazy." I was sobbing now, my fingers scrabbling across my face. "How could you even think such a thing? How could you? And Gavin, he looks *exactly* like you. *Everyone* says that."

Troy cursed again, louder, demanding to know who I was meeting. Who I had met today, where I had gone.

"I'm not lying, Troy; I promise I was there! On the beach, and there was a girl with a dog named Simon. Isn't that funny? Maybe I could find her, too. She showed me where she lives."

He sat down on the bed. "You'd like that, wouldn't you. Did you get her in cahoots, too? Oh, and by the way, if my husband phones tell him I was here, would you?"

I would say nothing more. It would not help. The first time Troy accused me of this I was so shocked I could barely speak. Mary Beth was a year old, and I was seven months pregnant with the twins. I was feeling heavy, swollen, unattractive, and out of sorts. We were driving home from a Bible study at Ken and Cheryl's when at a stoplight he reached over and slapped my face. Hard.

I gasped and looked at him.

"That's for tonight," he had said.

Was this a joke? But he was not smiling.

"I told you, that's for tonight."

"Troy, what…?"

"Don't pretend all innocent with me."

"What are you talking about?"

"I saw the way you were looking at Ken. I saw that look in your eye. You'd like to get him into bed with you, wouldn't you?"

I gasped. "Troy, you're joking! You're talking crazy! Why are you saying this?"

But he was talking fast, cursing, using language that baffled and frightened me. I had never heard him speak like this before. He was calling me names, using words I barely knew the meaning of. "I see the way you look at men, Sadie. Don't think you can hide anything from me. I see everything and I know all about you. You can't hide one secret, dirty thought in your head, because I know what a slut you are."

Oh, I knew Troy's rages, I knew them well. I had seen him throw things, break things, but this was the first time his rage had been directed toward me. Always it was against other people: that "idiot" of a client, that "poor excuse" for a salesman, that "jerk" of a boss. Maybe I should have seen it coming, but I didn't.

I cried all the way home while the babies kicked at my insides. I cried when I handed the baby-sitter her money. I cried when Troy drove her home and I sat with Mary Beth and rubbed her back while she fell asleep. I cried all night and all the next day, because I knew things between Troy and me would never be the same again.

Sometimes at night I wonder if there is maybe a kernel of truth in what he says. Maybe Troy can see something in me that I try to hide, even from myself. Because I *do* notice the way other husbands look at their wives, at the way they smile at them, the private, intimate looks; at the way Ken will reach out and touch his wife's shoulder with one finger, a gesture so intimate it has me yearning for something I have never had.

Troy was still shouting at me as I crouched against the headboard. "Do you know what my news was, Sadie? Do you know why I was early? Why I was so desperate to talk to you? Why I wanted Ham to pray with me? Do you have any idea what it's been like for me these past few months? Do you even care? With Federated breathing down all our necks. A call center? I'm supposed to work at a call center? Getting people to sign up for credit cards when they buy our computers?" He cursed again. "Well, I refused and as a result I don't have a job anymore." He spat the words at me, little drops of spittle in the air. "That's right, I don't have a job anymore. As of the end of this month we will have no more income. Are you satisfied? But does she care? Does my wife care? No, she's off with her lover."

He was sitting on the bed, his head in his hand. His voice was quieter now, and I opened my eyes. "Money is going to be tight, as if it isn't tight already, until I can find something else." He was teary eyed now. "We might even lose the house. I'm sorry, Sadie." He was whispering. "I just don't know what to do. Oh, God, I don't know what to do. I've never been a good husband." And he got up and walked out of the room.

I must have slept because when I woke, the house was dark, and Troy was in bed beside me. I thought it was the music that awoke me, but when I opened my eyes, all I heard were the peeper frogs in the distance.

I heard Simon whimper. I rose, nursed him, and he fell back to sleep almost immediately. I placed him in his crib. Gavin was asleep, his covers twisted around him. I walked past Mary Beth's cubbyhole of a room, where she lay sleeping on her back, her covers tucked neatly under her chin, her night-light on. I looked in on the twins, together in one bed, two blond heads together in a tangle of sheets and blankets.

The Sunday school papers and bulletins were still scrunched in the pocket of the baby stroller, which was in the van, so I put a thin jacket over my nightgown and went outside. The other houses were asleep too, their windows dark squares, and I stood for several minutes in the coolness of the driveway. It was still too early for a lot of bugs, which makes this, in some ways, the nicest time of the year. I listened for the music. I even prayed to hear the music. But I did not.

My bare feet crunched on a piece of paper. I picked it up and recognized it as one of the posters of Ally Buckley. I smoothed it out between my fingers. Have You Seen This Child? I had helped staple these up on lampposts and billboards around Coffins Reach. By now they were mostly torn down, as people went back to their lives. The life of a small girl snuffed out and everyone goes back to work.

At the back of the van I retrieved the papers from the stroller and took them inside, along with the crumpled poster.

I closed off the doors to the kitchen, retrieved Mary Beth's school scribbler from the piano bench, drew a series of staffs on the empty pages, and began transcribing my rapid and scrawly notes into something that made sense. I could hear the music in my mind as I wrote.

Unfathomable. I could no more imagine PJ or Tabby using a word like that than Gavin asking if he could help set the table. But that little girl with the dogs spoke to me about the music. Ghost music. Angel music. There had to be an explanation.

If I could get the music properly transcribed, I would send it to my old music professor and ask him if he knew where it came from. Ham said he wanted help. Well, this was something tangible that I could do.

After I had finished, I closed the book and buried it again in the piano bench.

Chapter Thirty

*T*here's a disease called Tourette's syndrome that I've done some reading on and even watched a television program about. Once I asked Troy to go to a doctor to get tested for it, and he threw the telephone across the room and we had to get a new one. I used to be convinced he had it. I used to think Gavin had it, too. I used to tell the children that sometimes Daddy gets sick and he can't help the way he behaves or the words he says. I don't think they ever believed me. I don't anymore.

In the morning I noticed new lines on Troy's face and bags under his eyes. There was more gray in his hair, too, although when that occurred I can't be sure. I got up ahead of him, and when I came out of the bathroom, he was sitting on the bed looking confused.

"Sadie," was all he said. "Sadie."

I sat down beside him. He took my hands in his and looked at me. For a long time we didn't say anything.

"I think I was asleep when you came in last night," I finally said.

"I went outside. I got working in my shop. I lost track of time."

"That's good. Working in your shop, I mean."

"I'm going to build a set of beds for the twins. They're getting too big for their junior beds. I found a Web site with some interesting designs. I printed it off and started drawing up plans. These are bed units that can be separated in case we want to separate the twins. But I was thinking, maybe you're right. Maybe we shouldn't separate them. Not right away, anyway. In school maybe, but not here. Not at home."

I felt relieved. I smiled actually. "Can I see the plans?" I asked.

He shook his head. "Not until they're finished."

"I'm glad you're doing that, Troy. You're so good with wood. Maybe you could find a job in that field."

He let go of my hands. "Yeah, Sadie. Great idea. I could make little bird feeders and sell them at the market on Saturday." He stood up. "Or how about I make a whole bunch of them and put them all over the lawn with price tags on them?" He was roughly pulling up his trousers and I didn't like the way his voice was becoming. "Or maybe I could make lawn ornaments of those fat ladies bending over, little boys peeing—the back view, of course. And sheep. I could make lots of sheep. You think we could live on that, Sadie? Wooden sheep?"

"That's not what I meant." I pulled my hair up into a red scrunchy. "I mean cabinets like the ones you started for the kitchen. Or big furniture. Like this bed unit you're talking about. Or remember that dining room table? The one you started out of oak? That would have been beautiful, Troy. You should finish that one. Those legs you made for it with that special tool thing you have? Well, those are just beautiful. And the lawn chairs, too. All you need to finish on those are the arms."

He sat on the bed and furiously pulled on a pair of black socks. "Get real, Sadie. There's no future in that. Just forget that idea. Put it out of your mind. It's just about as stupid an idea as you ever making a career out of that music of yours."

The phone rang and Troy answered the bedside one and handed it to me. "It's Judith," he said. He stared at me the entire time I was on the phone.

She told me she was going away for a couple of days. She was driving to Vermont. Her mother had a cottage on Lake Champlain and she was going to spend a couple of days there. "To get away," she told me. "To think things through."

"That will be nice," I said. "It will be nice for you to get away."

When I hung up, Troy demanded to know what she said.

"Just that she's going away."

"You said, 'That will be nice.' What did you mean? What would be nice?"

"Her going away. That's all."

"Are you sure that's all?"

"Yes, that's all. What else would it be?"

"Sadie, I've told you, you must leave that woman alone. You must not encourage her. I've told you that. We've talked about this many times. I wish you'd listen to me on this."

"She's just lonely. She has no one else."

"She's a killer, Sadie."

"Troy!" I stood square in front of him.

"I'm just saying that I know things about her. Things you don't."

"What things?"

"Has she ever told you about the child, Sadie? The one in the hospital?"

"What child? What are you talking about?"

He was carefully tying his tie in the mirror. "The *other* child. The reason, the real reason she's no longer a nurse, the real reason she will never work as a nurse again? The reason a lot of people think she had something to do with Ally? Has she mentioned that other child to you?"

My mouth felt dry.

"I thought not. How about her first husband? She ever mention *him* to you?"

I shook my head.

"See, there's a lot about your new friend that you don't know. Her first husband was killed in a car accident. But there was some mystery surrounding his death. It wasn't as cut and dried as all that. Plus, Sadie, she was responsible for the death of a child in her care in a hospital."

"Troy!"

"This is true, Sadie. For a long time Judith has been the subject of a criminal investigation."

"Who told you these lies?"

"These are not lies, Sadie. These are facts. Being on the deacon's board I'm privy to certain things. Bud and Irma are quite concerned. Let's just say, Sadie, that I don't want you near that woman. I don't want my children anywhere near her, either."

I stared at him as he tied his shoes, straightened his tie, and walked out.

I spent the morning sweeping and mopping the kitchen floor in a fit of energy. I put through a bunch of loads of laundry and folded them when they came out of the dryer. I worked quickly, my steps taking on a rigidity that my children were unaccustomed to. I vacuumed the living room, the hallway, the stairs. I got six loaves of bread rising. Was Judith really dangerous? A child killer? And why had she lied to me about working? Or was Troy making this whole thing up to take suspicion off himself?

I placed a load of whites in the washer, grabbed the knob, and turned it to Normal Cycle. It freewheeled around and twisted off in my hand. Oh, great! Just what I need! I closed my eyes, leaned against the washing machine, then sat down in a kitchen chair, and squeezed the tears away, the knob still in my hand. I turned it over and over in my hands and decided that maybe I could put it back on myself. I rooted through the junk drawer for a screwdriver and came up empty.

"You stay put," I said to Simon who was sleeping in his playpen. I grabbed the workshop key from a board of keys (shaped like a key—Troy made it) nailed on the wall beside the back door, and went outside. Gavin was sitting in the middle of the sandbox throwing handfuls of sand into the air. He was absolutely covered in it. Well, if he wasn't tormenting the neighbor's cat or killing more hamsters, I'd ignore him.

The key didn't fit. It wasn't even close. I looked at it. This was the key. It had always been the key. Am I going crazy? Has pregnancy and Judith and Troy and my kids finally taken me over the edge? I sighed and tried again but it didn't fit any better the second time around.

"Gavin, don't throw sand. You'll get it in your eyes."

"I won't. I won't. I won't. I WON'T!"

I walked back to the house with determined steps. I swiped all the keys from the board, every last one of them, and was back out and tried them all. None worked, and I stared at the door uncomprehending. Closer to the lock I noticed the scrapings of wood. I bent down and examined it.

"Daddy was hammering the door." Gavin was standing beside me.

"What? When?"

"I he'ped Daddy."

"You helped Daddy?"

"I he'ped hammer the door." He ran off again toward the sandbox.

So, Troy had changed the locks. Maybe it had something to do with the time Mary Beth and Emma had gone inside. And he forgot to tell me. Clutching a handful of jingly keys, I walked around the small building. I'm locked out of my own garage, and all I need is a stupid little screwdriver to get my laundry done.

In the back, the side that faces the woods, one of the windows was opened half an inch. I struggled with it, finally pushing it up to full height. I threw all the keys into the pocket of my jeans and climbed inside.

Boards were stacked beside the woodstove and a coffee mug, kettle, and a container of instant coffee were on a shelf behind the workbench. Chisels, hammers, and screwdrivers were neatly arranged on the pegboard behind his bench; his power tools were on high shelves still in their boxes.

It was the detached garage which attracted us, or at least Troy, to this house in the first place. There are not too many garages in these old row houses, but we were lucky. Ours is a corner house. When we first went inside the musty, damp garage, I could see the light in Troy's eyes. "This will be a perfect workshop," he said.

"A workshop?"

"For my tools. And wood. For making things."

"What about a garage?" I said teasing. "For the car."

He shook his head. "We'll leave the car out front. This will be a workshop. This will be perfect. This is what I've always wanted, what I've always dreamed of."

And it has become his workshop, a place where he starts projects and doesn't finish any of them. Over the years he has collected some quality tools. My parents and his father usually buy him tools for Christmas which he oohs and ahhs over. But sometimes I think he likes the tools themselves, rather than what they can do.

I wiped my finger across Troy's workbench. Cleaner than my kitchen counter.

On a shelf next to a stack of sandpaper was a framed photograph of us, his family. Half a year ago we had family pictures taken when our church hired a local photographer to make a church directory. There we were, all seven of us, looking so happy and normal—Simon, a tiny infant on my lap, Troy wearing his church smile, the children scrubbed and grinning. I turned away from it. Behind me, on a separate table Troy had made, was his computer underneath a clear dustcover.

When he first brought the computer home I thought it might go into a corner of the living room, or even in our bedroom, but no, he wanted it in his workshop. I was briefly disappointed. I had visions of the kids using it for schoolwork, printing off reports and using the Web for research. But I really didn't have much of a say in it. It was Troy's money that bought it, after all; it was purchased through a payroll deduction plan at work.

"And your guts will come out like ketchup!" I could hear Gavin in the backyard. I reached across the bench for the smallest of the screwdrivers and shoved it into my pocket.

I was about to leave when an oversized manila envelope next to the computer caught my attention. Plans for the twins' beds? I sat down at his computer, untwisted the little string around the fastener, and pulled out several sheets.

A sound came out of my mouth, a sound unrecognizable to myself. I was looking at the painting, the precise painting that had been on Judith's fridge, the one with the hedge and pathway and the trees dripping red fruit. There were several others in the envelope, all brightly painted, all done by the same hand, all with Ally Buckley written across the bottom right. One of them had a blue ribbon attached. First Prize, it read. For several minutes I sat with these pictures on my lap. Staring at them, hands trembling, until I heard Gavin screaming. I put the pictures back, put the envelope beside the computer, made sure the back window was the way I had found it, and let myself out of the workshop.

"Gavin! What is it?"

He was standing beside the sandbox, screaming, his plastic shovel raised above his head as if ready to strike.

"Gavin!"

On the edge of the sandbox was a long worm, neatly segmented into four parts. "Gavin! What are you doing? It's just a baby worm!" But he brought down the shovel yet again and cut one of the remaining pieces in half.

I walked into the house, screwed the dial on the washing machine, got a load of whites going, said hi to Simon who was standing up in his playpen grinning, and then went and threw up in the downstairs bathroom.

Then I sat at the kitchen table for a full ten minutes without moving. *If you need to talk, just to talk, I want you to call me.* Why had Bernice said those words to me? I dug out her card from the box of Bounce and punched in her number quickly without thinking.

"Bernice," I said. "You said…you said I should call you if…if…"
I couldn't go on.

"What is it, Sadie?"

I wanted to tell her about Ally's pictures next to Troy's computer
and about how I'm always afraid and about how Troy hits me
sometimes and calls me terrible names and about how I have a
stomachache that won't go away and about how Gavin kills hamsters and worms and about how I feel like I'm going crazy. Instead,
I told her I was pregnant and Troy had lost his job and that we
couldn't afford another child.

She was quiet for a while on the phone. Outside, Gavin was still
growling in the sandbox, and Simon lay on his back on the kitchen
floor playing with a Tupperware lid. I put my hand on my stomach
and waited.

"A woman came to me once," she finally said. "She had married
a man, a wonderful Christian man, an educated man, a lay minister.
Everyone thought this man was wonderful. Her parents certainly
did. And other women thought she had a wonderful life, married to
such a godly and good man. He was well known, you see, and
preached the most wonderful messages. He was even called on to
speak at other churches and retreats. He was a real man of God.
That's what everyone said."

She paused. I waited, wondering why she was telling me this.

"But this woman still has bruises from where he hit her, and her
nose is permanently disfigured. There were times when he beat her
senseless and then had to take her to the hospital, explaining to the
doctor that she fell off her bike or down the stairs or tripped on the
cement pavement. So many little stories he came up with."

I chewed on a fingernail while I listened.

"It took her a long time, a very long time, but finally she made
the decision to leave him. This wasn't easy for her. She grew up with
the idea that marriage is for life. But in the end, when she began to
be afraid for her children, for her own life, that's when she left.

"There were days, however, that gave her hope, days when he was good as gold. He'd treat her oh so sweetly then and bring her flowers. Oh, he'd bring her flowers the day after he beat her. Full of apologies, he was. Full of promises. He'd spent the night in prayer, he told her once, and God helping him he would never hit her again. But it never lasted. A week later, a month later, some rage would overtake him and he would beat her again."

I held the phone close to my ear and watched Simon chew on the lid. I felt a catch in my throat. I remained quiet.

"But finally she left. She left because her husband had broken the covenant of their marriage once too often."

"You mean he was having an affair?" I surprised myself by asking.

Bernice chuckled a little bit. "There's more than one way to break the covenant of marriage. Husbands and wives are to love each other the same way that Jesus loves us—with the same intensity, with the same kindness, with the same intimacy and friendship."

"Why...why are you telling me this?"

"I'm telling you this because this woman felt there was no hope for her, but God provided a way. He was that light in the darkness. And I know that now you can't see the light at the end of the tunnel."

She kept talking, then, about God's grace and forgiveness, about God meeting our needs through surprising circumstances. Sometimes through people and friendships we can't even imagine. This woman's tunnel was dark, Bernice said. She had to pretend. She'd hide her bruises at church where absolutely no one suspected a thing, and where she had no one to talk to. If she started to even hint at the subject, she was promptly told to submit to her husband no matter what. How dare you say such things about an anointed man of God? someone told her.

But this woman's light was a neighbor who knew everything that went on in that house. Neighbors do, you know. And one day this neighbor came and said that her family had a fully furnished cottage on an island off the coast of Maine, a private place, a beautiful place, and if she wanted, the neighbor would help her and her children go there when she was ready. She would drive them. She would provide for them. She would keep the secret of where they were. And that's what happened. This woman and her three children spent six months in a beautiful house, getting their lives together. They received counsel and prayer. This woman doesn't live there anymore. She has found good work and her self-esteem and her worth before God.

"I'm telling you this story, Sadie, because God always provides a way. Six children and no job is difficult, *will* be difficult; no one will say that it's not. But just like this woman, God will provide a light for you and your family. Right now you don't see any kind of light at the end of your tunnel. But I'm going to pray that God's light and love surrounds you, that not only will you know it, but that you'll feel it, and realize that God has a way of escape for you. There is light, not at the end of the tunnel, but in the middle and all around you, even with six children and no income."

After I got off the phone I sat for another five minutes at the table and thought not about light at the end of a tunnel but about the woman who had left her husband after he had broken their marriage vows.

Chapter Thirty-one

I had planned to make a batch of brownies for the kids' lunches. That was on my To Do list for the day. So I pushed myself away from the table, handed Simon an arrowroot, looked outside where Gavin was burying himself in the sandbox and got out the cocoa, shortening, flour, mixing bowls, spatula, and spoons.

When Troy and I decided on an early marriage, I had been only mildly disappointed that I wasn't going back to school. Following after my own plans was beginning to seem more and more selfish. And I hadn't wanted to be selfish anymore. I was giving my life to God and to my husband. My old career was musician. My new career would be wife and helpmeet, and eventually, I hoped, mother. My parents gave me a piano (my graduation present now became a wedding gift). But I was beginning to look at the piano differently. I was a "helpmeet," and if teaching piano helped Troy and his ministry, that was okay. But if it was just for me, well, that wasn't okay.

My wedding day was full of sun. My bridesmaids were lovely, and everything went smoothly. It was a big wedding, and Mrs. Scott, who taught me piano from the time I was eight years old until I entered college, was there, along with Professor Petersen from college. Troy's roommate Larry was the emcee and did a great job. (We haven't seen Larry since.) Troy's father and grandmother came and both were pleasant. At one point during the reception, I saw my father and Troy's father sitting on chairs facing each other and chatting amiably. I smiled. Things would work out.

Only one small thing marred it. While Troy and I were mingling at the reception, hugging, shaking hands, and receiving congratulations from well-wishers, Troy took me aside and told me that my wedding dress—the wedding dress my mother and I had driven all over Michigan City for, the one she and I had declared the most beautiful dress in all of the Midwest—showed too much cleavage.

"I'm just telling you, Sadie, so you'll know for the future. A woman of your size has to watch that."

"My size?" I tugged at the bodice.

"Your size."

"My *size*, Troy?"

"Your size."

Even then Troy made suggestions about my clothes. He seemed to have a knack for knowing what looked good and what didn't. But my wedding dress—this one I'd saved my piano teaching money for and picked out with the help of my mother—he had had nothing to do with. I thought it accentuated my good features—my smile, my eyes, the color of my hair, and the twelve pounds I'd managed to lose for the wedding.

"You don't like this dress?"

"I'm not saying there's anything wrong with the dress. The dress *itself* is beautiful. All I'm saying is that I don't want every guy gawking at you. You're mine now."

In the ladies' room I asked Clarice, my maid of honor, if she thought it showed too much cleavage.

She looked at me. "What a silly thing to say. Of course not! Not in the least!"

"You're sure?"

"Whatever gave you that idea?"

"I don't know. I looked in the mirror a little while ago and got this idea that it did."

But I had been miserable for the rest of the reception and kept tugging at the bodice, conscious always of Troy's captious eyes.

Troy picks out most of my clothes now. Some things are just not worth arguing over.

Simon was asleep on the floor now, the plastic lid clutched in his fingers. I dumped the chocolate mixture into the greased pan and thought for the first time ever in my entire married life about leaving Troy. How would a thing like that be managed? No one I knew had any magical cottages on islands. Would anyone from church understand? Troy was the respected one in church. Church was his domain. I was just the mousy wife who barely even made it to all the services because of one sick kid or another.

At my wedding I had promised to love him till death do us part. Only a few weeks ago I had sat beside Troy on the bed and renewed that vow. I could never break that promise.

But if Troy had really done something with Ally, if he was really dangerous, didn't I owe it to myself and to my children to leave? I shivered and felt a taste on my tongue like a mouthful of ashes.

Chapter Thirty-two

*I*t rained last night, and this morning there were dozens of worms on the sidewalk. I tried not to look at them as we ushered the kids into the van for church. I tried to ignore the fact that Gavin went out of his way to stomp on several before he climbed, growling, into the back of the van. I tried not to think about worms on the way to church as the children chattered and argued and Simon fussed and the van rolled over them.

I was thinking about worms as I sat in church on this Palm Sunday, this prelude to Easter, this prologue to the most important day on the Christian calendar. Troy was beside me, his suit-jacketed arm across the back of the pew, the weight of his hand on my shoulder. We were alone, the two of us, in the pew. Simon was in the nursery and the other four were standing in the back of the sanctuary in a clump of Sunday school kids holding palm branches, waiting for the cue to march forward. Silently I prayed that Gavin wouldn't start a fight, that he wouldn't start yelling.

I read through the bulletin, and one announcement in particular caught my attention. "Safe Harbor House (a shelter for battered women) is looking for volunteers to answer the twenty-four-hour hot line. Training will begin next month. If interested, please contact Betty Frost or Troy Thornton."

The youth worship band was playing and invited us to stand. I tried to pay attention to the words, which I know are supposed to lead us into worship. Most of the time they do, but not today. Not for me, today. Today I was thinking about worms. Today I was thinking about leaving my husband.

Last night I dreamed about worms. There were worms on the kitchen floor, worms on the counter, worms even in the fridge, climbing up the milk container, crawling across the butter. I closed the fridge in haste. Ally's picture was magneted to the front and was crawling now with worms. I woke up sweaty and so terribly, terribly afraid and it was raining.

What a mighty God we serve,
What a mighty God we serve,
Angels bow before Him…
You can't hide one secret, dirty thought in your head.

Beside me Troy was singing loudly in his church voice, the way he does. I felt weak, faint. I needed to sit down. I put my hand to my stomach and did. When I looked up, Troy was glaring at me. Slowly I forced myself to my feet and stood weakly, nauseated, shoulders slouched, my hands braced on the pew in front of me, my hair falling forward and hiding my expression.

Hosanna, hosanna, hosanna in the highest,
Hosanna, hosanna, hosanna in the highest.
You can't hide one secret, dirty thought in your head.

The children were marching forward now, each with a real palm branch. I smoothed my hair behind my ears and watched. The smallest children led the procession, followed by bigger ones, and ending with the oldest. Gavin was in the middle, and directly behind him were PJ and Tabby. He was walking calmly, waving his palm branch up and down, up and down, gently, like he was supposed to, like they had practiced. Good for you, Gavin! Behind him the twins were looking at him and whispering, making signals, and I wanted to scream, "No!"

And now PJ was poking him with her palm branch. When he

twisted around she would look away. I saw his mouth say, "Quit it."

Lord we lift up your name
With hearts full of praise...

And then Tabby bopped Gavin on the head with her palm branch, and Gavin turned, his face a little redder than before.

I touched Troy's arm. "Troy..."

But he was singing loudly, looking straight ahead at the words on the overhead. I could see Gavin's face, eyes bulging, cheeks puffing out. I didn't want this to be like last year. He was allowed to be in the procession this year if he *promised* to be good. So far, he hasn't been in any Sunday school Christmas programs because he can't be trusted not to misbehave.

The children made a semicircle at the front of the church, and an older boy stepped between Gavin and his sisters. And Gavin's face settled down. I would have to praise him later, out of earshot of Troy, who thought no one should be praised for something they should be doing anyway.

The worship band ended, the children turned and sang one song to the congregation. Even Gavin was singing—frowning, but singing. Then they were finished, and we made room for our children in the pew. We put Gavin between us, the twins on one side of Troy, and Mary Beth next to me. We sang a few more choruses, the offering was passed, and there was a duet by sisters who sang something about God loving all people. And I felt proud of my son.

And then Pastor Ken prayed for the sick people in our congregation, for the missionaries, for our government representatives. He also prayed for the Buckley family. At the end I heard Troy murmur amen, and I thought about Ally's paintings in an envelope in his locked workshop. I thought of the receipt from the gas station in Ellsworth.

In the afternoon my parents called, the way they do every

Sunday afternoon and I told them everything was fine. Just fine. In this little life of mine. And then we put the kids on the phone one at a time to say hello.

Chapter Thirty-three

The following morning Nick, Gavin's old van driver, rang the doorbell. And when Gavin saw who it was, he began running around in circles, holding a plastic airplane above his head.

"Hey, little big guy," said Nick. "I'm here to pick you up."

"I'm gonna EAT YOU UP!" Gavin said growling. "This worm is gonna eat you up!"

"Hey, that's no worm. That's a plane."

"Gavin, settle down," I said. "You'll get dizzy."

"You ready to go to the beach today?" Nick said to him.

"The beach?" I looked at them. "Well, okay then. That's fine. That's nice. Gavin, do you want to put your bathing suit on? And take a towel?"

I followed him upstairs and helped him into his bathing suit and found a beach towel in the closet. "You be a good boy now," I said.

"Oka-ay."

"Gavin, you'll hurt your voice if you keep talking like that."

When they left, I folded laundry in the living room in front of a television cooking show. Simon had pulled himself to a standing position by holding on to the couch. He was grunting in concentration as he stood there uncertainly, grabbing fistfuls of couch with chubby hands.

"Where're you going to go, mister?" I said. "Now you're stuck." I reached for him, and set him beside me.

When the laundry was folded, I switched off the television and dug out Mary Beth's notebook from the bottom of the piano bench. At church yesterday Ham had given me a photocopy of my original music. I told him I had heard it again on the point by the lighthouse and I had written more of it down. He said he had had a musician play it. The musician didn't recognize it. He was now sending it to someone at the music department at the university.

So someone had played my music. Someone was actually trying to figure out where it came from. I looked at my piano. It really would help if I played it, if I could *make* myself play it. I knew from the few times Gavin had plunked away at the keys that it was terribly out of tune. That was reason enough not to play it.

I decided to recopy the music and pulled out a couple of sheets from the back of Mary Beth's scribbler, took them into the kitchen, and spread my work out on the table. I drew a series of staffs with the help of a ruler and rewrote it. Then I laid the sheets I had originally written from memory. It was similar, too much the same to be a coincidence.

I love doing this work. I've always been good at math, but I also have a creative side that loves getting lost in a melody. Music composition is the happy marriage between the two. Music is all a matter of arithmetic. Back when I was studying theory, I remember becoming so absorbed in it that all else was forgotten. In my head now, I was hearing the music, all of the different instruments, all of them coming in at different times.

I heard a sound behind me. "What are you up to now, little man?" I said as I turned.

But it was not Simon. Bernice stood outside my door, large tote bag over her shoulder and clad in a bright orange caftan.

"Bernice!" I got up and went to the door.

"Hello there, Sadie," she said cheerily.

"I didn't expect you. Come in," I said.

"I know you didn't, but I was driving by. I have a few more bits and pieces of clothing that I managed to round up. Baby things this time. Tiny things. I wondered if you could use them."

"Oh, that's nice of you, but you didn't have to."

"I figured if you're anything like most of the mothers I work with, by the time you get to baby number six, your stash of hand-me-down baby clothes has pretty well had it."

I had moved my music over and was piling it up, my sharpened pencils next to it, while she spread out some brand-new infant clothing on the table. Most still had price tags on them.

"These are brand new," I said.

"We get new things sometimes. But we have so much, and most of our demand is for clothing for kids maybe aged five to ten. That's our biggest demand at the shelter." She looked at me. "How far along are you?"

I put a hand to my stomach. "I don't know for sure. I haven't been to the doctor."

"You haven't?"

"I was going to buy one of those pregnancy tests at the store, but I haven't gotten around to it yet."

"You're afraid, aren't you?"

"I have a friend who says she believes in God, but she's not sure God believes in her anymore. I've thought about that. Sometimes that's the way I feel. That God's given up on me somehow. Because how can I manage? How can we possibly manage?"

She put her hand on my shoulder and prayed for me right then. I stared at the floor, not sure whether to close my eyes or not. I didn't. She prayed that I would know God's love, that God would fill me with His love, and that I would know it. I didn't say anything for a long while. Even after she said amen, I waited. She squeezed my shoulder and then let go.

"You'll see," she said. "You'll see that God does believe in you. He does have a plan for your life, even now."

Simon was standing up, both of his hands on a kitchen chair.

He was slapping the top of it with his palms. He grinned at us. Bernice bent down and picked him up, and he squealed in her arms. Then she looked at my papers on the table, the top one scrawled with music notes.

"My word, child, what are you doing?"

"Oh, it's nothing, just something I've been working on."

"It looks like music."

"It is music. I'm a musician. Well, I used to be. I studied it for a while." And then I told her about the music I heard on the beach. I told her that one night I woke to the sound of it, and the melody was so haunting and so compelling that I wanted to get it down on paper so I would remember it always. I told her I heard a slightly different variation of it again one afternoon on the point. I told her about the girl with the dogs. I told her someone else had heard the music the night the other little girl's body was found, and that our friend Ham from the police department was having it analyzed.

"Ham. I know Ham," said Bernice.

"He and my husband are friends."

She nodded and stroked Simon's hair. We were sitting at the table by this time, and Bernice eyed the piano.

"Can you play it for me? Can I hear what it sounds like?"

"I'm afraid I won't do it justice. Besides, that old piano in there is hopelessly out of tune."

"I probably wouldn't even notice that."

"It's hard to explain. I just can't seem to play it anymore."

"Because the music has gone out of you."

I looked at her.

"It looks like a good piano, though. A nice grain to the wood."

"Oh, it is! It's a wonderful piano. There's a long history to that piano. My parents were going to give it to me when I graduated with my music degree, but it ended up being a wedding gift instead. I had this piano picked out since junior high school."

"Does your husband play, as well?"

I laughed at the idea. "Troy doesn't like music much. The only music in this house comes from that cassette player my parents gave me, the one on the counter over there. I have drawers full of cassettes that I listen to, but Troy doesn't care much for music. He would rather watch TV. That's why we have such a huge one that takes up half the wall in the living room."

"One day, Sadie, you will sit down there and you will start playing. I know you will. Your music will come back to you."

I nodded and looked away. There was so much she didn't know.

We spent the next hour going through the baby clothes. I wanted to ask her about that woman who left her husband. I wanted to hear more of Bernice's thoughts on marriage vows, but we talked about music and babies instead. Just being with her made me feel comforted and calmed.

When she left, Gavin was still out with Nick, and I was able to vacuum and even sort through some old magazines.

Chapter Thirty-four

Before I met Troy I had a boyfriend. His name was Ben. He was Canadian, although he'd never lived there much, he said. He grew up on the mission field somewhere in South America. I used to know where. He was fluent in Spanish, plus he spoke some tribal language I can't remember the name of.

And he knew how to squat. Nobody sat on chairs down there, he told me. Everyone just squatted on their haunches. Squatting around the dinner table, squatting beside their mounds of corn and beans at the market, squatting while they shelled their peas, squatting around the campfire while they told their stories of the day's hunting, the day's gathering. Even at church they would all be squatting in rows.

"I never sat on a chair until I was eleven," he said, and then he would wink at me.

He also told me they ate with their hands. "They'd just scoop everything up with their fingers, like this." And then he showed me. "The first time I ever saw a spoon I was ten. A missionary brought one in from the outside." That's what he called Canada, the outside.

"They had to have spoons," I said. "What did they stir stuff with?"

"Stir sticks," he told me, pushing his glasses up on his nose. "Every morning the women of the tribe would go out into the forest and gather the stir sticks for the day. That's where we get our word for stir stick, like for paint? It comes straight from the tribal language. Stir stick."

And he would wink at me. And I would wonder, did that wink negate the last sentence only? The last paragraph? Or everything he ever said to me?

Ben and I went out for pizza every Friday night. We'd button our coats up to our chins, and walk down Michigan Avenue to the lake, our faces into the wind, and continue talking. He told me people in Canada never wore coats because they were so used to the cold.

"My Uncle Bill? He never wears a coat. Doesn't even own one, as far as I know. Middle of a snowstorm, there he is, out there milking cows in his shirt sleeves." And then he would wink.

"Then how come you wear a coat?"

"You forget, I grew up in South America where you can put a kettle of water out in the sun, and you come back in ten minutes and it's come to a complete rolling boil. In fact, that's how we used to make tea."

"You're lying," I said, laughing.

"You're right. I am. It really takes twelve minutes."

Everyone referred to us as a couple. Will you and Ben be coming to the party? You and Ben should go out with Tom and me sometime. What're you and Ben doing over reading week? And I would answer enthusiastically, because that's what I wanted more than anything, to be a couple. But the truth was that Ben never touched me, except accidentally. He never kissed me. He never held my hand.

When I first started going out with Troy, there was a part of me that wanted Ben to be jealous. See, Ben, see, I can be a girlfriend. I can be somebody's girlfriend.

That there seemed to be no change in Ben's attitude toward me was what astonished me the most. He still expected us to go out on Fridays for pizza and Cokes.

"But I'm with Troy now," I said.

"And what? That means you can't hang around with old friends anymore?"

Once, when Troy was working, we did go out. We ordered the pepperoni special and Cokes, and he told me more stories about South America and about Saskatchewan. I tried to laugh, tried to be the same, but I couldn't. I had finally figured out that all we were all this time were good friends, buddies, pals, chums. And that's all he wanted.

The summer Troy and I were married, Ben went back to South America or Saskatoon or someplace, and I never saw him again.

A few years ago Clarice told me in a Christmas card that Ben had married someone from his hometown, and they had only one child, a little girl with Down's syndrome they had named Grace.

Chapter Thirty-five

*B*y the time Troy got home, I was frantic. Gavin was still with Nick, and I had no idea where, nor when they were expected. I didn't even know Nick's last name! Troy was standing behind me where I was slumped in a kitchen chair, his hands on my neck. He couldn't believe I had actually let our son go with someone who was almost a stranger.

"This is what I don't understand about you, Sadie. This is what baffles me about you."

Earlier in the afternoon, I had sent the twins down to the beach to see if they could find him. Stay on the sidewalks, I told them. Don't go anywhere else beside the beach and the park. An hour later they were home, their pockets full of rocks and shells, but no, they couldn't find Gavin or the man anywhere. I thought of phoning the Christian school to find out Nick's last name. I had even punched in the number, but I hung up before anyone answered, embarrassed that Troy and I had never gone back to meet with the principal.

When the twins got back without Gavin, I packed Simon into the stroller, gathered up the twins and Mary Beth and Emma, and the six of us walked down the hill toward the wharf. We walked the length of the beach and didn't see Gavin. We walked up to the swings and didn't see Gavin. We walked toward the storefronts and along the sidewalks. No Gavin. In the distance I saw a little boy who looked like Gavin riding a bicycle, but when I got closer I saw that it wasn't. The boy's mother, a skinny thing in a tank top and bleached hair, told me she hadn't seen anyone fitting the description of my son and Nick, and she'd been here all afternoon.

I raced toward groups of children, but couldn't find Gavin. I saw a young couple walking with their arms around each other, some elderly people sitting on the park bench, some dogs on leashes, seagulls, a few people down at the docks working on boats, but no Gavin, no Nick.

Despite a Members Only sign, I ushered the six of us through the open fence gate to the marina and walked down a wide dock. A man in a white hat shaded his eyes and said, "Beautiful day."

I asked him about Gavin and Nick. He told me he hadn't seen anyone fitting that description, and he'd been here most of the day.

"But I can't find my little boy." My hands were shaking, and I was trying to keep all the children close beside me. "Mary Beth don't go over there. PJ, Tabby, no, come back. You're too close to the edge."

"I can help you look for your boy," the man said. "Come on down to our boat for a minute. I'm sure he isn't far."

The wooden boards woof-woofed underneath us as we made our way down the wide dock. "Hazel!" he called. A woman emerged from the depths of a sailboat, wiping her hands on a towel.

"Excuse me," she said, smiling. "Just cleaning up some messes, the inevitabilities of living aboard. Hello. What a lovely bunch of children."

"Hazel, can we get these kiddies a drink?"

Around me four girls stared wide-eyed at the boat.

"Is that like a house?" said Emma in her boy voice.

"Oh, maybe a wee bit," the woman answered. "Do you want to come inside and see?"

"Yeah!" said Emma. "Could we?"

"Wait." I put up my hand.

The man turned to me. "They'll be safe with Hazel. And we'll find your boy. My name's Tom, by the way." He extended his hand. "Tell me, when's the last time you remember seeing him? Was he with you here on the beach and then disappeared?"

I was quiet for a moment. "No. He went with someone. They were supposed to be down here, and they're not."

"What's your little boy's name?"

"Gavin. It's Gavin and he's five and has curly red hair and freckles. He's with a man who's really big. Huge, in fact, and his name's Nick. They were supposed to be here. I thought they would be here. Now I don't know where they are. And my husband will be home soon."

Down in the sailboat I could hear the excited voices of four little girls.

Hazel stuck her head out. "I'm happy to look after the girls while you go with Tom. And I'm going to be praying that you find him."

I left, feeling a little better.

As we walked, Tom said, "You know, I have a strong feeling that your little boy is just fine. Just fine."

"Maybe he's home by now," I said. "Maybe I should go there. What if Nick was dropping him off and nobody was there. I'm so sorry to have bothered you with all this. You must think I'm an idiot."

"No, you're not an idiot, and don't keep saying you're sorry. You're a mother with lots of responsibilities who happens to be worried because her son didn't get dropped off when he was supposed to. You don't have this Nick's phone number do you? We could call from the cell phone on the boat."

I shook my head.

"Why don't we all head to your house. In case they're home by now, waiting. If you'd like, Hazel and I could come, too."

And that's how Hazel and Tom, two sailors who had most recently sailed down from Canada, happened to be in my kitchen making tea and phoning the Christian school. Nick's last name was Baldwin. When they phoned his home, they were told that Nick had dropped Gavin off at his home at least an hour ago and that Nick was out back mowing the lawn already.

I slumped into my kitchen chair and could not drink the tea. Just like Ally, on her way home, never making it there. Just like Ally.

When the phone rang, Hazel answered it and handed it to me. It was Ham.

"Ham!" I said. "Did you find him?"

"Find who?"

"Gavin."

"What about Gavin?"

And then I told him the story of how Nick had taken Gavin for the day and dropped him off when I was out, and no one had seen Gavin since.

"I'm going to head over to this Nick Baldwin's house," Ham said, "and find out when he dropped Gavin off, and why he would drop him off without making sure he was safely inside."

"Ham, if it wasn't about Gavin, why did you phone here? Did you want Troy?"

"Actually, I had some information about the music that I wanted to talk to you about. Plus, I know you have Emma there, and I wanted to arrange to pick her up."

Ham and Troy arrived around the same time. And that's how Troy happened to be in the kitchen, standing behind me and rubbing my neck and shoulders as I sat shaking at the table. "It's okay," he kept saying. "How were you to know? How was anyone to know? It's not your fault, hon."

And then Ham went outside to his police car for a minute, followed by Hazel and Tom. It was just Troy and me, and his hands were around my neck, squeezing, squeezing. "How could you be so stupid? This is what baffles me about you. I'm totally puzzled…"

And then Hazel and Tom were back in the kitchen, and it was just Troy's hands rubbing my neck, massaging my shoulders and saying that I wasn't to blame, that this sort of thing could happen to anybody and that he was as concerned about me as he was for Gavin.

"They found him," said Ham, walking in with a smile. "He and Nick are on their way here now. The person who answered the phone at Nick's was mistaken. It was Nick's brother who was mowing the lawn. Apparently the two look so much alike."

A few minutes later Ham brought Gavin in by the hand, followed by a miserably blubbering Nick Baldwin, who kept looking from Ham to Troy to me and back to Ham again.

"And what's your story?" said Troy.

"I spoke with you, Mr. Thornton, don't you remember?"

"No. I do not."

"I called you up on the phone. I specifically asked—"

"I did not speak with you, Mr. Baldwin, and what I know is that you had my wife just about out of her mind with worry, and I will not allow anyone to upset my wife."

"But don't you remember? Don't you?" He was near tears.

Troy stared at him, his face solid stone.

"Don't blame yourself, Mr. Baldwin," I said. "I probably didn't get all the information perfectly clear before you left. I'm just so happy you and Gavin had such a nice time. I hope you come back again. Gavin seems to really like you."

"Well, I like him, too," he said, wiping his brow with a handkerchief. "It's like, I sort of know what he's going through. I was like that as a kid too. I was always trying to be so tough, but inside I was so mixed up. The other kids used to make fun of me."

Troy made a deprecating noise and turned away. "No one is particularly interested in your childhood, Mr. Baldwin. And can you pretend to think you know what Gavin is going through, as you say?"

Gavin scooted under the kitchen table.

"Just with school and all. That's all I'm talking about here. I really like Gavin. Always have. I never let the kids make fun—"

"My son is *my* concern. We handle matters like this within our own family."

After everyone left, Troy turned on me. "What do you know about that man?"

"He drives the van for the Christian school. He seems nice."

"Just showing up like that, unannounced, and you merrily let him take off with our son. I'm shaking my head in amazement that you would do that, Sadie. If someone drove in the driveway with a moving van and said they were going to take all the furniture away, what would you do, just sit by and say, 'Oh fine, just take everything'?"

"It wasn't like that."

"Plus, that man seems slow to me. Maybe retarded. What does he want with a boy like Gavin?"

"He's not retarded. He drives the school van."

"I don't trust that man. I don't like people wheedling their way into our business. If anyone takes Gavin to the beach for the day, it will be me."

Simon woke in the middle of the night. I climbed over all the toys in the boys' room, changed him, sat in the rocking chair and fed him, then put him, sleeping, back into his crib.

On my way out, Gavin called to me softly. "Mommy?"

"Gavin, you're awake?" I knelt down beside him, stroked his carrot hair away from his face. "Did you have a nice time today with Mr. Baldwin?"

He nodded. "You know what?"

"What?"

"We saw fish."

"You saw fish, wow! Gavin, I never told you this, but I was really proud of you in church last week. You waved your palm branches really nicely—"

"But Mommy, the worms are going to get me." There was fear in his blue eyes.

"You're just having a bad dream."

"Daddy said they would get me if I'm bad."

"Well, that's just not true."

"Daddy said."

"But you're not bad, Gavin."

"Daddy says I am."

"You're not."

"Mommy?"

"Yes?"

"Worms are under my bed, Mommy."

"Just a minute. I'll look." I bent down. "Nope. No worms here."

"Yes, Mommy, they are. I could hear them."

"Why don't you come out of your bed and look with me?"

"No-o-o."

"I'll be right beside you. How about we look together?"

He climbed out of bed and we crouched down.

"There. Over there," he said.

"That's just a piece of dust. Here." I reached in. "See, it was just dust."

He backed away. "Worm!"

"Shh, you'll wake everyone up."

But he was crying, and I held him close to me on the floor for several minutes. "Let's pray," I said. We crouched there in the darkness, and I prayed for Gavin. Then I lay with him in his bed, cradling him in my arms until he fell asleep, praying that the worms would go away.

Chapter Thirty-six

Three days later Judith phoned me.

"Did you have a good time with your mother?" I asked her.

"I never saw her. We didn't hook up. I stayed in Bangor. I've hired this private investigator. Greg doesn't know."

"You did?"

"To find Ally."

"Judith, would you like to come over?"

After we hung up, I went out onto the back porch and stood there looking at the workshop. Locked up. With Ally's pictures inside. Would I tell Judith about that? Would I ask Judith about her work at the hospital? About her first husband's accident? Secrets, I thought. Everyone, including me, with all these secrets.

Under our one shade tree were the two armless wooden lawn chairs that Troy had started to make five years ago. I moved them closer together in the shade. It was a nice backyard. Small and cozy.

Later, when we were both sitting there, she with Simon in her lap, our iced teas on the ground, I said, "Judith, someone told me a rumor about you and your, um, work at the hospital."

She stared at me then, and maybe I only imagined that her eyes became slits. Or maybe it was the sun. She had been stroking Simon's hair, and she stopped in midstroke.

"My work," she said.

"You told me you work at the hospital."

"No. I don't think I ever told you that."

I stared at her. "I thought—"

"I never said I worked at the hospital. I'm quite sure I didn't. I don't know what you're talking about. I work for Greg part time. At SmartSystems. I'm filling in for one of the secretaries on maternity leave."

"I thought you said you worked in pediatrics."

She was quiet for a moment. "That was a long time ago. I haven't been back in a long time."

Even though we were in the shade, I felt hot. Why was I grilling her? Me, with so many secrets of my own?

"Okay," she said. "I guess I owe it to you to tell you, since I've told you so much, and you've been so good to me through this, and so honest. I used to work in pediatrics. I'm a trained nurse, an LPN, and was taking courses toward becoming an RN when everything crashed. For the second time in my life. Ally makes the third.

"There was a certain mother and father with a child in the hospital. There was nothing we could do for their son. He was dying. Well, I loved that little boy more than anything. I would have taken him home if I could have. He loved me, too. That's part of the reason I think those parents blamed me. Because that little boy responded to me more than to his own mother. Children generally do, I don't know why. The little boy was in a lot of pain, excruciating pain. It's so sad when children are dying, and he was in more pain than most. When he died, she just had to blame someone, and that someone was me. I'm totally cleared of any charges, Sadie, you can check that out. It's all a matter of public record. Greg stood by me. So did the hospital. But I fell apart."

"Oh, Judith."

"There was a hearing. It was in the papers. It was thrown out of court with all charges dropped. You can check yourself if you don't believe me."

"I have no reason not to believe you."

She flicked an imaginary piece of dust off Simon's T-shirt. "I had a nervous breakdown after that. I spent some time in the psychiatric ward. If it wasn't for Ally, I would have died. I'm sure I would have. Ally and Greg. Then we moved here and things were supposed to be better."

"That must have been terrible."

She was smoothing Simon's hair. "My first husband, Ally's father, died in a car accident. And then the child in the hospital, and now Ally."

"You were married before."

She nodded. "Rob was not a good man. He did not treat me well. But according to his mother and sister, he could do no wrong." She looked away from me. "When they told me he died, you know what I felt?"

I shook my head.

"I felt relief. He beat me, Sadie. He would come home drunk five days a week and use me for a punching bag. I was so fearful for Ally…"

I felt a catch in my throat.

"He died in a car accident when Ally was two. Which everyone blamed me for."

"Why would people blame you?"

"We had an argument, just one of many. He hit me. I told him to get out, and he left and got himself killed. He was so drunk that night, and I sent him to his death. His mother said, 'You shouldn't have let him drive under those conditions.' Notice, she didn't say, 'You shouldn't have let him drive drunk,' it was 'under those conditions.' After he died, my mother-in-law tried to get custody of Ally. But the courts threw it out."

"That must have been horrible."

"Then I met Greg. Greg is a good man. He's a hard worker. He has given me a good home, and he's the only father Ally has known. He stood by me totally when I had that trouble at the hospital. Got a good lawyer…" She was twisting a piece of ribbon on Simon's shirt between her fingers. "Greg asked me again to go into counseling, but I'm afraid. I don't want to end up in the hospital again." She looked at me through watery eyes round as saucers. "I miss Ally. How can I go on without my daughter?"

Chapter Thirty-seven

About five minutes after Judith left, Betty Frost was at my front door.

"Sadie," she said, jangling her car keys from one hand to the other. "How are you doing? How are you really doing?"

"Fine."

She smiled, that broad, in-your-face smile of hers. "I was just sitting at home, and all of a sudden I just thought about you. The Lord just brought you into my mind. So, I just had to pop over to see if you're all right."

"I'm fine," I said a bit cautiously.

"Well then."

She stood there. Finally I said, "Would you like to come in?"

"Oh, that would be nice." And she stepped into my kitchen.

I looked at the room through Betty Frost's eyes then: lunch dishes still on the counter, a food-spattered high chair, laundry in piles next to the washer. I ran a hand through my hair, trying to remember the last time I brushed it. Betty Frost on the other hand was wearing a pale blue pantsuit with a pearl necklace and matching earrings, silver hair coiffed meticulously.

I cleared a place for her. Before she sat down, she examined the chair and wiped a few crumbs away with her hand.

"Would you like some coffee or some iced tea or something?" I asked.

"Coffee would be lovely."

So I made coffee while Betty talked about her grandchildren.

Did I know that Ashley was walking? And Marvin and Elaine were expecting again. Of course, how would I know that, she said, since Marvin and Elaine live in Boston? Well, not Boston really, a suburb, Peabody, but close enough.

When the coffee was ready I poured two cups and put the cream and sugar on the table. Betty would have poured the half-and-half into a china cream pitcher, I was sure of that, but all I did was put the carton out. One less thing to wash that way.

I looked at her mauve fingernails around the coffee cup, and then Gavin came in and demanded a glass of apple juice, which I gave to him. He went back to the television.

"So much television," said Betty, shaking her head. "Makes you wonder, doesn't it?"

She started talking about her latest project: the Safe Harbor House and all these poor women.

"Is it lots of work?" I said.

She smiled. "Oh, it's work. It needs some organization, that's for sure. I was there yesterday and set up some files for Bernice."

"Do you have enough volunteers?" I put Simon on a blanket on the kitchen floor.

She looked at me for a long time without answering. Finally, she put her mug down and said, "You're thinking of volunteering, Sadie? Is that why you're asking?"

"Well, I don't know. I could, I guess. I know Bernice a little bit. She's nice. Very easy to talk to."

"Nice, maybe, but totally disorganized." For the next fifteen minutes Betty described just how disorganized Bernice was, and how she, Betty Frost, was going to reorganize things over there.

"It must be interesting," I said.

"Oh, it's interesting work. That it is," she said, picking up her mug.

"Well, keep me in mind for Safe Harbor," I said.

She looked at me dubiously again, and said, "Well, I'm sure there's *something* you could do there."

"If I can help in any way."

She put her coffee cup down on the table. "Sadie, Sadie, I can't stand to talk around things. It's just not me. I have to talk to you about why I'm really here. Why I really came."

I waited.

"It's about Troy. I need to talk to you about Troy."

My coffee cup was halfway to my mouth. I put it down on the table. "Troy?"

"People are concerned, Sadie. There's been some talk. Actually it's more about Judith."

"Judith?"

I watched her take a deep breath. "It's about your relationship with Judith. I know, I know." She put up her hand. "I know she was here earlier. I sat across the street and waited in my car until she left."

"You did?"

"You need to be careful of her. Wary of her."

"I took food to her once. Merilee and I were supposed to. She's been through so much."

She waved her hand. Her rings glinted in the light. "This has to do with Judith and with you. Troy was over to see us on Sunday night after the evening service. He said he needed to unburden himself. Those were his exact words, Sadie: *unburden* himself." She paused as if for effect. "Judith has had some—how shall I put it— some problems in her life, and Troy is concerned that you are getting too close to her. And with your history, a relationship with Judith right now might not be doing either one of you any good."

My whole body became very still. "My history?"

She reached forward and touched my arm. "Sadie, we all love you very much. You are so special to us."

I moved my arm away.

"Troy asked me to try to help you, dear, to keep an eye on you, so to speak. He's so worried about you. He asked me to maybe visit you once or twice a week, that sort of thing. Make sure things are all right. That's why I'm here. That's why I came. And then when I saw Judith…well, you can't imagine."

She paused. I kept staring at her.

"He's so worried about you. When I came over here and saw that Judith was here, I just sat in my car and prayed for you. That's all I did, pray for you. The whole time."

I put a hand to my stomach. Simon started whimpering, and I picked him up off the floor and sat him on my lap.

"We all understand how you aren't able to get out to the evening service much…"

"It's really hard with the kids."

"We all know how difficult it is with children. And we've all been there, believe me. We all understand." She smiled. I was coming to hate that smile. "Well, the evening service, as you know from the few times you've been there, is a much smaller, more intimate group. Well, what I want to say is that Troy has really opened up to all of us there. It's been good for Troy to have this group to feel a part of. I just want you to know that those of us who are there pray for you every single Sunday night."

I spilled coffee on my hand.

"Sadie, that man loves you so much. He is *so* concerned about you. He makes every decision with your welfare in mind, including his decision about not going into the ministry."

I opened my mouth to say something, but no snappy replies were there and only one word came out: "Ministry?"

"We know all about that. About why he had to get out of it. Well, no, he just shared that with Jim and myself and Ken and Cheryl. What a sacrifice he made for you. You have no idea."

I wiped my hand with a dishcloth clumsily, shaking, wiping the spills off Simon, wondering if I had burned my hand. I felt nothing.

"I know this makes you nervous, and maybe I shouldn't have said this much. Troy would probably kill me if he knew I was telling you all of this. You know how Troy is."

"Yes, I know how Troy is." I kept my voice even.

"Well, his biggest concern right now is your relationship with Judith. Especially considering the problems in her past."

"I know all about the problems in her past. I know about the child in the hospital. I know about her first husband beating her up. I know about her nervous breakdown…"

Betty was smiling smugly and shaking her head. "Ah, I see she's told you only what she wanted you to hear. Sadie, Judith was not acquitted. She was convicted of that crime, of killing that child. Of giving that child a fatal overdose of morphine. It's all there in public record. She was ruled temporarily insane and spent a year in a psychiatric unit." She paused. "So you can see why Troy is concerned about your friendship with her."

I stared at her glasses. In the living room Big Bird was singing a song about having a friend and being a friend.

"She needs a friend." It was all I could think of to say.

"I don't think a woman like that is capable of having a friend. Troy has described your friendship as the blind leading the blind. Two emotionally fragile women. Well, it's just not healthy. You can see that, surely?"

I looked down at Simon's head. He was reaching for a crust of bread on the table, and I grabbed his hands.

"Sadie, I'm here because I love you. So does Cheryl. And Merilee, too."

I looked up. "Merilee's in on this too?" I got up from my chair, sat Simon on the floor, and walked toward the window. I kept my back to her.

"No one's *in* on anything. It's just concern. It's just love. Plain and simple love. I want to pray with you, Sadie. I came over here because I wanted to pray with you. I wanted to tell you that I love you and hold your hand and pray with you. You should have seen Troy on Sunday night. He was actually in tears. During the service we could tell something was wrong. All of us could. He could barely keep from crying; then he asked the congregation to pray for his wife, whom he loves *so* much. He didn't give the details in the service, of course. These are things he told Jim and me afterward."

A bird was standing on the back of the armless lawn chair, and Betty Frost kept talking. Her hands were on my shoulders. I could smell her perfume, a cloying mixture that reminded me of worms. The bird ruffled its feathers a few times.

"There's help," she said, "for women who abuse their children."

I spun around, flung myself out of her grasp and backed toward the sink, tripping over a plastic truck that went skittering across the floor. I steadied myself on the counter. "What? *What* did you say?"

"There's help, and no one hates you. And no one blames you. We've all been there. We all know what it's like to feel overwhelmed."

"Troy said that about me? That I abuse my children? He said *that?*"

"Sometimes life gets overwhelming. Everybody knows that." She was smiling that smile again. "I only had three children, but I remember days when I felt like throwing all of them out the window one at a time. And sometimes when life gets so full of stress, rational thought goes out the window." She was smiling, smiling, smiling. "We do things we don't mean. Even to people we love. We can also have strange things happen to our senses. It happens."

"Troy is lying! Lying! I would never—" Strange things happen to our senses? Dear *God*, what was going on here?

"He told us about some music you were imagining, music that no one else heard. You can see why he's genuinely worried."

"It's him. It's not me. He's the one." I spat out the words. "If he loves me *so* much, how come he calls me such terrible names? And look at this, look at my leg here. That's where Troy threw a book at me. And there's more—he had something to do with Ally. Because of his job…" I was talking rapidly, but it felt good to say these things out loud. To admit them to someone, even if it was to Betty Frost.

She was looking at me oddly. "Troy said you might react like this. Might accuse him of things. Sit down, Sadie."

I closed my eyes.

"Sit down, Sadie. Sit down."

"I don't want to sit down."

She came over to me and put her hand on my arm. "God, You know how concerned we all are about Your precious child, Sadie— how much her husband loves her, how he is just so concerned that he came to see us. How he cried. God, we just pray that Sadie will find help, that you will just strengthen her, help her. Strengthen their marriage."

And then she left, and I stared at the bird on the chair with no arms. I stood there for a long time, trembling, able to breathe only in gasps, unable even to think, unable to feel. God, I prayed, help me out of this. If You are there at all, *help me out of this.*

The bird flew away and I turned away.

Chapter Thirty-eight

When I think of myself growing up, when I remember being a girl in a normal house with two normal parents, I wonder if there was something I missed, some clue, some moment in time I could look back on and say, ah, that's it; that's where it happened; that's why things are the way they are for me.

Growing up I felt different than most of my friends. While they were riding bikes and playing with paper dolls, I was content to sit long hours at the piano and make up songs, playing the tunes I heard in my head. Art, my mother called it, and God-given creativity, but maybe I was hovering, even then, on the brink of sanity. Hearing things. Maybe I was on the brink of disaster, even then, on the edge of some dark place, and if I stepped too quickly or took too broad a stride, I would fall, reeling head over teakettle, as my mother would say, before I reached the bottom.

"Listen to this one, Mom," I would say back then in the innocence of my childhood, and she would come in from wherever she was and sit on the edge of the sofa, her knees pressed together, head cocked slightly to the side, eyes closed. She wasn't one of those mothers who believes that everything her children does is wondrous and perfect. She was a fine musician herself. "What you just played, Sadie, play it again. Especially the ending. I want to hear that ending again."

And I would play it, and then she would come over and squeeze in beside me on the bench and put her hands over mine, and they would be soft and smelling like Jergens, and we would play, our two hands together. "It needs a seventh here, Sadie. Not a major. No, I don't think a major. Try the minor."

And then she might say, "And what about your practice pieces? Have you got them ready?"

And I would play for her the Mozart or the Czerny or the Chopin, and she would listen, eyes closed, and offer suggestions.

I took piano lessons from a tall rangy woman named Mrs. Scott, who wore on a chain around her neck a gold timepiece she would hold like a stopwatch, like a nurse checking the pulse of my songs or an athletic coach timing my scales. She was the best piano teacher in Michigan City, according to my mother. My own mother could have taught me piano. She had a few private students of her own, besides her daily teaching job, but she believed I'd get a better music education from someone else. To prove this, she pointed to all the pianists she knew whose children couldn't play a note.

When I reached junior high school, my band teacher introduced me to the clarinet, and eventually I moved to the more difficult oboe. My school years were filled with travel to music festivals and competitions, adjudications and concerts, the way some families travel for swim meets and Little League.

But for all my festivals and competitions, I never placed higher than second. There was always someone just a little bit better. Maybe that was it. Maybe the constant disappointment took me to the edge.

And the music has made me different. I think of things in terms of sound. I listen to the way birds sound on a spring morning. (I have actually been known to figure out which notes they were singing and once even wrote these down on score.) I listen to the frogs at night, the howl of the coyotes, the neighbor's dog, the timbre of certain voices. Even the hum of the refrigerator has a note that can be quantified and written down.

But all this music, all this imagining, all this dreaming, all this listening has made me different. My mother calls it the artistic temperament, but I call it the brink of sanity. And maybe now I have, indeed, fallen over the edge.

Chapter Thirty-nine

I do not like them, Sam-I-am. I do not like green eggs and ham."

I was sitting on a single bed, a twin on either side of me. Their skinny bodies were leaning into me, the bony nubs of elbows and knees pressing into my side while I continued to read. I don't often read to my twins. Usually they don't ask me, usually they don't need me. So when tonight they said, Mommy, read us a story, I agreed.

By the time Troy arrived home after work, I had already retreated into silence. I would be even quieter now, even more with-drawn in church if that were possible. I was, even now, trying to come up with excuses not to have to go on Sunday, Easter Sunday. How could I work it so I would never have to go to church again? For how could I face all those people who thought this of me? How could I face the people who listened to Troy's tearful request for prayer for his poor, disturbed wife? More importantly, how could I face God with the new thoughts I was thinking? When Troy left for a board meeting, I didn't even say good-bye.

When I finished the twins' book, I closed it and said, "Well, that's that. You guys brush your teeth."

"We want…"

"Another story."

"Read us the cats one, Mommy," said PJ, pulling her nightgown over her knees.

"You'll stretch out your nightgown," I said.

Tabby did the same thing, sitting on the bed, nightgown over her knees. "Yeah, the cats one."

"It's getting late. I've got to get your brothers ready for bed."

"Read, read, read."

PJ got up and grabbed a book from a pile on her desk. "This one," she said. "It's only a short one."

"Okay," I said. "One more if it's short."

Downstairs Mary Beth was whining, "Mommy, Mommy, Mommy."

"Maybe we should invite Mary Beth to come up," I said.

A look passed between them. "We can't," said PJ.

"Mary Beth is our enemy," said Tabby.

"She's not your enemy. She's your sister. I don't like you girls talking about Mary Beth that way. And I also didn't like the both of you teasing Gavin. I saw how you were bothering him with your palm branches on Sunday."

"But we can't help it."

"They're both aliens."

"We're the only true people…"

"In this family."

PJ placed the storybook faceup on my lap. "Read, alien mother."

Alien mother. I opened my mouth to read, but when I looked at the page my breath caught in my throat. I was unable to go on. There was a line drawing of a girl holding about a dozen cats. And the girl looked exactly like the girl on the beach with the dogs, from the wispy hair blowing across her heart-shaped face down to the too-big sweater with the sleeves that ended halfway down her fingers.

"What is this?" I asked.

"The cats one."

"But where'd you get this book?" I picked it up, closed it, looked at the cover.

"Our reading book, alien mother."

"From school, Mommy."

They both collapsed into giggles, hugging their nightgowns around them.

My hands trembled as I turned to the page:

Cats on the ceiling, cats on the floor
Cats on the back porch, climbing the door.

Downstairs Gavin was growling; Simon was calling for me; and Mary Beth was saying loudly, "No, no, no! MOMMY!"

But I kept reading, page after page, about a little girl who collected the cats that nobody wanted from all the countries in the world. And on every page the girl on the beach was in a different pose, and I began to wonder if even then, sitting in my daughters' bedroom, I was falling head over teakettle toward the bottom of some place that I would never be able to climb out of. And I wondered if I even had the energy to try.

Maybe Betty Frost was right. I was hearing things. Like phantom music. I was seeing things, like a girl on the beach. I kept on reading, robotlike. Alien motherlike.

"Come out from underneath the piano bench, Gavin," I said when I finally got downstairs. "I'm only going to say this once."

"Simon's eating paper," said Mary Beth.

"Well, why didn't you take it away from him?"

"I was calling and calling, but you didn't come."

"Mary Beth, don't whine. You could have taken it away from him as easily as me. I want both of you cleaned up and ready for bed before Daddy gets home." I kept seeing the girl on the beach, pink sweater down over her fingers.

Simon had baby push-upped himself to Troy's briefcase, which lay open in front of the magazine rack, and was stuffing pieces of paper into his mouth. He looked up at me and grinned.

"Simon, what have you gotten into? Those are Daddy's papers!

Gavin, Mary Beth, why didn't you stop him? I told you to look after him, Mary Beth."

"Because," growled Gavin.

"Can you please talk in a normal voice? I can't understand one word you're saying."

"I'm a monster worm. Worms can't talk."

I picked up Simon, who was drenched, and plunked him into a corner. He grinned up at me, mouth blackened by newsprint. I then set about to clean up Troy's papers. And for the second time that night, I was stopped cold.

I was looking at a whole stack of newspaper articles—some originals, some photocopies—carefully labeled at the top in Troy's unmistakable capital letters in black magic marker. On each page he had written the name of the newspaper and the date. All of the articles were about the disappearances of Amanda Johnson and Ally Buckley. 'Amanda Johnson Missing,' read one. And underneath it, 'Girl's Body Found'; 'Second Girl Missing: Is There a Link?' And more. Mostly they were from the *Bangor Daily News,* but there were articles from the Augusta papers, and even a few from *USA Today.*

With shaking hands, I gathered them up and put them back into Troy's briefcase. Inside at the bottom I saw the manila envelope that contained Ally's paintings.

I felt something at my throat, and I began to choke and choke. I knelt there choking for a long time, my children staring at me, and prayed to wake up from this nightmare.

Chapter Forty

Two months after Troy and I were married I got a letter from Ben. Troy wasn't reading my mail in those days, not like now, so he never knew about the letter. Ben said he wanted to congratulate me on my marriage, that he didn't know Troy personally, but from what he'd heard about him, he knew I'd made a good choice. He hoped Troy would always treat me well, because I deserved it. Near the end he wrote: "I'm sorry that things didn't work out for us. I know it's wrong for me to say this, since you're married now and all, but there was always this little part of me that wanted it to be me. But I knew, deep down, that all you wanted in me was a friend, someone to talk to, someone to kid around with. Always remember me, Sadie, and the good times we had at Gino's."

I kept that letter for a long time at the back of the top drawer of my dresser. When I heard that he was married and had a little girl, I threw it out.

I read this short story once about choices and how seemingly meaningless decisions affect not only you, but whole generations of people who come after. I sometimes think about that. If I hadn't married Troy, I wouldn't have given birth to my five children. But beyond that it would affect their children, and their children's children and on down the line, hundreds of people, thousands of people, all making choices and marrying people and moving places and having more generations of people.

I was thinking about these things while I sat by the window and waited for Troy to come home from the meeting. As the night grew blacker, I began to think about dates. I was trying to remember the exact date that Amanda Johnson went missing. Keeping a careful ear out for the sound of our van, I opened Troy's briefcase and rummaged through the photocopies. Here it was, "Girl Missing," and the date, November 15.

When the phone rang, I put the photocopy back in Troy's briefcase and ran into the kitchen to answer it.

"Bernice!" I said, surprised.

"I hope I'm not phoning too late. Betty Frost called me and said you might be interested in volunteering for the program."

"Oh, she told you that?"

Bernice chuckled. "She's quite the organizer. She was in today, took all of my files out then redid the system. As soon as she left, I put them all back the way I wanted them."

While Bernice talked, I rooted through the junk drawer looking for a calendar. At the bottom of a stack of old bills, I found what I was looking for. The calendar square for November 15 was empty. The following night, November 16, however, was the monthly deacons' and spouses' dinner at Merilee and Phil's. I sat down, still listening to Bernice, and tried to remember. And I did. I remembered that Troy was unusually bad tempered that night. While we were getting ready, he asked me if I was going to embarrass him by wearing the skirt and sweater I had picked out. "You look huge in that," he had snapped. I was holding Simon, barely three months old, against my shoulder. I put him down on our bed and changed into a different skirt and sweater, to which Troy said, "Maybe it's just you. Maybe you're enormous in everything."

But the night before. What had happened the night before? I closed my eyes.

"You still there, girl?"

I put my hand to my head. "Just tired, I guess. I've had a sort of bad day."

"Do you want to talk about it?"

"I don't know."

"Would you like me to come there? I could be there in five minutes."

"No."

"The Lord brought you to my mind today. And I've been thinking of you and praying."

"Thank you."

I was remembering. The night before the dinner Troy had come home late from work. Just like the night Ally went missing. A sales call, he had told me when he had finally gotten in. A late sales call. These things happen. Was there a connection between Amanda and Ally?

"You remember," Bernice was saying. "If you want to talk, you just call me…"

I heard the van. Quickly I said, "I have to go. Troy's here." And hung up.

"Hi there, hon," said Troy, kissing me.

"Good meeting?" I tried to keep my voice cheerful.

He sighed. "As they go. If it isn't one fire it's another." He hung his jacket on a hook by the back door. "Were you on the phone when I came in? I thought I saw you through the window."

"It was someone trying to sell us long distance."

"At this time of night?"

I shrugged. "I forgot to tell you at supper, but Betty Frost dropped by this morning. She was just in the neighborhood so she stopped by." I was trailing the ends of my fingers across the top of the kitchen counter. "Wasn't that nice of her?"

He stopped and grinned at me. "So, what did you two ladies find to talk about?"

"Oh, nothing much." I shrugged my shoulders. "We just had coffee, chatted. Mostly about babies, kids, you know. Women stuff. She gave me her recipe for rhubarb cake." Cheerful. Cheerful.

"That's nice. You'll have to make that for me someday."

"Yes." But I was looking out the window, my back to him, my palms pressed together, wondering what I was going to do next.

Chapter Forty-one

*I*t's just this innocuous little story about a girl who has all these cats. Every time someone doesn't want their cat, they send it to her. So she has these cats from all over the world living with her. Chinese cats, French cats, Spanish cats, Dutch cats." I was telling this to Judith the following morning on our way to the lighthouse in her car, a leather-seated Volvo. She had called me in the morning after I had spent a fitful night, and I told her about the girl on the beach and the music. She surprised me by saying, Well, we should go there! And I was just mad enough at Betty Frost's comments to immediately say yes.

"Whew!" Judith said. "I wouldn't want to get a whiff of her house. When I was little there was this lady on our street who had five cats, but you could smell her house a mile away…" She was talking loudly, gesturing, and I got a picture of what she must have been like before all the bad things started happening to her—popular, talkative, pretty, outgoing, friendly, funny—just the sort of woman who would make a wonderful witty wife to a rich business type like Greg Buckley.

"It's a kid's story," I said. "Kids don't mind that sort of thing."

She turned to the backseat, almost driving off the road. "Well, we'll ask Gavin. Gavin, do you like smelly animals?"

"Smelly worms," he said.

"Oh, you and worms," I said.

"Worms," said Judith, shaking her head. "Now there's a pet to have. You should get one of those worm farms for Gavin. That's what they call them, worm farms. Ally had one from her school once. They're clear glass on one side so you can see what the worms do. They had it filled with these special worms that eat garbage."

"Garbage?"

"Yeah, you throw all your garbage scraps in there, and they eat them up. The ultimate in recycling, I guess it was. We had the worms' home at our house for a while. Ally was supposed to take care of them. Finally I had to call the teacher, come and get these worms, they're driving me crazy. I had visions of the little beasties crawling all over the entire house. I actually had nightmares."

I smiled. Then we were quiet for a while. The Maine country-side sped beside us.

Then she said, "What was the girl wearing?"

"What girl?"

"The lighthouse girl."

"She had on sort of poor clothes," I said. "A pink sweater that looked like it belonged to her grandmother, stretched out at the bottom and way too big. Her pants were wide and too short. Like she was clothed fully in hand-me-downs."

"Well, that makes sense. Perfect sense."

The day was mist filled, and the closer we got to the lighthouse, the heavier the air seemed.

"Sadie, see that bag on the backseat? Gavin, sweetie, can you hand that bag up to your mommy?"

"This little one?" he said.

"The little one is fine, honey."

I took it. "What is it?"

"Look in and see."

I did. I held up the box.

"Judith…"

"That's so you can find out if you're really pregnant or not. I got the box that has two tests in it." She was smiling broadly. "Because if you are pregnant, you and I, lady, have a whole lot of work to do.

Baby clothes to shop for, maternity clothes to try on. Gavin, do you want another little brother or sister?"

"Judith, don't say that. I don't know for sure…" But I did. I didn't need her pregnancy test to tell me so.

"Gavin, dear, there's another bag on the floor. Can you get that one, too? There's something in there for you. But first give it to your mommy. There's a good boy."

"What?" he growled. "What did you get me?"

"Oh, you just have to wait and see."

I pulled out a little red jacket with blue buttons and matching pants.

"Don't you think that will be adorable on Simon? I found it at this cute little baby boutique in Bangor. I'll pull over and we can try it on him right away. Should we?"

"Judith, I can't accept this. This is too expensive."

"Gavin, now it's your turn. Sadie, there's something in the bag for Gavin, too. It's at the very bottom. We couldn't leave Simon's big brother out, now could we?"

I pulled out a new Game Boy. I said, "Judith…" at the same time Gavin said, "Wow!"

"I saw the one you had at the house was cracked."

"Judith, you don't have to buy presents. This is so awkward."

"Awkward. Why?"

"Because I can't afford things for you."

"The Game Boy was less than half price. I couldn't *not* buy it. Where do I turn off? How much farther up?"

"The turnoff's up ahead. Do you know the one with the lookout point?"

A few minutes later we were dragging the stroller out of her trunk and unfolding it. "Boy, this thing has seen better days," she said. "Look at this wheel."

"That's what I get for pushing it over rocks the way I do."

It was misting and damp, not exactly rain, but the kind of day when particles of wetness hang suspended in the air. You could almost bat them away with your hand.

"Gavin, let's put your jacket on you," I called after him, but he had chased down the path to the beach. I shoved Gavin's jacket, my own, and Simon's into the diaper bag and flung it over my shoulder.

We followed the path down, and I pushed the stroller over rocks and shells and patches of water. Several times I lost sight of Gavin in the fog and called, "Gavin, come back. You have to stay where you can see us."

Judith took his hand. "We won't see anybody in this fog. That little girl could be standing two feet in front of us and we wouldn't see her."

I shuddered because it was in fog like this that the first body had been found. Several people had walked within a few feet of Amanda Johnson without seeing her. Foghorns groaned and mist enveloped us, and it seemed we were the only people on the planet.

To our right, I could hear the breathing of the ocean, long sighs on the pebbled shore.

"Don't you think we should be seeing the light from the lighthouse by now?" Judith asked.

"They don't use that lighthouse anymore. The one they use now is out on the water more."

"That's too bad. It could've helped us on a day like today."

"Maybe we should turn back," I ventured.

"Why?"

"Because it's starting to get steep. I didn't come this far before."

"It doesn't look that bad."

Ahead of us the path was veering sharply upward.

"We can't take the stroller up there," I said.

"Oh, sure we can. Do you want to find this girl or not?"

"I do," I said as I huffed my out-of-shape body up the steep path. Then I stopped. "Isn't this part of the path that's condemned?"

"No, that's on the other side. This one's perfectly safe."

"Are you sure?"

"Positive."

The cliff path was suddenly steeper, and there was no way of knowing how close we were to the edge.

"Gavin! Stay close to Mommy!"

Judith picked him up. "You're a heavy little man," she said.

The mist had turned to rain, and it spattered on the rocks beside us. Several times the stroller slipped on the mud and lurched sideways and I was glad that Simon was strapped securely in. Of all of us, he was the driest underneath the stroller's plastic rain cover.

"My turn," Judith said. She put Gavin down, then took the stroller from me and began to push it carefully up the path. I held tightly to Gavin's hand as we climbed.

"I'm tired," he said, and I could tell he was because he had abandoned his worm voice.

"I know," I said. "We're almost there."

We were quiet as we walked, each of us concentrating on our next step. The right edge of the path led down to the ocean in a series of jagged ruts that ended in midair, disappearing in the mist. The water was now far down on our right. I guessed we were just above the point where the Atlantic surged against the reef, the place which gave Coffins Reach its name.

Even though it was raining harder now, Judith seemed filled with a boundless energy. I held tightly to Gavin's hand. I was looking at the wheels of the stroller ahead of me, crudded with mud.

"Judith, that wheel's about to come off. The back one."

Judith unsnapped the plastic rain covering and lifted Simon into her arms. When she folded the stroller and stuffed it under her arm, the wheel went careening off into the mist and down the bank. We could hear it bouncing off rocks.

"We can get another wheel," she said. "They sell those wheels. Let's sing a song. Bad times go faster if you sing a song. Do you know any songs, Gavin?"

"Worms," he said.

"You mean, the worms crawl in, the worms crawl out, that one?"

"Judith, must we?"

"Okay, Gavin, your mother's being a crab. We won't sing." And in a few minutes she started chanting, "Dog girl, dog girl, we're off to see the dog girl."

"Dog girl, dog girl," said Gavin.

My foot slipped and I fell forward landing heavily on my knee. I sought fingerholds in the mud and finally grasped a small root that seemed secure. I forced myself up.

It seemed forever, but finally the path opened up to an expanse of long soft grasses, bent over by the rain. We tromped through them, all of us drenched to the skin, except for Simon who was wrapped in the plastic covering of the stroller. I sensed rather than saw the lighthouse in front of us. And when we reached it, I said, "Well, we made it." I looked up the white sides and couldn't even see the top.

"It looks abandoned," she said.

"It is abandoned."

"I thought you said the girl lives here."

"That's what she said."

"Well, it doesn't look like anybody lives here." To our right the gazebo looked ghostly in the fog. The keeper's house, too, was empty.

There was a house nearby, a large gray stone one. The path that led to it was lined with thick hedges we could barely make out in the mist. As we walked down the path, Gavin clung to me, dripping wet, shivering. In Judith's arms Simon's face was wet and he was holding his tongue out to catch the drips. The rest of him was encased in plastic.

"It doesn't look like there's anybody here, either," I said. "And Gavin's shivering. Aren't you cold, Judith? And I'm worried about Simon. He'll get an ear infection, for sure. His head's sopping wet."

She moved the plastic up over his head.

A large dark porch yawned in front of us. There were a couple of lights on at the back of the house, but instead of looking like welcome beacons, they filled me with a dread I couldn't explain.

"Judith, maybe we should go."

"Go? Go where? Back down the path? Come with me. I'll do the talking."

At the back, her knock was answered by a small pink-faced man in a stretched-out, gray wool sweater.

"We'd like to speak to the little girl who lives here," said Judith in a crisp nurse's voice.

"Pardon me?" The man cupped a hand behind his ear.

"We're looking for a little girl and her three dogs."

"Mother!" The man turned and called. In a few moments a fuzzy-haired woman padded to the door in sloppy slippers.

"These here people are looking for dogs."

"You lost your dog, you say?"

"No, no," Judith said.

"What is it then? Are you lost?" she asked us.

"No, our car's over in the picnic area."

"Well, you should come in, my goodness. You all are soaked to your bones. Did you climb up the cliff path with those babies?" She clucked her tongue.

We walked into a kitchen that despite the light and the wood-stove in the corner seemed cold and cheerless. I let go of Gavin's hand, and he raced over to the table and grabbed the salt and pepper shakers, which were two fat people.

"Gavin!" I shouted and grabbed them from his hands. "Leave things alone."

"What we're looking for is a little girl," Judith continued, "around twelve years old, blond hair. A few days ago my friend met her on the beach walking her dogs."

"She was more like nine or ten," I said.

"Twelve," Judith said.

"Are you her granddad?" I asked. "Do you know about the music?"

At the mention of music, the woman stiffened. The man took off his round glasses and cleaned them on the tail of his shirt and then put them on again.

"What's this about music?" he asked.

"Dad, I'd say we've had enough about music."

"My friend met a little girl on the beach who said she lived here and that her granddad told her about fairy music. Or angel music."

"I don't want to talk about music. The police were here about music, and we've had enough about music."

I looked at the woman. "Are you the one who heard the music? I heard it. I was talking to the police, too."

"She doesn't want to talk about music," said the man. "She said there's been enough about music."

"But this is really important," I said. "It's important to me."

The woman said, "I've had enough about the music."

"Did you hear her?" said the man. "She's had enough about the music."

"Are you the police or newspaper people?" asked the woman.

"The little girl said she lived up here," I said. "Are there other houses?"

"Nope."

"I was sure she pointed up this way when I asked her where she lived. She said she lived in the lighthouse."

"Nobody lives in the lighthouse," said the woman. "Or the keeper's house."

"It's abandoned," said the man. "How could anyone live in an abandoned lighthouse?"

Judith was talking now. "She's almost twelve. She has very light blond hair, almost white. And she loves dogs so I'm not surprised she was walking some. She had a worm farm once. That's what they call them. Worm farms. And I'm not surprised to hear she was wearing an old pink sweater. You wouldn't believe some of the things she would want to wear to school."

I stared at Judith.

"Doesn't ring a bell," said the man. "Does it to you, Mother?"

The woman shook her head and looked away from us.

"But you must have seen my daughter! Is she with you? I was hoping maybe she was here. I was hoping she was with you. I was so sure. Because of the other one…"

"Judith…" I touched her arm.

"I know you," said the woman, pointing. "You're the lady from the television. The one whose little girl went missing," She paused. "I'm so sorry. And you thought your little girl was up here? You thought that was your little girl?"

Judith's lip was quivering. I looked at the way her wet jacket clung to her, her hair matted with the rain, at how tightly she held on to Simon. The old woman put a hand out. "Let me make a hot drink," she said. "Warm yourselves. Let me take the baby for a while."

"My kids'll be home from school soon," I said. "We can only stay a minute. Not long."

Judith had slumped into a kitchen chair. I took Simon from her and unwrapped him. I dried the three of us on threadbare towels in a tiny bathroom off the kitchen while the woman made tea and chatted on about how lighthouses work. When it was time to leave she said, "You'll drive these women to their car, won't you, Dad?"

"Sure, let me go fire her up."

On the way to the picnic area—and it did seem like a long way—I leaned my head against the back of the seat and listened while our driver pointed out landmarks and flora and fauna along the road. He told us he had never seen a girl with the three dogs, and he would have noticed about the dogs, he said. You couldn't have dogs in the area without him noticing. It's because of the cats. Mother loves cats, you see.

Chapter Forty-two

aybe you imagined the whole thing," Judith said to me on the way home.

"What!"

"I said maybe you imagined the whole thing. The music, the girl, the whole thing. It's not impossible you know. Think about it."

"The girl was as real as you sitting there talking to me. The music was as real as the music on the car radio now."

"All I'm saying is this—that the couple didn't have any idea what you were talking about. That's all I'm saying. And they said they would have noticed dogs."

"Because of their cats, I know. I heard."

"When I was in the hospital there was this woman there who heard music that no one else heard. There she would be, la la-ing all around the hallways to music that only she heard. She saw people, too. She'd get to the end of the hall and start talking to imaginary people who were standing there."

"I'm not crazy. I don't need to be locked up in a loony bin."

There was a silence. Finally she said in a quiet voice, "It's not that bad."

"Oh, Judith, I'm sorry. I didn't mean to offend you. I'm so sorry."

"No, it's me, too. I've been on edge all day. It's me. I'm probably more tired than I realize. Stressed. I sort of had this idea that it may have been Ally on the point. I don't know. It was just a thought that captured me and I went after it, and it's not there. Just all imaginings. Like that lady in the hospital. I prayed before we came. And now God has again not answered. It's just like God, you know, not to answer."

I looked at the rain on the window, little beads of it, breaking apart, the edges flying off in all directions.

In Coffins Reach, she turned to me. "I'd like you to come by my place. I'd like to show you something."

"The girls get home in about an hour. Just as long as I'm home for them."

When we got to her house, she dressed Simon and Gavin in some of Ally's dry clothes. Then she sat Gavin at the kitchen table with a piece of chocolate cake and a glass of milk. We laid an exhausted Simon on Judith's bed, and then she led me down a long hall to a part of her house I had never been in before.

In the office, she turned on the computer and while we waited for the screen to lighten she told me that the computer had saved her sanity.

"Do you have a computer?" she asked me.

"Troy does." I thought of Troy's computer, off-limits to everyone but him. It was because of the kids, he said. He didn't want them becoming glued to the thing. Besides, there was a lot of undesirable stuff out there.

"But what about me?" I asked once. "I know there's lots of information about music. My mother showed me the last time we were there."

"Sadie," he had said, "I think it's unwise for you to keep pursuing that dream. You're a mother now."

"Pay attention then," Judith was saying. "They aren't all that difficult to learn."

"I do know about computers, Judith. My parents have a computer. I'm not totally stupid about computers."

"Okay, then, so you know how to get onto the Internet?"

"Yep, I sure do."

"Okay, then. I want to show you something. This is important."

She fiddled with some more keys. "This is how I spend my days. This is what keeps me sane."

In a matter of minutes she was showing me a Web site she had made for Ally, and all the links she had made to various missing children's registries. She also showed me the police and FBI files. "I also link to other parents who've lost children. There's a whole network of us. We talk back and forth. We help each other. This is my lifeline. But I'm missing something for the Web site."

"It looks good to me," I said.

"I want to put her pictures up here. Not the ones of her, but the ones she drew herself. She painted all these beautiful pictures. She even won awards. I used to have them on the fridge, but then Greg told me to take them down. He wanted to take them to work, he said. I keep asking him to bring them home, but now he says he can't find them. What I want to do is scan them all into this Web site. It might help to jog someone's memory. I'm thinking that wherever she is she'll be painting pictures, and that maybe someone will recognize them. But they're gone. And that's something I can't explain."

I felt that hand again, like a choke. I rubbed my neck.

Chapter Forty-three

When I was a little girl I had nightmares. Not merely bad dreams where I woke up knowing that I had dreamed something unpleasant, but actual nightmares where I would open my eyes and someone would be standing in my room, or looking in the window from outside, or punching at the bottom of my bed from underneath.

For a long time it was the Chinese Lady who stood in the corner of my room beside the closet. She always wore a pale blue Chinese dress and waved at me with the fan she held. I would cower under my covers and she would laugh at my fear, her rose lips pursed, her white face nodding up and down. I never looked at her very long, because soon I would begin screaming and my mother would come and I would tell her about the Chinese Lady who by this time had disappeared.

In the morning my mother showed me how my blue housecoat hanging on the hook might look like a Chinese lady, especially if the window was open and a breeze was blowing.

"No, it was a real Chinese Lady. She was right there."

"How do you know she was Chinese?" my mother asked.

"Because she wore a Chinese dress."

Another time I woke up and Tom Sawyer was sitting at the foot of my bed leering at me. He was moving the piece of straw between his teeth, and when I opened my eyes, he tipped his straw hat at me. I screamed and he disappeared.

Once when I got up to go to the bathroom in the middle of the night, I stood at the head of the stairs and looked down. At the bottom was a lake of disembodied heads, eyes looking up at me. I screamed and screamed and screamed, until my father came this time, turned on the hall light and showed me that there were no heads down there. It was just a carpet. Our little dog Rambert wasn't even down there.

"But I saw them. They were there. All these heads. Millions of them."

I sleepwalked and sleep-talked, and sometimes woke up in a different place than I had lain down the previous night. I often woke up on my floor or on the couch in the living room. Once when I was seven, I woke up in the laundry room, the clean, warm laundry enveloping me.

My parents didn't worry about this, as parents today might (as I do when Mary Beth wakes screaming that she is being chased by Pokémons). My parents, especially my mother, said this meant I had been gifted with "imagination," and we'll pray to God that Mary Beth's imagination will flourish and be used by God for His kingdom.

My teachers said my imagination was "overactive." I imagined all sorts of fearful things happening to me on my way to school. And every afternoon when I safely walked through my door, I would breathe a sigh of relief, as much as if I had found my way home through a jungle of wild beasts.

I started piano lessons when I was eight and my nightmares gradually faded, until by the time I was ten, I never had another one.

Until now.

Chapter Forty-four

An hour after we arrived home Gavin began complaining of a stomachache. I laid him on the couch, wrapped him in a blanket, plugged in a video, gave him a cup half filled with room temperature ginger ale, and put a plastic bucket down beside him "just in case." The twins were in the playhouse, and Mary Beth was at Emma's today, working on a school project. Beside me in his playpen, Simon slept on his back, still worn out by the day's adventures. I had plunked in a classical music tape in my cassette player. With Vivaldi in the background, I could almost believe that everything would be all right. Almost. I was thinking about the phantom girl with the dogs. That's what happened to me. We read Tom Sawyer in school, and then I wake up and there he is, sitting barefoot at the foot of my bed. We study China in geography class, so I go to bed and see the Chinese Lady. I see that picture of the cat girl, probably lying open on the kitchen table, and then I see the girl, although now she's a dog girl, and she's on the beach. But whether I dreamed the music or not, it was there—real music, pages and pages of it at the back of Mary Beth's school scribbler, buried at the bottom of the piano bench.

With Simon sleeping, I opened the newest Idaho Pioneers. Get lost in something else, I thought. Get lost in a world where people are good to each other and everything makes sense and God is always in control. I read for twenty minutes and then I put it down. Those people prayed. Things went wrong, then they prayed and things became right again. That didn't happen in real life. I prayed for Troy, and then he would hit me. So I would pray harder and harder, and then a little girl is murdered and Ally goes missing and it's Troy. And I pray more, and I'm pregnant and Troy loses his job. And now I can't pray anymore.

I pulled out two pizza crusts and a package of hamburger meat from the freezer.

"Oh, Simon," I said out loud. "What're we going to do?"

"About what?" Troy was behind me. I twirled and stared.

"You're home early," I said, startled.

"And I'm glad to see you, too. Maybe Simon can tell me where my wife goes every day."

"What?"

"Or maybe I should hire a private investigator. But that costs money, and money's in short supply around this house these days. Or doesn't anyone but me seem to notice that? Where were you today?"

I didn't say anything.

"I asked you where you were today. What part of that question didn't you understand?"

"I was out for a little while earlier. Me and the boys. We went for a nice long walk."

"The boys and I. And you call yourself a college graduate."

"I'm not a college graduate." I could not stop my hands from shaking. I pressed my palms against my hot cheeks.

"And I can see why not."

I could hear little whispery sounds of growling from the living room. Maybe Gavin was feeling better.

"I repeat my question, where did you go today?"

"For a walk."

"You went for a walk in the pouring rain. Why do I find that hard to believe?"

"It wasn't raining when we started. Sometimes I feel like I want to get outside."

"So because you just have to get out, you risk my sons' health."

"It wasn't like that."

"I should think you'd have a little more sense than to go traipsing off in the rain, with Simon, who gets sick at the drop of a hat. And look at Gavin. What's the matter with him?"

"He wasn't feeling well when we got back."

"Sometimes, Sadie, I wonder if you have the sense you were born with." He looked around him and raised his arms theatrically. "Sometimes I wonder, how did I get into this life? What am I doing here? I phoned, Sadie. I phoned all afternoon. At fifteen-minute intervals."

"I'm sorry."

"I couldn't imagine where you'd gone. Naturally, I began thinking the worst. I knew you didn't have the van, so you couldn't drive anywhere. And it's pouring rain. I didn't know what to think. Is my wife seeing another man? Is that where she goes? I even began thinking…I began thinking that someone had come in for you. That killer. You don't know the things that were going through my mind. Didn't know whether I should get in the van and drive straight home."

"I'm sorry, Troy." I turned away from him, looked out the window at my twins' faces in the windows of the playhouse.

He came over and hugged me from behind. My hands were still shaking.

"It's just that I worry about you. You can't imagine." His voice was soft.

"I'm sorry."

"Sadie, it's just…it's just…well, I'll just come out and say it. I want you to be here when I call. I can't stand it when you're not." He grabbed my hair suddenly and turned me around to face him. I gasped. He held my cheek and jaw in his hand and pressed tightly. "Look at me when I talk to you! Why do you look everywhere but at me?"

"Troy…"

There was too much white in his eyes. After a while he let go. I rubbed my cheek and wondered if there would be a red mark. Like last time.

He sat down at the kitchen table and dissolved into tears, his head in his hands. "Look what you make me do, Sadie. Just look what you make me do."

"Went to the cliffs," said Gavin, walking in from the living room. I looked at him sharply. "I want more." He held out his glass.

"Feeling better, are you?" I asked.

"I want MORE!"

"Okay, okay." I poured him some ginger ale from a plastic bottle on the counter.

"What's this about cliffs?" said Troy.

"Oh, what Gavin calls cliffs and what are real cliffs are two different things. Kids exaggerate, you know that."

"I played with the fat people saltshaker."

"Okay, Gavin, you be quiet now." And I put my fingers to my lips and ushered him back into the living room, and got him lying down again.

"Big house, big house, big house." He was chanting.

I came back to the kitchen and chattered and chattered. "We just walked and walked. Didn't see anybody much. Just walked and walked. Simon's sure tuckered out, though. Look at him sleeping there. Trouble is, I bet he'll be up all night now. I should try to keep him awake, just so he doesn't stay up all night. Ever since we got home, he's been asleep. Fell right to sleep. But this is nice, to have this time to get supper on without him fussing. That doesn't often happen…"

Troy grabbed a Diet Coke from the fridge and headed out to his workshop. "You either say absolutely nothing, or you talk a blue streak and no one can understand you. I'm going out to my workshop. Come out and get me when supper's ready."

"I will."

Later that evening, after Troy had left for a church missions committee meeting, Bernice called to tell me that the Safe Harbor House volunteer training was going to be on six consecutive Monday nights beginning in about two weeks.

"I can't get out at night," I told her. "It's so hard with my family. If Troy happens to be working late there's no way I can get a babysitter. It's something we just can't afford."

"I understand," she said in a honey voice. "And on those nights when your husband isn't home, why don't you bring those children of yours on over to the center? We've got a whole slew of babysitters lined up for the training. Plus toys galore."

"I never should have volunteered. I don't know what possessed me. Troy's on the committee."

"Yes, I know that."

I was rubbing my cheek. There was a red mark under my eye where Troy had squeezed. I was running out of makeup. I buy concealer sticks two at a time at the grocery store, the cheap brand, but they work.

"Gavin can be difficult at times. He goes into these tantrums. Sometimes he's good as gold, and then he just gets in these moods. It's especially bad during the evenings when he's tired."

"How about this? How about if I come over there?"

"What?"

"To your house. We could talk about the program."

"You'd come to my house?"

"Sure I would, honey."

We made a date. She would come the following Monday morning at ten. I didn't write it on the calendar. When she hung up PJ and Tabby came in to tell me that Gavin was throwing up all over the place.

"It's really gross, Mommy."

"It's everywhere. It's even on his new Game Boy."

"All over the couch."

"Yucky, yucky."

They made throwing up noises as I wearily made my way to the living room.

Chapter Forty-five

The Saturday before Easter, I heard the music for the last time. I was boiling a dozen and a half eggs so that later in the day my children and I could sit around the kitchen table and dye them our favorite Easter colors. This was something I grew up doing on the Saturday before Easter, but now this enforced tradition usually ends in disaster. I had no doubt that today wouldn't be any different.

In the morning when the eggs were boiling on the stove, Judith showed up at my door with a brand-new stroller from Sears, still in a box.

I stepped out onto the porch. "Judith, you don't have to do this. You don't have to keep giving me things."

"But I broke your stroller. And I had this one lying around the house. It was a gift for Ally. But we had two. I never used this one."

"I can't keep accepting things."

Her arms were around the box, and she leaned into it as if for support. Her eyes were red rimmed.

"Judith, what's wrong? Did something happen?"

"It's the questions. They keep asking questions."

"Who does?"

"The police. I just get to thinking maybe it's over with, and then they're over and asking questions and we have to go through the whole thing again."

"That must be horrible."

"I know the parents of the other girl must be going through the

237

same thing. Especially since they're so obviously linked. That's what I keep thinking."

I perked up my ears. "Linked?"

"Amanda Johnson's mother was one of the principal shareholders in Federated. So now they're thinking the same person took both girls."

I was suddenly very still. "I didn't read that in the papers."

"The police keep some things out of the papers. That's how they work."

"I didn't know that."

Later that day Troy asked me where the new stroller came from.

"My mother sent it," I told him.

"Your mother?"

"The other one broke. The wheel fell off. I guess I mentioned it to her. So this one came in the mail yesterday."

"Next time they call I'll have to thank them."

"You don't have to, I already did."

He was putting on suit and tie and told me he was going into Bangor for the day. He was having lunch with some fellow from an insurance company about a job.

"Should we wait for you to come back to decorate the eggs?"

"No, I may not be back until early evening. Go ahead without me."

"Do you want to take one of the children? Mary Beth or the twins might like a drive into Bangor."

"Sadie, this is a job interview, not a trip to Disney World."

If he got the job, he told me, he would be selling insurance, plus helping people with investments. It was a real opportunity for advancement. He could work right up the corporate ladder with this one.

"Are you sure you want to do that again, Troy? Sell insurance?"

"And what, precisely, is that little comment supposed to mean?"

I turned away and went back to folding laundry.

In the afternoon Betty Frost called to ask how Gavin was. "Troy mentioned it at the deacons' meeting. How sick he was."

"He's fine."

"Did the rest of your children catch it?"

"No."

"Troy was concerned about the boys being out in the rain."

I gripped the phone tightly and said nothing.

"The other reason I called was about the Safe Harbor House training. I know you said you wanted to volunteer, and I wondered in what capacity?"

"What do you mean?"

"Well, there's the twenty-four-hour help line, which will be established. Then there are all sorts of things that will need doing. I was over at Bernice's just yesterday trying to help her get organized."

"She already phoned me."

"Well, why on earth would she do that? I'm the one who's setting it all up. Everything's going through me. Plus, I know all the candidates—I know who's better qualified and for what position."

I was beginning to feel hot.

"I'm thinking of you, Sadie, more along the lines of a helping capacity."

"Helping capacity?"

"Oh, folding brochures, bundling them for the various centers, that sort of thing. This would be something you could do right at your kitchen table. To be honest, Sadie, I really don't know how comfortable you'd be in the people end of things. I'm thinking of you along the lines of brochures here, Sadie, and maybe you'll have an opinion on this. No reason why I shouldn't ask your opinion about this. In her presentation to the board, Bernice said she wanted to put up racks with the new brochures in women's washrooms in community centers and churches in the area. I guess Troy didn't see women's washrooms in churches as a pressing need. And I have to say that I agree with him on that point because if their husbands are as abusive as all that, I can't see them *allowing* their wives to come to church in the first place. Plus, well, we just redecorated the ladies' washroom and frankly there's just no place for a rack and brochures."

"What about next to the paper towel dispenser?"

"Sheila's making this lovely artificial flower arrangement that will go there."

Gavin had opened the dustcover of the piano and was plunking loudly on the keys. "Gavin, please. Mommy's on the phone. Just a minute, Betty."

Betty Frost laughed. "You really do have your hands full, don't you? Just like my Michelle with her two now, but she's really enjoying moms and tots at the church. They even have aerobics twice a week. They've been hiring a baby-sitter, and they have an aerobics instructor, a Christian, so of course they use Christian music. It's so important to get into shape as quickly as possible, don't you think? And to meet other Christian moms who can become friends? Do you ever go to that group?"

"I did a couple of times."

"Well, I highly recommend it, Sadie. It might be a good place to make friends. Good, lasting, Christian friends, not to mention getting in shape. Now you let me know in what capacity you see yourself fitting in at Safe Harbor."

I cleaned furiously after that phone call. I sprayed some stuff on the rug where Gavin threw up (there was still a tinge of it in the air) and waited the required fifteen minutes, then vacuumed that up. I dusted the window ledges and sorted through old magazines. In the kitchen I put newspapers all over the table and got the egg decorating cups out. I would make us all sit here and decorate eggs. I am a good mother.

I stopped my frenetic movements for one minute and stood in the doorway. And I heard it. In the middle of the day with everyone home, just an ordinary Saturday afternoon, and there it was! The music. My music. I went outside and stood on the back porch and listened. Despite what Judith had said, despite what the dog girl had said, the music didn't frighten me. It filled me with hope. I rooted in the piano bench for Mary Beth's notebook and the sharpened pencils I had begun keeping there.

I carried Simon outside and plunked him down on a blanket in the shade, and I sat on an armless lawn chair and began transcribing what I heard. It was slightly different this time. But a wonderful tune. A glorious tune! Inside the playhouse Mary Beth and the twins were arguing.

"But I wanted that one!"

"Please, girls, can you please get along? I'm trying to listen."

"What're you doing, Mommy?" Mary Beth came and stood beside me looking down at the strange scrawls in the back of her notebook.

"Writing down music. Isn't it pretty? I just wonder where it's coming from."

"PJ and Tabby are making fun of me, Mommy."

"I'm trying to listen, Mary Beth."

"They said I took their Pokémon cards, but I didn't. What're you *doing*, Mommy?" She was pressing her warm body against mine, clinging to me.

"Mary Beth, please, it's too hot for that."

"PJ and Tabby say I'm stupid, but they're the ones who are stupid."

"Mary Beth, please. I want to get this down before it goes away."

"Can I walk over to Emma's? Please, Mommy. She wants me to."

"Will anybody be there?"

"Her dad."

"You can bring her back here if her dad's busy."

So for more than an hour, I sat in the backyard and wrote and wrote. And then looked at the pages I had filled. Dozens and dozens of them.

And then just as suddenly, the music was gone. In midnote, midsentence, midphrase it stopped. No fade out, no resolution, no ending.

I went back inside and buried the scribbler in the piano bench.

Chapter Forty-six

I drew the bowl of hard-boiled eggs out of the fridge and placed them on the table and thought about an Easter a dozen years ago. Troy and I had planned to visit both families over the Easter week holidays. We stayed with my family first for four days and we laughed, visited, told jokes, and decorated eggs. My brother was home from medical school that same week, and Troy shared a room with him.

"Well?" I said to my brother at the end of the visit, "what do you think of him?"

He looked at me seriously and said, "Sadie, I think I'd give this guy a wide berth if I were you."

"You didn't like him?"

"Who was that other guy you were going out with?"

"What other guy?"

"The other guy. The short one."

"You mean Ben?"

"Ben, yeah, that's his name. Here's my opinion, for what it's worth: Go back to Ben."

I stared at my brother who said, "You asked my opinion. I just call them the way I see them."

The Monday morning after Easter, we climbed into Troy's barely running Chevette and drove to his home, three hundred miles away.

His house was a very ordinary white bilevel with a minimum of shrubbery. I described it to Clarice as wide open. Now I call it stark.

No one came to greet us when we arrived, despite the fact that

Troy called out Hello, we're here! several times.

Troy's father was sitting in an easy chair watching television when we walked in.

"So, you're the girl," he said without looking up.

I smiled and nodded and nodded.

He looked up at me briefly and turned back to the television. I think those four words are the longest grouping of words he's ever spoken to me. Usually, it's *Hello,* or if we're outside it might be *Nice weather,* or *Lousy weather,* or *Interesting,* when he's got his head buried in a newspaper.

But Troy's grandmother more than makes up for her taciturn son. In the kitchen she was sitting at the table drinking iced tea, her fleshly legs wide apart, a hand on one knee. Her face was ruddy and soft and oily looking. Her first words to me were, "So you're the one our boy keeps talking about."

I smiled and blushed. "I suppose so."

"Well, I suppose we should get some supper on. I hope you're not fussy."

I assured her I wasn't.

She groaned and hoisted herself out of her chair. "We'll do up some eggs. You can help. Both of you. And let me tell you something about Troy," she said without looking at me. "If you can change him, Sadie, more power to you."

I laughed nervously.

"Boy's got no ambition. Never did, never will as far as I can see. Takes after his mother. He ever tell you about his mother? Just up and left one morning, never even a how do you do. Troy takes after her if you want my opinion. Woman didn't have the sense she was born with and neither does Troy and neither does his father. Troy'll never amount to much. But if that's what you want, well, that's what you'll get."

"Grandma…" said Troy.

"Don't *grandma* me. A few things got to be said here before this lovely young lady gets hitched to this family."

That was the only time she ever called me "lovely young lady." Now it's usually "the fat wife."

"I'm going into the ministry, Grandma," said Troy. "I'm going to be a minister."

She frowned and looked at me. I didn't know where to look. "I gave up my own life to move in with this here boy and his no-good father. Did you know that? Troy ever tell you the story of how his mother just run off, wanted nothing to do with him? I had to move in because that father of his couldn't manage on his own. Well, if he spent a little less time in front of the boob tube, I'd say he'd manage just fine. All the time watching those sports shows. I tell him you'd be better off watching the soaps. I gave up my own life. Do you think I wanted this? No, I had friends. We were going to travel, but instead I'm saddled with a five-year-old boy and his dumbwitted father. And for all these years I stayed."

"Oh," I said.

She talked while she worked, scrambling eggs into a pan and whisking them with a fork. "Troy, get out the bread, will ya? Make yourself useful."

"Grandma, I'm going to be a good minister. You'll see. I'll make you proud of me." He was lining up the bread for the toaster.

"What're you *doing?*"

"Getting the toast ready."

"Give me that. Can't you do one thing right? You got your hands all over that bread. I got to do for everybody around here. You and that dumbwitted father of yours."

Later in my room I cried and cried and cried for all Troy had to endure, and I loved him all the more for it. We will overcome this, Troy. The two of us, we will do it. We will show her.

That's what I thought then. What I never expected was that Troy would grow up to be just like her.

From the first, I knew my marriage would not be like my parents'.

For starters, Troy and I have always struggled with money. I grew up in a house with both parents working and money was never an issue. Not that my brother and I were given every single thing we wanted, but I never remember my own mother struggling the way I do, trying to feed and clothe five children on Troy's meager sales commissions. And now, even those would be gone.

I looked out the window. The girls, including Emma, were playing calmly in the playhouse with only half a roof. I looked beyond them to Troy's locked workshop.

On the counter a clear plastic container of homemade spaghetti sauce was defrosting in a patch of sun. The house was fairly clean for a Saturday, though the table was still covered with newspapers. The eggs could wait. I put Simon in his plastic baby seat and grabbed all the keys from the wooden board.

Outside, the twins said, "Where are you…"

"Going, Mommy?"

"How do you do that?" Emma said to the twins.

"Do what?"

"Talk together," she said.

"But Mommy, where're you *going?*" asked Mary Beth.

"I have to get something from the workshop. Mary Beth, can you let me know if you see Daddy drive up? Come and get me as soon as you see him. And don't provoke Gavin."

"What's provoke?" asked Emma.

"Get mad at," said Mary Beth.

None of the keys worked. I wasn't surprised, of course, and I found myself, like before, climbing in the back window, thankful that I was out of sight of the questioning looks of my children.

Once inside I unlocked the door and called to the kids, "PJ, Tabby, come let me and Simon know the minute Daddy comes, okay?"

"You already said that."

"Just don't forget."

"You asked *me* to do that, Mommy, not PJ and Tabby," Mary Beth said.

"Okay, Mary Beth, you come and tell me. You be the one."

"But we…"

"Want to."

"I asked Mary Beth first, and I forgot, so Mary Beth, you and Emma be the ones, okay?"

Inside I put Simon's carrier down and pulled the cover off the computer and turned it on. A few moments later I clicked on the Netscape icon and heard the internal modem dialing. Soon I was hooked right up to an Internet browser.

After a few false starts, I found the *Bangor Daily News* site, and began reading articles about Amanda Johnson and Ally Buckley. Most of them were the same articles that were photocopied in Troy's briefcase. I looked at a grainy black-and-white school picture of Amanda, and then I realized that what was in Troy's briefcase were not photocopies, but printouts from these sites on his computer. I read through them all, but found no link between the girls. It was just like Judith had said—for some reason the police wanted that information kept out of the papers.

I read the stories about Ally, most of which I had already read in the newspaper. I did a search for Federated, and with a thick carpenter's pencil, took notes on a notebook I'd brought with me. Again there was no mention of anybody named Johnson.

I learned a lot about Federated. It was a Georgia-based company that specialized in consolidating credit card debt with their own brand of low interest card. The company had started in the 1980s amid lots of controversy and several lawsuits. Words like *antitrust* and *monopoly* kept cropping up, and I didn't understand it completely. From what I could see, Federated charged a one-time start-up fee for their low interest credit card, but along with that fee, one got financial counseling and money management advice.

I went to one site called Federated Is a Scam! And I read one man's story about how Federated was worse than dealing with loan sharks, because it's fine if you keep up your payments, but if you miss one, the interest rates skyrocket. A medical emergency forced him to miss one month's payment, and now he was paying far more to Federated than he was previously paying to MasterCard and Visa combined. That article was dated 1996.

"New Face Still the Same Old Scam," read an article in a 1997 newspaper. This one outlined the success of businessman Greg Buckley, who owned a chain of restaurants in the southeastern states and had bought most of the shares of Federated. His plan was to raise the profile of the company with glossy brochures and "down home" ads appealing to families. And it was working. There were five call centers in the eastern United States and more being built. Federated credit cards were quickly becoming an alternative to MasterCard, Visa, and American Express. I scanned down the names again, but still no mention of anyone named Johnson.

A fairly recent article talked about Federated's newest acquisition, SmartSystems, a small computer company in the small town of Coffins Reach, Maine, where Buckley grew up. On the verge of bankruptcy (I didn't know that!), SmartSystems' claim to fame was debugging the Y2K problem. Since then, however, the company had fallen on hard times. They had sunk most of their financial resources into developing antivirus software, but just as soon as it was ready, another company came up with similar software and a more strategic market plan. Federated's plan for SmartSystems was to keep a small contingent of software developers, but to sell most of the assets to Bangor-based ComputerTech. They also planned to expand the present building into a 300 employee call center, bringing jobs and new life to the picturesque fishing town.

A letter to the editor in the same paper decried the fact that the modern expansion would infringe on some of Maine's wetlands, threatening the habitat of "peeper" frogs.

I scanned the notes I had taken. They didn't really tell me a lot, so I decided to change directions and went back to the *Bangor Daily News* site and searched for articles about Judith's trial. "Nurse Accused" was the headline of the first one I read. Judith had been arrested for the death of Noel Gunn, five years old. He had died of a drug overdose at the end of Judith's shift one morning. The grainy picture was Judith, but it was a Judith I didn't recognize—wild hair, handcuffed, head down, Greg on one side and her lawyer, presumably, on the other. There was a picture of a freckle-faced, five-year-old boy named Noel Gunn. He had been dying from an aggressive form of leukemia that was not responding to treatment. Mercy Killing or Outright Murder? one paper asked. Judith and her lawyer maintained her innocence throughout, and from what I could read, the hospital backed her. The parents of the child seemed to be on a smear campaign. They claimed Judith had purposely increased Noel's dosage. She claimed he needed it for the pain. In the end she was convicted and suffered a nervous breakdown and was hospitalized for three years.

I shifted gears and did a search on the news site for "music," and it yielded millions of articles and links, none of them relating to the crime.

A sound behind me made me jump. I turned, my hands in fists. Ham stood there.

"You startled me," I said. "I thought it was Troy."

"I'm sorry."

"I was concentrating."

"I can see that. You jumped a mile."

"I was looking up about Amanda and Ally. Reading articles. I was looking up various newspapers. That's what I was doing."

"Sadie, you don't have to give me an explanation."

There was an awkward silence. I'm not good with silences.

"I'm sorry for startling you," he said again.

My hands were shaking. I put them flat on the table. "Ham, I have to ask you something. Why was it kept out of the papers that the mother of the girl who died, Amanda Johnson, is one of the shareholders in Federated, the company that's buying out SmartSystems?"

"Because she isn't."

"Yes, she is. She's a principal shareholder of Federated."

"Whatever gave you that idea?"

"It was something I heard."

"Amanda Johnson's father is an employee with the city of Bangor, and her mother's a secretary in a real estate office. Neither one of them has anything to do with Federated. The little girl's body happened to be found here, but that's their sole connection with Coffins Reach."

I shut the computer down the way Judith had done, and then put the cover on it.

"Did Troy tell you this?" he asked me.

"Not Troy, no."

"Who then?"

I didn't say anything.

"Is there anything you're not telling me, Sadie?" His voice was gentle.

I smoothed my hair back. I swallowed.

"What happened to your cheek?" he asked.

"My cheek?" I put my hand there. "Sunburn. I was outside and forgot my sunscreen. My face gets all blotchy sometimes. If I forget my sunscreen."

He looked at me for a while and I couldn't read his expression.

"Is Troy around?" he finally said.

"He's in Bangor. At a job interview."

"How's that going?"

"I don't know. Don't tell Troy about this, okay? About me being on his computer."

"I won't."

"He's kind of touchy lately. It's the job thing. Being out of a job,

I mean. But I came in here because I wanted to find out about Federated. He keeps things from me, because he doesn't want to worry me. But I worry anyway."

He peered at me. I was conscious of the blueness of his eyes. I didn't know where to look.

"Would you come and tell me if something were wrong? I mean really wrong?" He was still looking at me. I nodded.

I had a sudden thought. *He suspects Troy. That's why he's friends with him. That's what police do. They become friends with the people they suspect.*

Chapter Forty—seven

*T*he birds woke me on Easter Sunday, and I was up and out of bed well before Troy was back from the sunrise service. He always goes to that. I never do anymore. Getting five kids ready for church when it's just Sunday school at 9:45 is hard enough, but to try to get them all ready for a service almost three hours earlier is something I don't even want to think about. Troy said he would be back at nine to pick us up for our church's annual Easter pancake breakfast.

In the kitchen five little Easter baskets sat on the table. No one had wanted to decorate eggs yesterday, so I had done it by myself late last night. I had closed all the doors, put a cassette in the player, and by the time the cassette was finished I had decorated eighteen eggs and placed them along with chocolate bunnies inside the baskets.

At 7:30 I stood in front of the kitchen window trying to come up with an excuse to stay home. The sun was up and the armless chairs looked golden in its eerie sheen. Abuse my children? What did all those people think of me? My hands felt cold and I ran warm water over them at the sink. I couldn't face Ken and Cheryl and Karen and Merilee, and I wasn't even sure I wanted to see Bernice, sure that Betty Frost had given her an earful about me.

But by 7:45 I was shaking kids awake, getting them to brush their teeth, yelling at them to brush their hair, get dressed, helping them find missing socks and shoes and hair ribbons.

After eating the head off his bunny, Gavin started complaining of a stomachache again, and I thought, oh good, I won't have to go to church. I told him to hop right into bed, but he perked up when he found out we were having pancakes at church.

At five after nine, Troy pulled into the driveway, and by 9:30 we were lined up with our paper plates for pancakes, eggs, sausages, bacon, hash browns, and coffee. Pitchers were filled with the new season's maple syrup, which would be generously poured over and into everything, including coffee.

I was in line behind Teresa, a woman about my age who had a four-year-old and was pregnant with her second. We talked about doctors and babies, hospitals and pregnancies. Her little boy would be going to kindergarten in the fall, she told me, and they still hadn't decided whether they should be sending him to the Christian school or the public school. I told her we sent our kids to the Christian school for kindergarten, but to the public school for first grade on. Then she smiled and commented on Simon's cute Easter outfit, and I said, yes, it is adorable, isn't it?

I could be open and friendly with her because I was fairly certain she wasn't a Sunday evening service attender. Then she surprised me by saying, "Ted and I have been enjoying your husband's contributions to the evening service. Especially last Sunday night when he preached. We both enjoyed that. You missed a good one."

He preached? Troy preached?

Imperceptibly, I backed away, looked down, letting the sides of my hair cover my face as I fiddled with the buttons on Simon's shirt. In the distance I could hear Betty Frost calling Irma and Bud to come sit with them, that she and Jim were saving them a place. Cheryl came and put her arm on mine and said hello, it's so nice to see you, Sadie, I hope you are well, how are you, fine, how are you, busy, you know, always busy, so much to do.

Merilee was next and asked about Gavin. Troy said he was sick, I hope it's not the same flu that we had, it went through our family a couple of months ago and you would not believe how sick we all were well, I must get over to where we are sitting or I'll lose my place, we must get together sometime, call me okay?

Lillian from the library made a point of coming over, too. Well Sadie, how are you enjoying that next book in the series? Fine, I said. Well, I have a new one I think you'll be interested in, just came in. It's about Christian families. I'll put it aside for you. I look forward to reading it. Thank you very much.

Rhonda and Charles walked in, he holding their baby, and Lillian turned from the duty of talking to me to the joy of talking to her family. Phyllis from the prayer chain was sitting with a group of white-haired ladies at a table over by the coffeepot. She looked in my direction. I looked away. They always went to the evening service; most of the older people did. Millie Dennis was there. Michelle and her little ones.

When my plate was filled, I couldn't find where Troy had gone. For several seconds I stood there, flustered, bewildered. The room was teeming with people, all smiling, all rejoicing on this Easter Sunday morning, the most important holiday in the Christian calendar, a day of praising God for His grace. But suddenly all the faces were foreign, the language they spoke unintelligible. I finally spotted Troy and made my way carefully to where he was saving a place for me at a far table. He was already deep in conversation with Phil. And they were all strangers to me, even my husband.

That it should happen to me in church is not so strange, is it? This realization that there is a God, and that He has loved me all along? No, it is not so odd. Church is where I have always encountered God.

I was seven and it was Christmas and the organ was playing *Silent Night* while the Christmas tableau was acted out: Mary, Joseph, the baby Jesus, the shepherds, the angels. I looked at the figures around the stable, sang the music in my loudest voice, the way I always did. But when I looked behind the tableau at the wooden cross on the back wall, all at once I realized that this Jesus, this baby Jesus, was the same Jesus who died on the cross. This new thought filled my eyes with tears I could not explain. He loves me. He *loves* me, a fact I could not explain, nor could I explain how I knew. I just did, a little girl holding on to her father's hand on Christmas eve.

It was Jesus, I said to my father later, *wasn't it? The real Jesus. He was here, really here.* I don't know if my father understood fully what I was trying to say, but he nodded. And there were tears in his eyes, too.

Ten years later it was a very ordinary Sunday morning that I met God yet again. The minister was talking about becoming one with the will of the Father. Not my will but thine be done. Not my will but thine. The words became like a mantra to me that morning. Not my will but thine, again and again. And I looked beyond the minister to the cross on the wall behind him and I surrendered my music, something I had been fiercely holding on to, to God. Not my will but thine be done. My music, my life, all my songs will be for You, and You alone. "All to Jesus I surrender, all to Him I freely give."

When Robin died and there was no solace anywhere on earth for me, it was in church that God found me yet again. When people said, You're young, you'll have another, it was worse than if they had said nothing at all. That there had been no funeral, no graveside ceremony for my little baby was a grief I felt I would carry for the rest of my life. Robin had never really lived, Troy reasoned, so a funeral was uncalled for. He told the senior pastor this, told him it was a decision we both had made. But Robin *had* lived, my soul cried. I had felt him alive within me. It was a grief to me that I didn't know where the nurses had taken him after I had held him briefly. They never told me. And so, on that day two months after Robin died, I was sitting at the church piano and going over the songs for Sunday. And suddenly my music became much more than music. "Be still my soul, thy God doth undertake to guide the future as He has the past. Thy hope, thy confidence let nothing shake…"

My music had become my prayer. And it was then that I knew where Robin was. He was safe with God. And I would see him again.

So it is not so strange that today, this Easter Sunday when I am afraid of the man I am sharing a hymnbook with, afraid of what he is and what he has done, that God would reach down to me again. We were singing, and I listened to the organ: "When I survey the wondrous cross on which the Prince of glory died." There were tears in my eyes when I sang those words, tears I couldn't explain or understand. But I was beginning to believe that God was listening to those tears. It wouldn't be like Judith said. God doesn't forget people. He doesn't.

Tears tracked down my cheeks at the beauty of it all, the awesomeness of the music, this adoration of God. And I didn't know what was going to happen, or how it was going to turn out, but I looked at the cross and I felt in that instant that God knew me, that He cared, and that He understood my pain.

ou should have been in church," I told Judith the following
morning. "The service was beautiful."

"I don't go to church. You know that."

"We prayed for you."

"And has anything changed? Has it? Did Ally walk mysteriously
back into my house because you prayed?"

"I'm sorry…" I didn't know what to say. "There's so much I
haven't told you. My life is not all that perfect…"

"Sadie, I would really love to chat." There was a hard edge to her
voice. "But the detective I hired is coming over. I really have to go."

"Maybe we'll get together soon."

"Maybe."

When she hung up, I looked around my kitchen, wondering
why I could never get it right. I begin to think God is answering my
prayers, and I try to tell someone about it, and I get put back in my
place.

A knock on my door. It was Bernice Jacobs. Bernice had come!
I was so sure in light of what Betty Frost had, in all likelihood, told
her, that Bernice wouldn't come. After all, all I would be doing for
Safe Harbor would be folding brochures, all I would be *allowed* to
do was fold brochures. Because of my *history*.

The kitchen was still a mess, cereal dishes still on the table,
Simon still in his sleeper, Gavin without his teeth brushed and hair
combed, still in his pajamas, and I didn't look all that great either.

"Oh Bernice, come in," I said. "I wasn't sure you were going to make it."

She smiled warmly showing a lot of teeth. "I wouldn't have missed coming here."

"I'm still so disorganized this morning. But sit down. Would you like coffee? There's some still warm. Sorry about the state of the kitchen. Here, let me clear a place at the table." I piled plates and dishes in a rickety heap and carried them to the counter. At the sink I wiped my eyes clean.

When I turned, Bernice had a wet dishrag in her hand and was wiping the table.

"You don't have to do that," I said.

She chuckled. "I've done this many, many times."

I poured two mugs of coffee and explained that mornings, especially Monday mornings, were chaotic. Plus, I never quite felt well in the morning. I never felt like I had really had enough sleep the night before. I apologized that all I had to go with the coffee was two percent. I needed to get out and get some groceries and I hoped she didn't mind two percent in her coffee. I sat down across from her.

"Wasn't that a wonderful church service yesterday?" she said.

"Yes."

"God was there. Did you sense it?"

I nodded.

"So much musical talent for such a small church," she said.

"Yes."

She looked at me thoughtfully and I suddenly felt shy. "Sadie, is there something wrong?"

I looked down at my coffee and said, "I was wondering if you could tell me something… Can you tell me more about that woman who lived on that island? The one you told me about? You said that God always provides a way, but this is what I want to know: Why would God provide a way for her to leave her husband when leaving your husband is so against the Bible?"

"What do you mean, 'against the Bible'?"

"What God joins together let no man put asunder. That verse." She leaned forward. "That woman on the island was me."

I'm sure my mouth gaped open a foot. I clamped it shut.

She seemed to look past me when she said, "He was a fine man, my husband. An educated man. A professor. A lay minister in our church, too. A wonderful Christian man. Both of us, educated people. At least that's the picture everyone else had. But I still have scars from where he hit me. And my nose," she said, touching it. "My nose has lost its original shape for good."

I reached for my mug and spilled coffee all over my hands and onto my shirt and at the same time Simon started bawling. I reached for a dish towel. "I don't know what happened," I said. "The whole cup just slipped out of my hand. Clumsy me. You can dress me up, but you can't take me out…"

She didn't smile. "It's what I do now, help women in these situations." She had picked up Simon, and was rocking him on her shoulder. He had quieted. "Especially Christian women."

I got up and poured myself another cup, my face turned away from her, carefully, carefully, so as not to spill. I poured in a bit of milk, spooned in half a spoonful of sugar. I tried to keep my face expressionless as I sat down across from her. "What do you mean, especially Christian women?"

"Christian women are experts in hiding abuse. They've learned to hide it so well that they even hide it from themselves. The lies they tell over and over to themselves every day. They expend so much energy in hiding it, they have no energy left to get help or to get out."

I forced myself to drink some coffee. Then I said, "His sleeper's covered in cereal. He'll get you dirty."

"I'm just fine." She smiled, again a flash of even white teeth. She truly was a beautiful woman. "My husband was a pillar of the church. He was on the board of our small black church, and he sang the loudest. Oh my, he loved music. And treated all the ladies so fine, and everyone said he was such a gentleman, and he raised his hands and praised God louder than anyone in church. Such a gentleman, Bernice. You have a treasure there, Bernice. What a man you have there, Bernice. But at home, when we were alone, he would beat me. I can't tell you the times he drove me to emergency with all kinds of stories—she walked into a wall; she fell down the stairs; she fainted in the bathroom. And everyone would pray for clumsy Bernice. Is there something wrong with her that she falls down so much? We really must get some help for Bernice. Bernice really needs our prayers, here she is in emergency again. What's the matter with her?"

I began to choke. "I'll be all right," I said, holding up my hand. "Coffee just went down the wrong way."

"I had a master's degree in counseling. That was the ironic thing. Physician heal thyself. But he would ask me to forgive him. He would cry and say he would never do it again, and we would pray. We would sit there on the couch in the living room, Bible opened on our lap, and pray together. He would ask God to forgive him, he would ask me to forgive him. And then a day later, a week later, a month later it would start all over again."

I didn't say anything. I couldn't trust my vocal cords.

"Abuse takes all forms. Some husbands never lay a hand on their wives, yet their wives are abused just the same. Those are the saddest. Those women will probably never seek out the services of Safe Harbor or any kind of counseling. They'll begin to believe that they are too fat, too skinny, too stupid, too smart for their own good, too quiet, too talkative. My husband told me I was fat and lazy even though I was caring for three young boys, teaching part-time, and working on a Ph.D. in psychology. And the surprising, awful thing was that I believed him." She paused. "In some ways I had it better than a lot of abused women. I had a job. I had my own car. Some husbands keep their wives virtual prisoners at home. They aren't allowed to go out, aren't allowed to have any friends. They have no money of their own and are virtually powerless. And then the worst part is, their husbands try to prove they have this authority by pointing to Bible verses they take out of context."

"But doesn't the Bible say that people should never get divorced? That women should stay and pray through it, and eventually, if they pray hard enough, their husbands will change?"

"That passage is talking about unbelieving husbands, not Christian husbands who *know* the truth, yet continue to abuse. And as for the divorce passage, a marriage is a partnership; it is a sacred, intimate partnership between two people who love each other, like Christ and the church, and submit to each other. That's the biblical model, not one person lording it over another, completely controlling the other, putting down the other. I've heard that old 'two wrongs don't make a right' argument, too. My pastor, even when he heard what John had done, counseled me to stay with him. John was committing a wrong, he told me, but I would be committing a greater wrong by leaving. I listened to that for a while, until I ended up in the hospital unconscious, with possible brain damage. When I realized he was capable of killing me, I knew I had to leave."

I had to concentrate on my breathing. Breathe in, breathe out. God would take care of me, I knew that. Was I putting myself willingly in danger? My father always told me that God gave us common sense, and we were to use it.

"Is that when you went to the island?" I heard myself ask.

She told me her next-door neighbor came over one evening and helped her pack. Then she drove Bernice to their island cottage where she stayed for two months. Bernice told me about other women she had helped out of abusive marriages. She told me how Safe Harbor worked, how women came, how the twenty-four hour help line would work. I made a fresh pot of coffee, and we talked through that. We talked while I nursed Simon, while I got Gavin dressed, while I cleaned up the kitchen. We talked while she helped me fold laundry we placed in neat piles on the kitchen table.

And I felt for the first time there was someone who might understand how it was with me.

I have no explanation for what happened that afternoon. There are nice people in the world, I thought to myself when Bernice left, and Bernice is one of them. Ham is nice, I thought, and so was the young man who quieted Gavin in front of the Rite Aid. And Nick. Nick was nice, too. And Nick was at the door for Gavin now, and this time I did know where they were going. A local animal shelter had an afternoon program that taught children how to take care of animals. Nick had talked to me yesterday after church about the possibility of taking Gavin. He fiddled with his fingers when he asked me, and I had beamed a smile and said, "Oh yes, you may take Gavin. That would be nice." Troy had glared down at me.

When Nick arrived, Gavin had immediately begun to spin around and around on the floor, finally letting go of a Fisher-Price person that flew out of his hand and clunked on the top of the piano. Then he growled and grabbed at Nick's knees.

"Gavin, don't. Please behave," I said.

"Oh, I don't mind, Mrs. Thornton. He has lots of energy, that's for sure. I'll have him home by three, three-thirty at the latest. This time I promise. Here's the number where we'll be." And he handed a slip of paper to me. I stuffed it into the pocket of my jeans.

And so Simon and I were alone on a warm, sunny afternoon. He was standing up and holding onto the couch, grunting and calling.

"I hear you, Simon. I hear you." And I laughed and picked him up, lifting him high above my head. He giggled and I giggled and tickled him and he baby-giggled some more, and I reflected that I hadn't laughed with my baby for a long time. I hadn't laughed at all in a long time.

And on the couch we played peekaboo with the corner of his

blanket. "I see you, Simon, I see you. Peekaboo." Finally we stopped laughing, and I held him on the couch and cried until there were no more tears.

I put Simon on the floor then and went over to the piano. He push-upped himself toward me. Simon gurgled at me. I gave him a plastic teething toy, which he put in his mouth. Then I sat down at the piano, lifted the lid, and pressed my first finger on middle C. Just one note. I pressed it again. A noon breeze ruffled the curtains behind me, and a square of light seemed to settle on the keys of the piano. Then it was gone and the curtain ruffled back to its original shape.

With that same finger I played the G above middle C. Then I tried the E between. Then with my thumb, third finger, and pinkie I played all three notes at the same time. A chord. I played it again. Then I tried a scale, the simplest scale, eight notes from C to C. Scales and chords, I could hear Mrs. Scott say, all music is made up of scales and chords. The two most elemental of musical configurations—I was now hearing my composition teacher—yet all the music in the world is built on them, and like snowflakes, the patterns are endless. There will never be a time when all the songs have been written, when all the melodies have been used up.

The piano was tinny and off-key, as I knew it would be. I played another chord. Another scale. This time with my left hand. I added my right hand and watched my fingers venture farther up the keyboard, almost as if they were being moved by another. Yes, it was out of tune, but suddenly it wasn't, and I was crying. I was playing chords up and down the piano. And I was crying.

And then I was playing old hymns from memory: "Great Is Thy Faithfulness," "Amazing Grace," "Be Still My Soul," "There Is a Fountain Filled with Blood," "I Surrender All." At first the notes felt strange and clumsy, my hands too large and lumpish for the keys, like a barely remembered language.

And then it was time.

I stopped playing, my fingers lingering on the keys, the sound of the last chord still reverberating in the room, and I reached for Mary Beth's notebook and opened it to the first page of my music and began. The haunting melody filled the tiny living room. Even Simon seemed to be listening. And I was back there, wandering down the beach after the girl with the dogs. I was sitting on the rocks, furiously transcribing note after note on scraps of old Sunday school papers while the tide sighed against the shoreline. I was sitting in my backyard with my children surrounding me. I was standing beside the window, my nightgown wafting around my knees in the breeze.

Tears washed down my face as I played the piano I hadn't touched since Gavin was a baby. And then, on that warm afternoon in spring, my music stopped being music and became a prayer. Like that afternoon in church when I mourned Robin, my music became a meditation without words—praise, worship, adoration. And I had a feeling God was listening to me, that there was Someone who knew what I was praying, even when I did not.

In my mind I was hearing the oboe, the flute, the passage with the violins, the reprise with just the recorder, the sound of the harp. I played the entire score twice, from the beginning to the end, until I felt spent and finished, but filled with a hope I could not explain, a hope that defied everything I knew to be true about my life.

Chapter Forty-nine

All that week I played the piano whenever I found a free moment. I was working on the composition, refining it, improving it. With grocery money I had bought a folder of blank score and a bunch of pencils. I was painstakingly recopying all the music, adding harmonies and countermelodies. And when I would finish my practicing, I put the lid carefully down on the piano and shoved the sheets of music to the bottom of the piano bench. I was playing other pieces, too, practice pieces from college that had lain dormant and dusty in the piano bench all these years. I played hymns and choruses from memory. I played the songs from Gavin's videos, and he laughed and clapped and danced around the living room.

The following Sunday I sat in church and thought about my music, trying to come up with a name for my composition (for I was beginning to think of it as my own): "Ocean Song," "Song of the Sea," "The Lighthouse," "Tide of Hope." It seemed that each day I came up with a new name for it. My music was like a secret, like the first time you're pregnant when no one else knows, and you walk down the street thinking, I'm going to have a child. And you try to act nonchalant and normal as you put your groceries into the cart, as you casually pull into parking places.

During the offertory the pianist played a difficult Bach prelude. I listened, eyes closed, smiling slightly, my head cocked to one side. I was smiling because I reminded myself of my mother, leaning her head to the side while she listened to music.

Troy leaned down and whispered, "What's so funny?"

"Nothing."

"Then why're you smiling like that?"

"Just listening to the offertory. It's beautiful."

The secret was making me stand up straighter, making me pull my stomach in, making me do my work more quickly—my hands moving in the sudsy water or lining up cups in the cupboard. Always with a song, always thinking about how I could improve page five, second measure, maybe that's where the oboe solo should go. No, where it is is fine. Tomorrow when I get to the piano I'll work out that detail.

On Wednesday, I had climbed into Troy's workshop and spent some time on Troy's computer looking on the Internet for schools where I could finish my degree. What I really wanted was to contact my old music professor. (I had found his name and number on the Web.) I wanted to send the music to him, see if he had suggestions. Maybe he could tell me who composed it.

As my world grew brighter, Troy grew steadily grumpier. Sometimes he looked as if he were holding back his rage, saving up his anger.

I looked up at him now, his eyes steely and staring straight ahead. I was called out of the service to the nursery then. Simon was fussing, the nursery worker bent down and whispered. When I stumbled past Troy's knees, he looked up at me with a smile, but I saw something else there, something glinting and sinister at the back of his eyes. I had been seeing this look all week.

He hadn't touched me in a couple of weeks. Even brushing past me accidentally caused him to flinch—except in church, of course, where he kept his arm around the back of the pew, the tips of his fingers pressing into my shoulders.

But when he reached out to steady me that morning, I felt a sharp pinch on my thigh. To the casual observer Troy was smiling as he helped his wife get past his knees, but to me he was saying, "I don't know what you're up to, but I'm going to find out. And remember, I'm the boss." I shut my eyes fiercely against the pain and followed the nursery worker down the center aisle.

Our church nursery is a colorful place, organized and clean. Each child's name is calligraphied on fancy tags above hooks on the wall where each child's diaper bag is hung. Underneath is written each baby's schedule plus any special instructions. There's nothing written under Simon's name, even though I know he must be allergic to things, the way he's so cranky and sick. But Troy has never wanted to waste money on allergy testing.

I volunteer in the nursery about once every two months, but I'm in here more often than that. A middle-aged woman named Carol Connery is in charge and she's a stickler for organization and cleanliness. She's good at finding helpers, raising money for toys and furniture, and organizing baby showers. She believes every baby should be on a carefully written-out schedule. That there's nothing written under Simon's name disturbs her greatly. And Simon has never taken to her. Whenever she picks him up he wails, and I'm always making excuses. "It's not you, he's just tired." But it is her.

When Melissa, the teenage helper, and I walked in, Carol was holding a wailing Simon stiffly and upright in her arms. Next to Carol sat Rhonda with her baby on her lap, and I couldn't help but notice the contrast between her chubby pink-skinned baby, complete with the little elasticized ribbon around her hairless head, and red-faced, drooling Simon. I slipped my shoes off at the door—another of Carol's rules—and walked in my nylons to Simon, who held out his arms to me.

"It's not you," I said. "He's just hungry."

In the far corner, Blair and Todd's newborn lay sleeping peacefully, covered in a teddy bear blanket.

I carried Simon to a comfortable rocker, faced away from the others, shielded myself with a blanket, and began to nurse him. I was never sure that Carol altogether approved of breastfeeding in the church nursery. I noticed that Rhonda was holding a plastic baby bottle in one hand, testing it against her wrist.

"What a little character," Carol said, smiling at Rhonda's baby. "She gave me the biggest smile just then, didn't you, little punkin face?"

"Sadie, I wanted to thank you for the sleeper set you bought for Regan," Rhonda said.

"I'm sorry I couldn't make it to the shower."

"That was a lovely shower, wasn't it?" said Carol. "And I'm so pleased with this new idea of having the fathers along. Such a nice touch."

"There were so many people, I was just so overwhelmed," said Rhonda.

"We had a wonderful time," Carol said. "And there is no one more deserving, considering what you've been through to have this little one."

I finished nursing Simon and sat him up in my lap and rubbed his back while Rhonda and Carol talked about making baby food in blenders. Carol said she used to make all of her own baby food, and froze it in tiny plastic Tupperware containers. One serving at a time.

"But that was, oh my, twenty-five years ago now. Maybe the quality of baby food has improved, but in my day it was simply dreadful. Not good for the babies. Loaded with salt and sugar and preservatives. People know better nowadays." She surprised me by turning to me. "Do you make your own baby food, Sadie?"

I swiveled the rocker around and faced them. "Simon mostly just gets what we eat, little bits of this and that I cut up for his high chair. He likes bananas and pudding."

"And you're still nursing him?"

I nodded my head.

"How old is he now?"

"Eight months."

She clucked her tongue. "All of my babies were weaned at four months."

"Oh, but you're so lucky to be able to nurse," Rhonda said. "I couldn't. I tried and tried, but Regan was losing weight, so the doctor had me put her on formula."

"Well, she's certainly turning into a fatty now, aren't you, Regan?" said Carol. "Oh, let me hold her, Rhonda, you've had her for too long." Carol held out her arms. "Come here, little sweetie pie. Oh, you're such a cutie, you are. Look at her smile. Isn't that something? I've never seen a baby smile so young. My goodness, when is that man going to be finished?" said Carol. "He does go on, doesn't he?" The sermon, piped into the nursery, was a continual drone to our conversation. I had figured out long ago that the only reason they piped in the service was so that we could hear the closing hymn and start picking up toys and packing up the babies.

In the corner, Melissa was reading a story to three toddlers, and something about it made me perk up my ears.

"Cats on the ceiling, cats on the floor…"

I turned to her suddenly. "Melissa, what are you reading? What?"

"Cats on the Ceiling."

"Can I see the cover, please?"

"Sure." She closed the big, square picture book and handed it to me. And there was the girl again, right there on the front cover, the girl I'd seen.

"Do you know this book, Mrs. Thornton?"

"My twins have this story in a reader," I said.

"I have all her books. I read them to my cousins."

"All whose books?"

"Tuppy Malone. The writer." I looked down at her name in big letters across the bottom. "She came to our school once. She's really neat. I want to be a writer like her. I have all these ideas. My favorite is the monsters one."

"Do you know if she lives around here? This Tuppy Malone?"

"I don't know. I guess. I have one of hers signed. The monsters one."

She talked on, but I wasn't listening. I was looking through *Cats on the Ceiling*, reading it carefully, every word, looking at all the pictures.

Chapter Fifty

I wasn't pregnant. The little swab came out blue instead of pink. I stared at it, certain that either the test was wrong or I had taken it wrong. But Judith told me the tests were 99 percent accurate. I put the box back up in the cupboard and went to the piano. And that's where Bernice found me about an hour later. I heard a movement behind me, and when I turned, there was Bernice. And she was crying.

"Bernice," I said. "I didn't hear you come in."

"I'm sorry. I knocked. Then I heard the piano, so I just opened the door. That was simply extraordinary, Sadie. I didn't know you could play. Your music. It reminded me of…" But she didn't finish.

I was suddenly shy. "You have to excuse the piano. It would have sounded better if it was in tune."

"I didn't notice the piano. I only heard the music. It was truly magical. What is that piece? I have to admit I'm not up on my music, but I've never heard that one before."

I told her.

"And now you're curious about where the music came from."

"I am."

"Music is in the deepest part of your soul. Music is your soul, Sadie."

"But where did it come from?"

"Instead of analyzing it," she said, "why not merely accept it as a gift from God? You told me that the girl called it angel music. Well, maybe it is. Maybe it just is. Sometimes God does extraordinary

271

things. I once counseled a terribly abused woman. She had to get out of her house or her husband would kill her, of that I and the police were absolutely certain. But she wouldn't leave. She couldn't, she said, because her husband would come and find her wherever she was. We made escape plans for her many, many times. And even when the escape plan was foolproof, she always backed out at the last minute.

"One night she showed up at my door, suitcase in hand, carrying her baby and holding the hand of her little girl. She told me that the two women I'd sent over to help her pack were very persistent. She tried to argue with them, she told them she didn't want to leave, that she and husband were working things out, but they wouldn't take no for an answer. They were so insistent that she finally went along.

"I was confused because I hadn't sent any volunteers to her that night. I asked her where they were, and she said they'd dropped her off in their car. In the morning we found out that her husband had come home only minutes after she left, with a gun that he'd gotten somewhere. He shot up the whole house looking for her. He finally turned the gun on himself. I questioned all of my volunteers. Not one of them had been there that night to pick her up. To this day we don't know who it was."

I felt chills. I rubbed my arms.

"Sometimes these little miracles happen. We can't explain them, and why should we even try? Maybe this music was sent to you."

"Why me?"

"Why not you?"

Magical? Sent by God? But there was a little girl in Tuppy Malone's book who had talked about the unfathomable music. And there was a woman on the point who had heard it and was now so frightened she didn't even want to talk about it. No, there had to be an explanation.

—◊—

Later that afternoon Judith phoned and told me to turn on the television right away, that Amanda Johnson's murderer had been arrested.

"What!"

"Turn it on right now."

I grabbed for the remote on Troy's bedside table and switched on the television.

"You were right. Amanda Johnson's mother had nothing to do with Federated. I finally got Greg to admit that he lied to me. He said he told me that so I wouldn't keep hoping about Ally, that I would accept the fact that she's gone. He thought if I thought there was a connection, I would think it was the same guy. But it wasn't."

I sat on the bed and looked at the screen and listened to two voices, Judith's and the news reporter's. Amanda Johnson was murdered by a pedophile who was out on day parole. It had nothing to do with Federated. It had absolutely nothing to do with Troy.

"The good news," said Judith, "is that he couldn't have anything to do with Ally because he was back in prison before Ally went missing."

On the screen a handcuffed young man in prison garb, head down, was being led toward a courthouse by two police officers. His name was Vince Whitehouse and just this morning he had confessed to the brutal rape and murder of ten-year-old Amanda Johnson, whose battered body was left on a secluded Maine beach. This arrest ends an intensive investigation. This case has renewed interest for some in calling for reinstatement of the death penalty in the state of Maine.

On the news, I saw a few protestors with signs. I saw the face of Amanda's father who said he hoped justice would be done. In the background I saw Ham, walking behind the prisoner.

"So this had nothing to do with your husband's work," I said. "Or with Federated?"

"Ally could still be alive," she said. "My Ally could still be alive. I'm going to get onto the Internet right away and tell my friends."

In the evening I asked Troy about a key to the workshop. "I needed a screwdriver and couldn't get in."

"That's because I changed the locks."

"Why?"

"To keep out nosy intruders."

"But what am I supposed to do when I need to get something?"

"You wait until I get home, or—" and he sneered at me—"you could climb in the back window like you did those other times. Let me ask you this—why all the interest in Ally and Amanda Johnson? And looking up information about Judith? Shame on you, Sadie. And college music programs? What's that all about?"

Chapter Fifty-one

*J*udith called me the next morning and told me she'd found a whole Web site on Tuppy Malone. When she began reciting the Web address on the phone, I put up my hand and said, "Whoa."

"What's the matter? I thought you'd want to know this."

"I do, but I don't have use of the computer anymore."

"Why not?"

"It's in Troy's workshop."

"Outside?"

"Yes."

"Well, I don't understand…"

"I don't have a key."

"Why not?"

"I can't find it."

She didn't say anything for a while. Then, "Okay, then, how about if I print out what I have and bring it over?"

"I'd like that."

Judith arrived with a thick file folder plus a bag which she handed to me. It was from an exclusive shop in Bangor. "I bought you something on my way."

"This wasn't on your way."

"It's for you."

"Judith…"

"I don't want to hear it. Open it. Open it up. I want to see the expression on your face."

I pulled out a hand-embroidered maternity dress. I looked at her. "This is beautiful, but I'm not pregnant."

"You took the test?"

"Twice. Yesterday and then again this morning. It was negative both times."

"You must be so disappointed."

"Actually, I'm not really."

"I'll have to take this back then, get you something else."

"No, Judith, you don't need to get me anything. Really."

She folded the dress, put it in the bag, and then laid the file folder on the kitchen table and spread the sheets out. On the first sheet was the picture of a woman with a little round face, gray curls, and huge owl glasses. Across the top of the page was her name, Tuppy Malone, in a stylized childish script. I read that she grew up in Presque Isle, Maine, but now lived in Bangor with her husband and three huge dogs. I learned that she had received a Newberry Award for *Fishpies for Hannah,* her book set in colonial Maine.

I flipped through the sheets and found a picture of Tuppy and her dogs. They were sitting next to the lighthouse (the lighthouse on the point!), and the dogs were named Simon, Jody, and Dorry.

"Those are the dogs," I said, pointing. "The very ones. The same names and everything."

"Wait till you see this." She handed me a sheet she had kept behind her back. "This is the prize."

I took it and stared down at the little girl, the one I had seen, the one who had spoken to me. "This is her."

"Well, this girl is Tuppy Malone's niece!"

I read that her niece, Samantha Malone, is a frequent visitor, and the illustrator used her for the popular *Cats on the Ceiling.*

"So you see," said Judith, "the mystery is solved. It wasn't magic. You weren't seeing things. There was a real little girl all the time."

"But there's one problem," I said, putting down the paper.

"You're going to say the music."

"It doesn't explain the music."

"Well, I looked. I looked everywhere. I couldn't find anything about music."

"She called it angel music. Another person told me I should just accept it as a gift from God."

She leveled her eyes at me. "God doesn't work that way. God never works that way."

"I don't know. I don't know what to think."

"It was someone's stereo or something. That's all it was. There are no miracles, Sadie."

Chapter Fifty-two

Something was wrong. Even before I came in through the door, my arms laden with grocery bags, I could sense it. Something about the way Gavin eyed me from under the kitchen table, growling quietly. Something about the way the twins stood silently in the doorway, not giggling, not even looking at each other. Even Simon, on the kitchen floor quietly chewing on a Tupperware lid, didn't yell for me the way he normally did.

"Give me a hand, you guys," I said. "There's still a bunch of bags out in the van."

No one moved.

Mary Beth was sitting at the table, sucking loudly on her hair and trying not to look at me.

I went back out for the rest of the groceries.

"What's wrong, guys?" I said when I returned.

No one looked at me. Under the table, Gavin turned and faced the wall.

I could hear the television in the living room and could see the back of Troy's head as he sat in his chair watching it.

I started putting the groceries away, keeping a bagged salad out for supper. I wiped Simon's hands and face with a dishrag and handed him a cookie and set him in his playpen.

"What's up with you two?" I said to the twins. They didn't answer. Mary Beth continued sucking on her hair.

"What's the matter? What's going on here?"

From under the table, Gavin growled, "Piano."

I bent down. "What did you say?"

A loud growl. "PI-AN-O!"

"What about the piano?"

"Gavin, no!" said Mary Beth.

I walked into the living room.

And stared. And stared.

"Troy…" But I was barely able to speak. I could only stand and stare at the space against the wall where my piano used to be.

"Troy, where…?"

He turned and faced me, grinning, his hands on his knees.

"Where's my piano?"

"I sold it." His voice was cheerful, hearty, as if he had done a good thing.

"What? What?"

"Calm down. I said I sold it. It's halfway to Augusta by now. I got a good price for it, too."

I had to sit down. I slumped onto the floor and hugged my knees to my chest.

"The money, Sadie. Money's going to be tight. I only have three more weeks left at work, so I've got to be thinking ahead. Someone at work said they were looking for a piano so their kid could take lessons, so I jumped at the chance." He waved a check in the air.

"That was my piano. My parents gave me that piano."

"They gave *us* that piano. It was a wedding gift to *us*. *Us* is the operative word here. And I made a decision to benefit our family. All of *us*."

"You could have asked me, Troy. We could have at least discussed it." I was pulling at a stray thread in the carpet.

"Sadie, don't pick at that. You're always picking at things, and we don't have a lot of nice things as it is."

My hand stopped. "You still should have asked me. You should have asked."

"Sadie, you haven't touched that old thing for years. It was so out of tune it wasn't funny."

"But that was my piano, Troy. I wanted the kids to take lessons."

"None of our kids show the least bit of interest in the piano. Frankly I'm surprised you're reacting this way. The money we got will pay the mortgage for two months. That should make you happy. But then money never seems to be an issue with you."

"I could have given piano lessons."

"I made a decision, Sadie. As head of this house I made a decision that will benefit my family."

"But you should have told me." And then it all made sense. An hour ago Troy had smiled and told me to go get groceries. "Go on out by yourself," he had told me. "I'll look after the kids. You need to get away. You just go, get what you need, stop for a coffee if you want, take your book with you, there's no rush." And before I left, he smiled and kissed me on the forehead. He hadn't kissed me in weeks.

"But it was mine. My parents—"

"Sadie, I thought you'd be pleased. Not only does it give us groceries for another couple months, it also frees up more space in this room. I think that table looks nice there, don't you?"

I could barely look at it.

"I made that table. I've been working on it. The least you could do is offer a comment on it."

I didn't say anything. I was afraid to say anything, afraid that I would become like Gavin and scream and scream and scream until I had no more breath left.

Then I had another thought. A more horrible thought.

"What about the bench? What did you do with the bench?"

"The bench?"

"The piano bench." I was working hard to keep my voice even.

"Sadie, you can't sell a piano without a piano bench."

"But what about the things in the bench? There was music in there. Did you get that?"

"There was nothing in the bench."

"There were music books in there."

"Nothing of importance. I told the people they could look through the stuff and keep what they wanted and throw the rest out."

"There was music in there, music from college. And there was some music in there that I was working on for Ham, for the police department. It was important."

"You were working on music for the police department? What does the police department want with your music?"

"It was for Ham. Remember when we had dinner with Ham?"

Troy was laughing now. "Oh, my poor little disillusioned wife. This is really funny. That little conversation over supper? Ham seems interested in some phantom music by the lighthouse and you go off on your high horse thinking he really *wants* music. This is quite funny. I'm enjoying this."

I got up and walked out of the room and through the kitchen and out the back door, ignoring the five little faces that peered at me. The pain in my heart was a physical thing. I could put my hand to my chest and feel it and if I pressed hard enough the pain would burst and go all through my body, and my soul, just newly revived and still so fragile, would die.

A part of me wanted to continue walking. To walk and walk and never stop. But I couldn't. I wouldn't. The thought of my children stopped me at the tree. So I sat down in the armless chair under the tree and stayed that way for a long time.

I looked up, and Mary Beth was standing in front of me, shifting her weight from foot to foot, sucking the sides of her hair.

I held out my arms. "Come here, sweetie." She came into my arms and I held her. "Mommy's just sad right now," I said.

"I know."

She rubbed my head with her little hand and said, "I liked it when you played the piano when I came home from school."

"I'm glad."

"It was pretty."

"Daddy didn't realize this would make Mommy so sad or he wouldn't have done it. He didn't know Mommy was playing the piano again."

"Daddy knew."

I moved her away from me slightly and looked at her face. "What did you say?"

"He knew."

"What do you mean he knew?"

"Gavin told him. Daddy asked Gavin what was making you so happy, and Gavin told him that you played the piano every day. I heard him."

I held her hand and we walked back to the house.

I had no tears. One has tears when one has emotion, when there are things to care about, when there is hope. As I put the fish sticks in the oven and got the salad ready and set the table, I realized my husband had pressed against that black spot in my chest, and it had burst. God had played a cruel joke on me by offering me hope. I was even beginning to believe that this music was a special gift for me only. But Judith was right. There are no miracles.

Chapter Fifty-three

I am dead. I have no more soul.

I am a piece of wood when I serve the fish sticks, two for Mary Beth and the twins and Gavin, half of one cut carefully in little pieces for Simon, five for Troy, and three for me. I am silent when I scoop out the peas, a spoonful for each plate, and as I dish out the salad, a forkful for each. I look at my hands and marvel that they do not tremble, not in the slightest, when I lean over Troy. He looks up quizzically at me, and I stare into his eyes. He will see nothing there. For there is nothing to see. My spirit has gone.

I take my seat and we eat in silence. All of us. Even Simon does not squeal the way he does at supper, his little hands reaching for more. Instead, he looks from me to Troy then back to me again.

There has been a small, black place in my heart since the day Robin died and Troy didn't want to see him. No, it was there before that, miniscule but there, a cancer too small to be detected, but growing. One cell. It has to start with one cell. It was there the day of our wedding reception. It was dime sized by the time we'd been through two churches and Robin was born.

It was there when the senior pastor's wife at the church in Joliet put a hand on my arm and said, "Sadie, if you stay with that man, you are guaranteed a life of heartache." By the time Troy slapped my face in the car and called me a slut, the black spot was baseball sized.

Sometimes the black spot is scabbed over, and I can forget it's there. But it reopens and bleeds every time Troy pushes my shoulders against the wall and calls me a whore. It bleeds when Troy prays in church in his praying voice, and I know that none of these people know he once unplugged the phone and threw it at my head and knocked me unconscious. He took me to emergency and told everyone I'd fallen down the stairs and hit my head on a wooden train. After that Troy has modestly kept my bruises to places where no one sees. My back, my legs, my heart.

During the evening Troy goes out. (I don't know where. His workshop? A deacon's meeting? A missions committee meeting?) I get the children into bed, the way I always do. The way I will from now on, living here in this life that I have no escape from. Even the Idaho Pioneers can't help me now.

I marvel how easy it is tonight. My children obey. They brush their teeth without argument. They climb under their covers without protest and look at me strangely. Maybe they realize their mother is a dead woman. Alien mother. The twins were right. I pray their prayers with them to a god that is no god. Like Judith, I have prayed and prayed. I have prayed that Troy will change, and he doesn't. The little pieces of joy and hope get snatched away as soon as they take hold in my heart.

In the living room that evening I see that by mistake Troy has left the check on the coffee table. I pick it up and put it in my jeans pocket. Tomorrow I will take it to the church and rip it up in little pieces and throw it at the feet of Ken and Cheryl and Betty Frost and Merilee and Jim and Carol and Lillian and all of the Sunday evening service people. Judas money, I will tell them. I want no part of it. I have been betrayed.

Out of curiosity I take it out of my pocket and look at it. This is all he got for it? This paltry amount? I laugh. Oh, Troy, you got duped! You could have gotten twice that amount. Well, the joke's on you!

I sit on the couch for a long time staring. Then I get up and look at the check. I look at the name in the upper left: Brent and Claire

Moskony of 1114 Florence Lane, Augusta, Maine, 555-7476.

I punch in the number and tell Claire Moskony of 1114 Florence Lane, Augusta, Maine, that my husband has inadvertently left some music books of mine in the piano bench, and has she seen them?

"Well, I don't know. The piano just arrived. I haven't looked in the piano bench yet. There are things in there that you want?"

"Yes."

"Well, your husband *did* say to throw everything out. My husband may have done just that. I don't know. I can't promise anything."

"Can you look? I'll hold while you look."

"Well, okay then."

She comes back and tells me she is sorry but the bench seems to be completely empty, and her husband never saw any music in there either. I don't trust myself to speak. I am about to hang up when the woman says, "I just want to thank you again for the piano. It means so much to us. Our daughter is just so excited about starting piano lessons. You've made one little eight-year-old very happy."

I slide my back down the wall and sit on the floor and look at my dead hands.

I will call Bernice next. I will tell her there are no more miracles. No magical houses on islands. No angels come to drive you away in their car. All the miracles have been used up before I got here.

You have reached the voice mail of Bernice Jacobs in Community Services, Center for Family Violence. Please leave your name and number and I'll get back to you as soon as I can. If this is an emergency please press 0.

I hang up without leaving a message and go outside and sit for a long time under the tree in the dark.

Chapter Fifty-four

The following morning Troy asked me where the check was, and I said I didn't know.

"That check means we can pay the mortgage for two months. I want to know where you put it. Where is it?"

I was microwaving one of those little oatmeal packets for Simon. "I don't know," I said.

"You're lying."

"I never saw it."

"It was right on the coffee table. I've looked everywhere."

"I'll look when you go to work."

"Look at me when I'm talking to you."

I looked.

"I need that check, Sadie."

"I don't have it."

"I don't believe you."

"Believe me."

"I don't know why I put up with you. You're insane."

He came toward me, eyes blazing, and I just stood there. There is nothing you can do to someone who's already dead.

I'm not insane, I thought after he left. Dead, but not insane. And Ally is still missing. And I know who took her. And he betrayed me. It was time to tell someone the truth. I could do this one thing.

I punched in Ham's number.

"If you knew someone who had done something really bad," I told him, "wouldn't it be your civic duty to tell the police that?"

"What happened, Sadie?"

"Remember when you told me to call you if anything really bad happened?"

"Are you all right?"

"It's Troy."

"Is he there now?"

"He's at work."

"I'll be right there. Stay where you are. Don't move."

And he was. He came with curly-headed Julie. Bernice came too, which surprised me. My hands were on the kitchen table and they were very still and white. "He's the one you're looking for," I said. "He killed Ally because of something at work. Greg Buckley laid him off, and he didn't want to work for Federated. I don't know the whole story, and I can't figure it out exactly, but that's what I know. Troy did it. I found all this stuff—first there was the Visa receipt for Ellsworth. He was the one who was there with Ally. Then there were Ally's pictures in Troy's workshop, and all the articles that he printed off the Internet. They were all in his briefcase."

Ham was looking at me oddly.

"It's Troy you're looking for, Ham. Troy's at work. If you want to, you can go and get him there."

"Sadie," Ham said gently, "Ally is safe and sound."

"What?"

"She's flying home today from Australia. They'll be landing in Bangor—" he looked at his watch—"in about four hours."

"Australia! What?" I put my hand to my face.

"Ally's aunt took her. Judith's late husband's sister. She never felt Judith was a fit mother, but that's another matter. We've been tracking her all over Australia for the last month. Judith hired a detective and worked with him on putting Ally's photo on a number of Web sites for missing people, and that's what finally clinched it. Judith tracked down her own daughter."

I stared at him. "But what about the Visa receipt and the pictures and all the computer printouts and everything?"

"First of all, Troy probably goes to Ellsworth three times a week. Secondly, the sighting was a false lead. Someone just made it up. Third, we wanted Ally's pictures, so Greg gave them to Troy to give to me, because he knew Troy and I are friends and get together fairly often."

"But what about the music? You said there was music! What about the lady and the music?"

"Turns out it was just someone's stereo, probably out on a fishing boat. You know how sound carries over the water. Well, the fellow in the house didn't hear it because he's deaf. We have a fisherman who confirmed that he was listening to a radio on his boat. When we made a recording of the music you wrote down, the woman said it very definitely was not what she heard that night."

"I don't understand. Nothing makes sense." I got up, turned my back to them, walked over to the window, and looked out at the half-finished playhouse and the armless chairs. My voice was even when I said, "Well, that's good news about Ally."

"It is, indeed."

"Judith and Greg must be very happy. The police must be happy."

Ham came up behind me. "Sadie, what's the matter?"

"Nothing. Troy sold my piano, that's all. That's why I'm not myself."

"Your music?" said Bernice.

"He threw it out."

"Oh, child." She came up and put her hand on my shoulder.

"That's what he did. He sold my piano."

"Is he hurting you?" Ham said.

"Hurting me?" I kept my head perfectly still and stared out at the workshop where Troy makes all his beautiful things out of wood. A sculptor's hands. So much talent. "Why would you ask if he's hurting me?"

And Bernice put her arms around my shoulders and she was

smoothing my hair and just the touch of her hands on my hair, the gentleness of it, the three of them there, burst something deep inside of me, something that wasn't dead after all but just dormant and silent, and I began to sob.

Bernice led me back to the table, sat down beside me, still not letting go of me, my hands in hers, and said, "Tell us, Sadie. Tell us."

"I'm so tired and I'm so afraid and I just want to get through one day without my stomach hurting."

"I know, I know," she said.

"He throws things at me. And sometimes they miss, and sometimes they don't. And once I had to go to the hospital. And he squeezes my face and pushes me against the wall and tells me he's going to kill me. Once he pushed me and I fell down the stairs. And he gets so jealous and calls me terrible names."

And she held me in her big arms and kept holding me, while Simon baby push-upped across the kitchen floor and Gavin sat in the corner where the piano used to be and growled.

"I thought Troy had taken Ally and done something terrible to her. He could do that. I know he could. He's capable of it."

"We know," said Ham.

I moved slightly away from Bernice. "You do?"

"Do you want to know why I've been so friendly with Troy?"

"I figured it was because you suspected him of Ally's disappearance. And maybe even that other girl, Amanda."

"That's not why. It was because of you."

"Me?"

"Right from the start I suspected that Troy was abusing you."

I didn't know what to say.

"It was that time I came to pick up Emma for the first time and I saw you. I watched you. There was something about your eyes. Even in the way you walked."

"If he's hurting you or the children," said Bernice, "you should not stay here."

"It's just me he hurts. Not the children."

"And you don't think they're being hurt by watching what goes on here, by listening behind closed doors?"

A fresh round of tears. "I would do anything for my children."

"I know you would."

"A couple of weeks ago I even told a lady at church that Troy hits me, and she didn't believe me. Troy is such a wonderful person, you know."

"He expends an awful lot of energy hiding this, doesn't he? Like an alcoholic," said Julie.

"Sadie, are you ready?" Bernice said. "Are you ready to come now?"

I opened my eyes wide. "What do you mean, come now? Come where?"

"To a safe place."

"Now? I can't go anywhere now."

"Sure you can, honey."

"But my girls will be coming home from school in a little while, and I've got stuff thawing for supper and laundry to do. I've been in such a state I haven't gotten anything done. Look at this kitchen. There are dishes—"

"We can pick up the girls from school."

"I can't go, Bernice. I can't. I just can't. Troy will kill me if he comes home and I'm not here. And what if he calls and I'm not here? He likes me to be here when he calls. You don't understand."

"Sadie, you have a choice to make," Bernice said. "This is your choice, and I'm going to pray that you make the right one."

In the end they left alone. But before they left, Bernice put her hands on my shoulders and prayed that I would be strong.

Chapter Fifty-five

I was not feeling very strong. No one in my family has ever left her husband. Family violence. Abused wife. Spousal abuse. Even the words sounded like they belonged to someone else. Like cancer. And if I leave, isn't that like giving up? Like I haven't tried hard enough?

I had been walking around my house since they left, thinking, thinking. Wondering what to do. Wondering what God wanted me to do. If I left, wouldn't that make me a failure?

I wanted my husband to be the one to stand up in church five years from now and say, *I did terrible things to my wife. I said terrible things to her. But she never gave up on me. She loved me with Jesus' love, true agape love, and eventually I saw how much I was hurting her. And praise God, He changed me. I want to publicly thank my wife for never giving up on me.*

How I have pictured this so many times in my mind! How I have prayed for this!

Troy didn't kill Ally. He had nothing to do with Amanda. And yet...and yet, for a moment there, I believed he had. That I might believe, even briefly, that he was capable of this, shouldn't that be enough for me to leave?

Leave. How can I even think such a thing. I worry about my children. I worry that they will be fatherless. Isn't it better to have a bad father than no father at all?

Troy called me in the afternoon. Just to say hello, he said, just to ask forgiveness about the piano, and to assure me that as soon as we got on our feet again, he would buy me another one, a better one, maybe one of those electronic ones, or even a grand piano if I wanted. We'd turn the attic into a kind of music studio, or he'd build an addition on to the back of the house. He'd been thinking about that for a while. "It's a promise. You have my word on it, Sadie." He also wanted to tell me about a job he might be in line for. "It's way more money. It looks so good!"

"That's good, Troy," I said.

"Just wondering…have you come across that check yet, honey?"

"It's mine, Troy."

He got really quiet. "I thought you said you didn't know where it was."

"I kept it because the piano was mine. I can't lie anymore."

He didn't know how to answer me, I could tell. "I don't like your tone," was what he said.

Later the girls came home and threw their lunch boxes on the table and grabbed juice and cookies. And then my twins flanked me on either side as I sat on the living room floor and hugged me.

"Are you still sad, Mommy?"

And I hugged them and told them that I loved them, and that no matter what happened, I would always love them and we would always be together.

They left me and ran upstairs. Mary Beth came in sucking on her hair and complaining about a poor mark in arithmetic, and how everyone said she was stupid.

"You're not stupid, Mary Beth, don't you ever believe that. I never want you to believe that."

"Clark says I'm the stupidest in the class."

"Well, Clark is wrong."

And I looked at her sadly because she will turn out like me unless I do something. Unless I make a choice.

I moved slowly the rest of that afternoon. Ordinary tasks seemed monumental. And so when Troy came home, supper wasn't ready and the table wasn't set. That's one thing I always made sure I did—had the table set before my husband came home. (I read that in a book once.) And Troy came in demanding supper, and I said it wasn't ready, that I wasn't feeling well and I had a lot on my mind, and he said that was obviously not true since my mind was too small to have a lot on it in the first place, and where was the check now that he was home? I said it was safe, and he grabbed my shoulders and pulled me around from the sink, which made a glass bowl filled with thawing hamburger meat for sloppy joes fling out of my hand and shatter onto the floor, barely missing Simon who was sitting in the corner sucking on a cookie.

"It almost hit Simon!"

"I want that check, Sadie." With his forearm he swept everything off the counter and onto the floor.

I scooped up Simon and put him in his playpen. He began squawking, so I gave him his juice cup with the plastic cover.

"You are such a little whore! Give me that check."

"I will put it in a bank account and I'll use it to buy another piano."

"You can't cash it, it's made out to me."

"I'll rip it up then."

"Don't get snippy with me! I'll just get the people to cancel it and write me another one."

"Go ahead."

He spun me around and slapped my face. I looked up and there were four little faces peering at me from the doorway.

"Mary Beth," I said, "you and PJ and Tabby, can you go to your rooms now? Gavin, you go with them. Mary Beth, can you come and get Simon out of his playpen and take him with you?"

She obeyed without hesitation, picking up Simon, herding Gavin up the stairs. How do my children know to scatter so quickly?

And you don't think they're being hurt by watching what goes on here, by listening behind closed doors?

"I don't know what you do all day. I come home and the house is a mess. Bicycles all over the driveway, toys everywhere. Nothing done around here. What do you do? Watch television all day? Soap operas? Or read your stupid books?"

"Troy…please. Why don't we get help? Why don't we at least try?"

"You're the one that needs the help."

I bent down and began picking up the debris on the floor. I took a dishrag to clean up the glass. I was sweeping pieces into my hand, and he stepped on my hand. I screamed as glass shards pierced my palm. Then he lifted me up by the shoulders and slammed me into the wall.

"That'll teach you to steal from me."

"My hand."

"Where's my check?"

Then he began pulling things from cupboards, throwing them onto the floor, not caring if they broke, pulling out all the papers from the junk drawer. I saw his Bible go sailing, pages open, onto the glass.

"Where's that check?" And he cursed and swore.

My back was against the wall, and I was cradling my arm. Blood dripped on the floor. Then he backhanded me across the face; his ring—his wedding ring, the one we had bought together in Michigan City with our savings—ripped open my forehead. I screamed again as blood ran into my eyes. He hit me hard across the back of my head. I fell against the edge of the counter and slid to the floor.

It was suddenly dark, and as if from a great distance I heard someone say, "Troy, drop it!" The last thing I remembered before slipping into unconsciousness was praying, *Please, God, save my children. Please take care of my children. My children…*

Chapter Fifty-six

The pain woke me in the hospital, a searing pain in my right hand that shot up my arm. I had only faint recollections of what had brought me here. I remember screams. My own? I remember hearing, Troy, drop it. I remember, Mommy, Mommy, Mommy. And then a lot of faces and people and being moved onto a stretcher and lights and then dark again. I remember seeing Bernice. Ham was there too, and Julie with the curly hair.

"Pain," I said. "My…hand…"

"You gave us quite a scare," Ham said.

"My children?" I leaned up on my left arm, but the pain forced me down.

"Your children are fine. They're with your mother. She flew in yesterday."

"My mother?"

Ham nodded. "She's here."

"My mother? When?"

"Yesterday it happened. Last night you were in surgery."

I looked down at the large white bandage covering my hand.

"What time is it?" I asked.

"Early afternoon. Around two."

I fell asleep again and woke up to a nurse pricking my left arm. I winced and looked at her.

"I know. A terrible thing to wake up to," she said. "Just taking some blood here. We'll give you your pills. How's the pain?"

I thought about it. "Not as bad."

When the surgeon came he told me a large piece of glass had penetrated my right palm. He had initially feared nerve damage, but he was certain he had reattached everything to its proper location. That was how he put it.

"We'll get you started in physical therapy in a week or two. You should have full use."

"My head hurts."

"Well, I'm not surprised. You have a major lump on the back of your head and four stitches on your forehead. Everything checks out, though. There'll be a bit of scarring for a while, but that'll fade in time. Scars usually do, you know."

My mother came in then with my children and bent over and hugged me for a long time without saying anything. I held each of my children in turn. Mary Beth was upset over another "bad" spelling mark of 92 percent. Nick was going to take Gavin to a pony farm on Saturday, and PJ and Tabby were going to be in a play, playing one person. When I took Simon onto the bed he squealed in delight. The nurse helped sit me up so I could nurse him.

No one mentioned Troy.

And then Bernice came with Julie who told me Troy was being held for assault. Julie had me go through the attack from beginning to end into a tape recorder. Bernice held my hand the whole time.

Two days after surgery my mother took me home. All of Troy's clothing had been removed from his closet and drawers—all of his jackets, computer salesman suits and ties, socks, shoes, boots, coats, everything gone. And my mother had covered the queen-sized bed with a rose-colored spread I had never seen before.

On top of the dresser was my music, all the books and all the sheets. I flipped through them and hugged them to myself and wept.

"Where did these come from?" I asked my mother later.

"They were out in the workshop. Next to the computer."

My mother stayed for a month. And we talked, late into each night, over cups of tea and coffee cake she bought at the market. Two o'clock one morning we sat in the kitchen and she told me, finally, what she and Troy had talked about when Mary Beth was a baby.

"That first time we just talked. I wanted to get to know him. He seemed so strange and moody, and I wanted to get to know this new son-in-law of mine. He told me all about his woodworking, and I was fascinated by it. I urged him to go into that as a profession. But the second time I came, he began to ask about you. He wanted to know what you were like as a child. I answered him; we continued to talk. But when he told me that he would be in the ministry today if it weren't for you, well, that did it for me, I'm afraid. He wanted to know why you seemed to have a problem with your weight, and did I think this had anything to do with your fragile emotional health."

Maybe it was the lateness of the hour, but when my mother told me that, I burst out laughing. And then we both started laughing. And we laughed until we were crying. Then she held me in her arms, and I was a child again and afraid of the Chinese Lady.

A week after my mother left, I went out to Troy's workshop. My mother had found the key. I never asked her where. All of Troy's tools were still there, along with his computer, his tools in boxes on the shelves, the picture of his family, and his half-finished pieces of furniture. I looked at the plans laid out for the twins' bed units. I ran my hand over three exquisite dowels he had turned on the lathe, fat legs for an old-fashioned dining room table. I touched the kitchen cabinets, ran my fingers over their intricate scrollwork, all done by hand, incomplete, raw, but showing so much promise. On his workbench were his books and magazines. I leafed through them. *The Fine Furniture Maker's Guide, Advanced Woodworking,* and piles and piles of *Woodworking* magazines, all arranged in chronological order and dating back to 1990, the year we got married.

I closed the magazines, put everything back the way I found it, turned out the light, and locked the door behind me.

Chapter Fifty-seven

*I*t has been six months since I got out of the hospital. I have decided to go back to school in the fall. There's a place close by where I can finish my degree in music composition. Also, and this is the most surprising thing, I have been offered a part-time job teaching music at the Christian school. I have five children that depend on me, and I have to figure out how I'm going to support all of us for the rest of my life.

Also, I now carry the stigma of "single mother," and there will always be people who don't understand. There already are. I must have driven him to it, they say. I heard secondhand about a few parents who have opposed my working at the Christian school because of this. But since no one came to me, I'm assuming I'll start in January. I need the work too much to worry about what people are saying. Bernice has said that will always happen, and to just walk through life, your head held high, and your heart and mind fixed on Jesus.

But my church has been amazing. Bernice and I had a long talk with Ken and Cheryl and some of the deacons and their wives—most of whom couldn't believe this of Troy, despite my scars. They do now, I think. You can imagine how all of this became the only thing people talked about for quite a while. I think we are over the worst of that now.

My children and I are beginning to heal, although at times I find life overwhelming. Even simple things—a plugged drain, a flat tire, shoveling the snow—are major efforts. I'm worried for Gavin, praying that he not grow up like his father and his father's grandmother, that the cycle of abuse be stopped. I'm thankful that Nick still spends a lot of time with him. To wean him from so much television, I canceled cable. And yes, he *does* have a worm farm! Judith and Ally brought one over for him.

Simon is less sick these days, and he's walking now. It looks like he did go straight to walking, never crawling. The twins are still the twins, but I notice they are kinder to their siblings. Mary Beth is still frightened and cries sometimes at night, but I think she is getting better, too. The church is letting me use a funny little piano that was in the church basement and that nobody wanted, and Mary Beth has started lessons.

Judith and I are still friends. She's on a lot of committees helping to raise awareness of missing children. She and Greg and Ally are back together as a family, and doing fairly well. They come to church occasionally. We've had long talks, and some of her bitterness toward God seems to be gone.

I have most things figured out about last year. Troy had nothing to do with Amanda Johnson or Ally Buckley. He didn't kidnap Ally because of the loss of his job. Those events were just a part of a long series of coincidences. About a week ago I finally asked Ham what Troy was threatening me with in the kitchen when Ham said to drop it.

"A knife," Ham told me. "Troy was holding a knife."

Troy is in a minimum security prison. For how long, I don't know. Ken keeps in touch with him, and has told me that Troy is getting counseling and attends a support group. Troy has tried calling me a few times, but I have installed caller ID on my phone (one of Bernice's suggestions), and I don't answer it unless I know who's calling. And I have instructed the children to do the same. Troy's not supposed to have any contact with me or the children, but there are still nights when I wake up terrified that I can hear him breathing, coughing, coming up the stairs. That happened to me a lot in the beginning; it doesn't happen so much anymore. But still, I wonder if my life will ever be free of fear. Bernice has told me to take it one day at a time with prayer.

I have moved the computer into my bedroom, and I sent an e-mail to the address at the bottom of Tuppy Malone's Web site. A few days later Tuppy Malone actually phoned me. She told me that her precocious niece—that's how she described her, precocious—told her she didn't hear any music that day on the beach, and that unfathomable was her word for the day.

"That little girl will be a storyteller one day," Tuppy had said. "She just loves to make up things. She would have heard you talking about music, and it wouldn't have fazed her a bit to say it was unfathomable."

I sent photocopies of the music I heard to Professor Petersen, who spent two weeks researching, but could not find where this music came from. He said he was going to get the school orchestra to begin working on it. That is so exciting to me! When they are ready to perform it, maybe around Christmas, he's going to send out plane tickets for all of us to attend the concert.

I volunteer with Bernice down at Safe Harbor now. I talk to women, telling them my story from beginning to end, like I have written it here. I want them to know that being married shouldn't have to hurt. That's not God's plan for marriage and families.

And I'm getting to know God again, too. I've actually started leading a Bible study at Safe Harbor, but I sometimes wonder if I'm the leader or a student. God is teaching me so much. More and more I am figuring out who I am. More and more I am becoming able to move forward. More and more, things are making sense to me.

But the music, the music remains a mystery.

Multnomah Publishers

The publisher and author would love to hear your comments about this book. *Please contact us at:*
www.multnomah.net/sadiessong

Mystery and intrigue in the islands...

Naomi and Zoe are distraught as police begin an extensive investigation of a friend's death. In a different state, Margot begins her own investigation. What she discovers shatters her to the core and intertwines the lives of the island-dwellers as they seek to make peace with themselves, each other, and God.

ISBN 1-57673-397-1

Discover the secret of the seashore

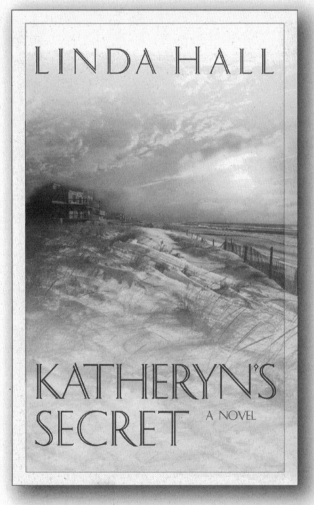

LINDA HALL

KATHERYN'S
SECRET   A NOVEL

While investigating a long-unsolved murder, mystery writer Sharon Colebrook and her husband, Jeff, find unexpected secrets, startling revelations, and dangerous truth within their own family tree.

ISBN 1-57673-614-8

The journey to peace...

a Novel

MARGARET'S PEACE

LINDA HALL

Margaret returns to her family home on the Maine coast in hopes of finding peace and the God she has lost. Instead she must relive the death of her sister and face long-buried secrets.

ISBN 1-57673-216-9